FEMMES
FATALES

IRON MAN

FEMMES FATALES

ROBERT GREENBERGER

BALLANTINE BOOKS • NEW YORK

Iron Man: Femmes Fatales is a work of fiction. Names, places, and incidents either are products of the author's imagination or are used fictitiously.

A Del Rey Mass Market Original

Copyright © 2009 Marvel Entertainment, Inc. and its subsidiaries. MARVEL, all related characters: © 2009 Marvel Entertainment, Inc. and its subsidiaries. Licensed by Marvel Characters B.V. www.marvel.com. All rights reserved.

MARVEL, IRON MAN, and all related characters and the distinctive likenesses thereof are trademarks of Marvel Entertainment, Inc. and its subsidiaries, and are used with permission.

Published in the United States by Del Rey, an imprint of The Random House Publishing Group, a division of Random House, Inc., New York.

DEL REY is a registered trademark and the Del Rey colophon is a trademark of Random House, Inc.

ISBN 978-0-345-50685-6

Printed in the United States of America

www.marvel.com
www.delreybooks.com

9 8 7 6 5 4 3 2 1

For Robbie,
who showed me an inner strength
worthy of an Iron Man

author's note

Growing up on comic books, I've had favorite characters and creators, and along the way I became a working professional in the field I love. To be able to write a novel featuring one of my all-time favorite characters is a dream come true.

Thanks have to go to Keith Clayton, who had faith in me from the outset. When he couldn't handle the editing himself, he turned me over to Steve Saffel, an old friend. Steve and I had never worked together before but found ourselves on the same page from outline to finished product. His contributions in terms of plot, pacing, and characterization were always enthusiastic and spot-on. He turned half-baked notions and dangling plot threads into a coherent story. Within Del Rey, I need to thank publisher Scott Shannon and in-house editor Tricia Narwani, who took over for Keith. Also a tip of the hat to Tricia's able right hand, Susan Moe.

It was a particular delight to base the story on comics from the era I loved best, the mid- to late sixties, when everything about Iron Man was new and exciting for a ten-year-old reader. I want to thank writers Stan Lee and Archie Goodwin in addition to artists Don Heck, Steve Ditko, and Gene Colan, whose stories enchanted me time and again. An additional thanks to Marvel executive editor Tom Brevoort, who helped me figure out some elements of the story's continuity.

Kenn Hoekstra, agent of S.H.I.E.L.D., appears thanks to his employer Robert Erwin's generous donation to the

Siegel & Shuster Society charity auction this past fall. Erwin wrote me, saying Kenn "is quite possibly the biggest Iron Man fan I have ever met . . . I would take the Pepsi challenge on that statement with any fourteen-year-old. His desk and office are adorned with memorabilia. He did a little dance when I told him of this amazing opportunity; I wish I did not have to see that."

Closer to home, I began this novel in the wake of my son Robbie's passing, and one of the last movies I took him to was *Iron Man,* which he loved. I think he would have enjoyed this story, as well. Writing this as I dealt with his absence was a good prescription for grief. My patient and supportive wife, Deb, made certain I got this done on time and in a much nicer home office. Kate, my vivacious daughter, cheered me on from her Maryland home.

—ROBERT GREENBERGER
January 2009

prologue

Richard Andrew Stoner sat at his desk and cursed.

The room was dark, lit largely by a desk lamp and his computer screen. The shadowy space was sizeable, with a meeting table, chairs, credenza, and a couch against the wall.

It was another all-nighter, and Stoner was certain he would hear about it from Caroline. But he had little choice. He was building an operation the likes of which had never been attempted before. As a result, there was no rule book to follow, nor mentor to guide him. Instead, he was entrusted to figure it out on his own, from scratch.

His wife had known what she was getting into, marrying a career military man. She would just have to understand.

And there were so many lives involved. . . . The very thought both exhilarated and terrified him—not that he would ever show it. It was not how he was trained.

That the budget was seemingly unlimited didn't hurt. If he needed anything—regardless of how exotic—he could have it delivered within twenty-four hours. Armed with that knowledge, he plunged ahead and hired, purchased, and delegated.

He ran a rough hand through his hair, which had started to go gray. He was powerfully built, and prided himself on staying in shape as an example to others. Every morning began with calisthenics and weight training, and Stoner made time for target practice each week, sampling all the new ordnance that had been arriving from around the world. He'd never imagined preferring a Glock to a Colt, but he adjusted.

He felt as if he hadn't left his office all day, and realized there was a reason for that. He hadn't. Reaching for his coffee mug that proclaimed "World's Number One Dad" in a colorful crayon typeface, he tasted the coffee and spat it back. Worse than cold, it was stale.

Stoner decided he needed an orderly, with standing orders to freshen the cup hourly.

Now that's *a great use of personnel,* he thought wryly.

No, he'd just need to have a coffeemaker installed in his office, with an ample supply of the strongest stuff money could buy. That was the only way he was going to make it through the late nights.

On his sleek desktop were folders bulging with information on potential recruits, requisition forms, status reports, phone messages, urgent notes from department heads, and catalogues to help outfit his army.

Why did I ever let them talk me into this?

He had resisted when called. He was a field officer, not a desk jockey, and he hadn't felt comfortable with the enormous undertaking the Executive Council had laid out for him. But they had persisted, and with good reason. A clear and present danger had introduced itself—one he recognized as a threat to freedom on a global scale.

That made it a military conflict, something with which he had experience, and no matter what the matériel he requisitioned, what he needed first and foremost would be troops he could trust. That Stoner could cull his team from the best armies throughout the free world still struck him as unprecedented—it made him feel as if he was assembling the ultimate all-star team.

That was how the Council had sold him on the idea, knowing from his record during the desert war that his men would follow him through the gates of hell. His greatest achievement was that he had brought the majority of them back alive. Giving him another opportunity to lead, and to choose from the cream of the crop—it was exactly the right thing to get him to take the job.

How could he say no? Clearly they had done their homework on him, much as he was studying his recruits now.

A view screen nestled in the far wall suddenly lit up, casting a glow that overwhelmed the other sources of illumination. Major Stoner glanced up and saw an agent waiting there. He marveled at the clarity of the image, considering the fact that the signal had been bounced off at least a dozen satellites from six different countries and scrambled to prevent any chance of interception.

The agent himself looked fifteen, but was listed in the records as nineteen. Baby-faced though he might have been, the man was a sharpshooter from the Italian army.

"Bianco, you need a haircut," Stoner grumbled.

"Aye, sir," the black-haired youth said in flawless English with barely a hint of an accent. To Stoner's silent amusement he remained at attention while Stoner gave him his marching orders and instructions as to where he would be stationed.

"And about that haircut—get it *before* you report for duty," he added.

"Aye, sir," Bianco replied impassively.

"Godspeed. Out."

He tapped a touch pad on his desk, and the image winked, instantly replaced with one of another man, closer to his own age. He had a weathered look that made him appear handsome in an untraditional way. When the man was aware that he had gone live, his eyes sparkled to life.

Women no doubt loved him.

"Lockwood," he said briskly.

"At ease, Lockwood," Stoner said, forcing his hand not to salute. They were both former U.S. Army, and had similar backgrounds—both having served in the Middle East before reassignment to the new company. But their Army days were behind them.

"I have a job for you, Colonel. There's a shipment leaving Cairo at 0800 Thursday. Take charge of it, and make sure it gets where it needs to go," Stoner said crisply. "At no time is it to leave your control."

The major was tired, thirsty, and ravenous. Still, he couldn't present anything but the image of a competent commander, despite visions of cheeseburgers that began dancing through his mind.

"Aye, sir," Lockwood replied.

"I'm sending the details to your CO. Pick them up within the hour. Stoner out."

Again the screen winked out, but this time it switched to black, looking like a hole in the wall. He decided he needed the company logo there, as a screen saver to fill the space and act as a constant reminder of this new operation. The design team had gotten the Council's thumbs-up earlier in the week, and the new insignia was being rushed onto uniforms, letterhead, ID cards, and just about everything but the toilet paper.

With a shrug he returned to his stack of files. Every department seemed to have its own demands and the endless hassles that came with them, but there were only so many hours in the day, and the priority was on staffing.

Each hire needed to be vetted. In the beginning the screening had taken six months, and they got it down to four over the past few weeks. The major wanted it down to six weeks, if possible, but that seemed to be a pipe dream given the languages, cultures, and varying infrastructures from which they were plucking the best of the best.

The organizations from which they were being plucked didn't always let them go easily, either. They continued to protest, but every Friday, before wearily returning to his home in Decatur, Stoner noted with satisfaction the charts that showed inexorable progress, as they kept inching toward 100 percent staffing.

He surveyed the mess on his desk, sat back in the comfortable leather chair, and sighed. Stoner was career Army and he still marveled that the Council had picked him out of the dozens of acceptable candidates they must have considered. They had told him—from behind opaque screens that hid their identities—that he had the right experience, training, and temperament to build this ambitious experimental program.

Caroline tried to be understanding, really she did, but since he had been reassigned, his absences had grown longer and longer. She was starting to grumble herself, while Willie and Emily were also making it known that Dad's presence was missed. Willie was still young, but Emily was a teenager now. Thinking about them gave him pause, their smiling faces replacing the mouthwatering cheeseburgers in his mind's eye, and it made him smile; his first real smile of the day.

But it didn't last. His mouth was pasty since he'd had nothing substantial to eat or drink in hours, and he thought maybe he could grab something from the mess and finish tidying his desk before calling it a day.

Stoner rose from his desk and felt a muscle strain in his right hip. Although he continued to work out, age was definitely starting to catch up to him. Maybe a desk job made more sense than the field, after twenty-three years in the service.

Of course, he observed, this wasn't an ordinary desk. It gleamed in the dim lighting, some sort of polished metal with a coating that left it feeling slick. He also noticed that it never left a trace of having been touched, no coffee stains or fingerprints, but no one could tell him what it was made from. Not the desk, nor the devices it hid.

Not even his CIO could fully explain all the gadgets that had been awaiting him in the office on his first day on duty. He had telecommunications technology that seemed to have been taken from an outlandish Sci-Fi Channel television series—*Stargate* or *Seeker 3000*. He'd been told that much of it was cutting edge, and as far from off-the-shelf as you could imagine.

Everything about the Atlanta headquarters felt larger-than-life, from the office furnishings to the gymnasium. What boggled his mind was the notion that the leadership continued to call this their *temporary* quarters. Then they had showed him the computer models for the real HQ, already nearing completion. He swore it was something the Japanese had designed, like those transforming robots Willie always watched on television.

Speaking of which . . . he looked at the digital readout on his computer screen. It showed Zulu time and Decatur time, and he saw that it was growing late. Maybe he could eat on the way home, risking crumbs in the car.

Yeah, time to call it a night. Lifting the handset from his desk phone, he had an instant connection to his secretary, who put in even more hours than he did.

"Lieutenant Adannaya, it's time to go home," he said.

"I'll call the motor pool," she said.

"I'll pick up the car around front," he acknowledged. "Better enjoy this while I can. I gather the commute to the real office will be a real bitch."

"But with no traffic to speak of," she countered. *"And given the parking lot they call the I-285 beltway, I have to say that I approve."* She clicked off.

He liked her soft Afrikaans voice, and thought they worked well together, even though she had been assigned to him without choice. In fact, she had been hired *before* him, and had spent a week readying his office while he was still being briefed by the Council.

He began scooping up the clutter, forming it into a single pile so he could quickly locate whatever he needed, placing other items in the outbox that he knew would be tended to the moment he cleared the doorway. Things ran smoothly here, and he never had to sweat the details, focusing instead on the Big Picture.

That must be why they pay me the big bucks.

So intent was Stoner on organizing his desk, deciding on a wrap or salad for dinner, rather than the greasy and tasty cheeseburger, and figuring out what lame excuse he could offer his wife, he didn't hear the door slide open.

As it softly locked into place, however, Stoner heard the click and looked up to see if the lieutenant needed something before he left.

There was no one by the door.

Instantly alert, he glanced around the office. By the couch was a shape.

A man-shape.

Stoner's hands moved. One reached for the Glock at his hip, the other tapped the red key that instantly deleted his hard drive and sent out an emergency signal. He knew his computer was backing up his data every forty-five seconds, so little could be lost.

The Glock 17 carried seventeen rounds but was also low weight with reasonable recoil, allowing him to fire it accurately with one hand. The pistol aimed itself at the couch but the figure was missing.

As thin gray smoke from the self-immolating disc drive wafted up from beneath the desk, a fist swung from the opposite side, connecting with the major's temple and sending him to the carpeted floor.

He couldn't imagine how the assailant had got past the building's state-of-the-art security, or how he managed to move so silently now, here within the office. But he brushed the thoughts aside, and crouched to defend his turf.

The smoke actually helped him frame the figure, and Stoner launched himself forward. His hands grabbed onto fabric and felt the realness of the man.

The intruder's hands were already in motion, clubbing Stoner's ears and causing concussive pain. The soldier refused to let go, though, and as the man tried to box his ears a second time, Stoner head-butted him.

The force of impact made the man fall back and Stoner raised the pistol, eager to gain an advantage. Instead, a swift kick knocked the gun loose from his hand, and a second connected with the major's right kneecap. An explosion of pain traveled from knee to hip, and he staggered.

The attacker pressed his new advantage and swung with lefts and rights to keep Stoner off balance. A thick, muscled man, Stoner stayed low and absorbed most of the blows, although he couldn't gain the upper hand.

He had to put this enemy down, and fast. His hand found the barrel of his Glock and quickly scooped it up. There was no time to reverse it, so he used the handle as a bludgeon. He felt metal connect with bone and the attacker grunted once—the first sound he had made.

Stoner rose to his feet, feeling the pain throb up his right leg, making standing difficult but not impossible. He focused on his breathing, keeping it controlled, and measured the distance between the two of them. His assailant passed into the glow from the desk lamp, and what the major saw made him pause.

The other man was wearing some sort of camouflage that let him flawlessly blend in with the wood paneling, patterned carpet, or even the metal desk. It covered every inch of his body, and had to be some sort of new material, he thought quickly.

But then the intruder crouched again. The techies could study the fabric once the assailant was in the brig.

Stoner launched himself through the air, a direct assault, his right hand still hefting the pistol; the left hand pulled back in a fist of granite.

They collided and rolled over the desk, scattering its contents, then went tumbling to the ground with Stoner smacking the pistol into the man's hooded head. He heard the glass goggles crack, just a little tinkle, but it caused him to grunt with satisfaction.

This low to the ground, the air was tangy with the smoke

of burning circuits, which were softly crackling from within his futuristic desk. They rolled away from it and banged into the desk chair, which in turn rolled to give them room. Over and over they went, grappling, with neither man gaining a clear advantage.

Stoner was on top for a brief moment, and raised his right arm to land a hard blow with the pistol, hoping to put the man out. Instead, he heard a soft metallic sound, then felt a very sharp blade slice through his starched white shirt and flowered blue tie and into his skin. He looked down and saw the knife blade extend from under the attacker's left wrist, attached to a bracelet of some sort.

The blood blossomed across the now-ruined shirt, a black stain in the murkiness, and he felt the cool steel pierce skin, blood vessels, and muscle, cutting deep.

He tried to cry out for help, but blood filled his throat, making it painful even to breathe.

The knife jerked in and up, gutting him like a freshly caught fish.

Within seconds, Stoner lost consciousness. His final clear thought was a flash of regret that he couldn't take Willie to the Falcons game that weekend.

Once Stoner was a lump of flesh on the floor, the intruder stood and surveyed the room. Not only had the computer fried itself, but the files were a scattered mess, and he didn't have time to glean their value. Still, that didn't concern him—any intelligence would be appreciated, but that had been a secondary goal.

His mission had been to kill Rick Stoner, and it had been successfully accomplished.

The assassin knew he had only minutes to retrace his steps and slip away before being caught by the night shift security detail—however many remained alive. He had to exit the brownstone and reach the spot where his transport awaited him.

Quickly, he left the office and strolled past the body of Lt. Adannaya, slumped over her own terminal. As he passed her cooling form he reached under his outfit for a small metal box. With one hand, he slid open the seal and depressed the single button. Then he set the box next to the lifeless woman.

He was safely three blocks away before the explosion that reduced the building to a heap of rubble. Without turning, the man muttered under his breath.

"Hail Hydra."

i.

The fall air was crisp outside the Long Island headquarters of Stark Industries, but no one in the conference room was thinking about the temperature, or the gorgeous foliage that could be seen on the grounds of the sprawling complex.

If anything, it was far cooler within the well-appointed room with its oak paneling, teak table, and deep leather swivel chairs. At the head of the polished table, around which sat a small group of men and women, was Anthony Stark. Standing six foot one, he was the very model of a corporate executive. As if summoned from central casting, he was young, handsome, and exceedingly well groomed in his handcrafted, charcoal-gray Hugo Boss suit. Every hair was perfectly in place, his chin clean-shaven, his mustache utterly symmetrical.

Stark looked entirely at ease, as if this was where he was meant to be. Yet, he had been in charge of his father's company for only a very brief time. And Tony Stark had never even wanted to be in charge. He had been perfectly content heading up the research-and-development division for his father, Howard, who had run the company until his untimely death.

Losing his parents to a freak car accident had upended Tony Stark's world, leaving him an orphan *and* the inheritor of the family legacy, all in a single instant. He was just twenty-one, and not at all prepared for either to occur.

After graduating with two masters degrees at the age of nineteen, he had dabbled in the R & D labs, but really preferred chasing women and drinking with either his pal Tiberius Stone or his cousin Morgan Stark—who also showed no interest in the family business.

Stark had grown up watching his father struggle to keep the company on the cutting edge of technology as the preeminent munitions manufacturer in America. Howard Stark had put in endless hours at the office, which had been fine for the teenage Tony, who preferred uninterrupted tinkering in the labs or dating fabulous-looking women who were attracted by his wealth and good looks.

His mother, Maria, had chuckled over Tony's excesses in both fields, often saying that the chip didn't fall far from the silicon factory.

How he missed them both.

Especially now.

This was the very room in which Howard had announced to the board of directors that he had become the majority shareholder, having bought out his brother, Edward, who failed to share his vision for the future. The board had liked having the two brothers around, letting them snipe at each other so that the chairman—now gone—could manipulate them freely and profit at their expense.

When Howard took over, he quickly maneuvered the chairman into emeritus status, thus becoming the CEO and chairman of the board. The directors had been cold-cocked, but shock turned to delight when Wall Street signaled its approval overnight with a twenty-five-point jump in the stock.

Howard had known how to read a spreadsheet, negotiate peace between feuding departments, and mollify a board that couldn't see past the quarterly dividend. Tony did not share those same skills. Not yet anyway. What they *did* have in common was a passion for technology and an ability to judge character. As a result, Stark Industries continued to recruit the best and the brightest, often sending the CEO to Stanford and MIT to personally recruit the most promising seniors.

Despite his look of calm, Tony would much rather have been on a campus now, sharing a beer with a promising engineer, instead of facing a dozen hostile glares.

"Well, Stark, what do you have to say for yourself?"

The speaker was Leticia Dandridge, a veteran member of the board and the one who usually led the pack when they were feeling rabid. She was well past sixty and had gone for one face-lift too many, as far as he was concerned. Her tightly tailored pants suit revealed that she was a gym hound, and he knew for a fact that she had little else to do with her life these days other than work out and bait him.

"Diversification is the answer," he said in reply. "You know that as well as I do, Leticia."

"Yes, but is it necessary to gut our most profitable programs in the process?" she countered.

All heads swiveled back and forth between the two. Dandridge always kept herself at the exact opposite end of the table, offering her a clear line of fire. All they needed was an umpire and ball boys.

"Munitions will no longer provide the predominant revenue stream for Stark Industries," he said, voicing a mantra he'd been forced to repeat several times since the beginning of the meeting, more than half an hour earlier. "The world is changing, Leticia, and we need to change with it. It's becoming a very dangerous place, and all too quickly a country we supply weapons to today can become our sworn enemy, without warning."

"I still don't buy it," she said dryly. "What prompted this alarming change of heart?" She wasn't going to give an inch, and the board was happy to let her challenge him. After all, munitions were what had placed the company on the map under Isaac Stark Sr. more than a century ago. For decades, they had been SI's bread and butter.

"Symkaria, for one," Stark said calmly. "Eastern Europe boasts several of our best clients, and the landscape there is constantly shifting. I, for one, don't like the idea of having our tech falling into the wrong hands. But by diversifying, and moving more heavily into electronics, aerodynamics, and engineering, we can cut back on arming countries that may no longer share our worldview."

Dandridge sipped from her crystal glass of water, letting the silence drag out longer than necessary. Then a voice came from his right.

"Really, Stark, is that our concern?" The speaker was a balding, heavyset man. "It's not as if we're responsible for the world's insanities."

That Calvin Handler spoke at all was noteworthy, and Stark glanced over at Pepper Potts, his personal assistant, who was taking the minutes. They quickly exchanged amused looks, then she returned her attention to the digital recorder and her steno pad.

"Cal, you know me—I'm an engineer. Get me started, and I can explain any technical issue you'd care to address, but you'd be lost by the third integer. This is even more difficult to explain—it's a vision thing. My dad . . . my dad had a vision, and none of you questioned him. I'd like to think you'd give me the same benefit of the doubt."

"That's the thing, Tony," Dandridge said, taking up the discussion once more. "Howard Stark grew up with the company, and was further along in his professional career before he took control."

Stark's dark eyebrows rose with that comment. "Are you saying didn't I grow up within the company?"

She gave him a long, appraising look—enough to make him want to squirm.

This is more brutal than ten rounds with the Titanium Man. He felt his calm beginning to fray.

Finally she spoke again.

"There's no question that your inventiveness has been instrumental in our continued growth," she began, "but your father certainly had more . . . corporate experience."

"You're kidding me, right?" Stark had to grip the table to control his rising frustration. "This is an age thing, isn't it? You think I'm too young to be trusted with the company's assets?"

"Did I say that?" She tried to look surprised, but failed at it, largely because her skin was too tight and not as flexible as it once had been.

"No, you didn't," he acknowledged, "but it sounds as if you're contemplating a change in leadership. A new CEO, perhaps?" He felt anger rising within him, but tamped it down.

He took a deep breath and paused. Then he noticed a scent in the air, at once of lilacs . . . and something else. Oil and grease, he thought.

Stark could tell the difference between the fragrance of twenty-year-old scotch and seventy-five-year-old single malt, but for the life of him he couldn't identify what went into the perfume that had caught his attention. He knew its source, though, and glanced once more toward his red-haired executive assistant . . . who was *not* meeting his gaze.

"Calm down, Tony," Handler interjected. "The board isn't seeking a new CEO." That earned the obese man a look from Dandridge, which confirmed that she was up to something.

It was time for him to take charge of the situation.

"Need I remind you all that I control the majority shares my father controlled, and I have no intention of relinquishing them," he said through gritted teeth. "So even if you *did* have something in mind, it would be doomed to failure from the start. Is that understood?"

Felix Alvarez, his corporate attorney, was seated nearby,

looking bored by all of the sniping. Yet he nodded his close-cropped head—a motion that wasn't lost on Stark's opponents.

"That's not what we were suggesting," Dandridge said, trying to snatch back the initiative. "Let me assure you, no one is questioning your position."

"You're damned right," Stark replied.

"There's no need for such language," Dandridge protested.

"Leticia, I'll use whatever language I feel is appropriate to the situation," he asserted, "much like I'll decide what we create, and what we sell."

"But see here, Stark," Linda Liang said. She was opposite Handler, and was a far sight prettier. Perhaps forty, she had built up an online auction company from scrap, and it was a rising star in the increasingly important World Wide Web. Tony had her added to the board after old Chip Ewing retired.

"We're getting requests for new weaponry from the Department of Defense," she continued. "Terre Verde is also seeking new missile designs, and if we don't act, the contracts will go elsewhere. Why ignore such lucrative deals?"

"I'm not saying that we get out of the field all at once, but that we shift our focus a bit," Stark replied, adopting a placating tone. "I want to *control* our growth, so we don't lose our ability to manage the operations. I certainly don't want us to become as bloated as Republic Oil."

"They've changed their name to Roxxon, you know," Handler chimed in.

"Whatever . . . that's not the point," Stark said. His mouth was dry, and he wanted a drink. Something stiffer than the lemon water in the pitcher that sat before him.

"The point is, from my time in R & D, I know that we're on the verge of significant breakthroughs that will help NASA get back to the moon, and enable the airlines to save on jet fuel. Those could be significant revenue streams, as long as we don't have all our resources tied up elsewhere." Peering around the room, he delivered the bottom line.

"I'm just asking that we stop making so many bombs, and build more useful stuff."

"Stuff?" Liang echoed with a hint of a smile.

Ouch, he thought.

"When we're done building it, I'll know what to call it," Stark declared, recognizing that he had at least one ally in the room other than Pepper.

"Look, Edison didn't have a roadmap. He just kept tinkering, and came up with innovations that changed the world. R & D will be the key to the next Big Thing." He paused, then continued. "This country's needs—in the wake of increased terrorism both at home and abroad—range from high-tech airport security to faster screening of cargo coming into the country's ports. Those concerns alone could keep us occupied around the clock. Just go with me on this."

He sat and studied the faces around the table.

Two looked bored. Two others stared at him, and clearly they wished they were looking at his father. Dandridge seemed thoughtful, and Handler nodded without expression. Liang and one other smiled.

He couldn't read the others.

Feeling somewhat encouraged, and ready to call the meeting to an end as soon as possible, he began speaking again.

"In fact, I've been giving great thought to global conflict and its resolution. Forces are on the move, and we have to be poised to provide assistance beyond identifying new ways to blow things up." With that he picked up his copy of the agenda, cleared his throat, and turned to the next item, which just happened to involve the Terra Verde missile request. As he read it out loud, he could see everyone relax just a bit, since this was something they could wrap their minds around.

Still, when the meeting broke up twenty minutes later, no one seemed particularly happy with the company's direction.

Especially Tony Stark.

ii.

The auditorium was huge, easily containing several hundred people, and yet every seat was filled.

Despite the numbers, the murmur of the crowd was curiously subdued.

They were dressed identically in military uniforms dominated by green-cowled tunics, the bulk of their faces masked and their eyes hidden by opaque yellow goggles. Facial hair was forbidden, so the only way to differentiate one attendee from another was by skin tone and physique.

All seemed fit—men and women alike—although the loose-fitting tunics and pants hid most of the musculature. All wore yellow gloves and boots, which matched the hue of the stylized *H* stitched into each tunic.

A sea of interchangeable soldiers, each known only by a number. They were an army, and they were hers to command.

The woman noted all this from her position in front of a monitor backstage, in the moments before the chronometer reached 14:00 EST. As the digits changed, she took a deep breath and strode forward.

Her own outfit was a modified version of the standard uniform, but as the leader she had the discretion to make such changes. After all, the man she had replaced had seen fit to do so, thus asserting his own authority.

She was tall and athletically built, so she chose a tight-fitting, sleeveless green unitard instead of the tunic of the rank and file. Leather gloves covered her otherwise-bare arms to above the elbows, complemented by calf-length boots with spiked heels. Twin pistols hung at her hips, held there by a leather belt and holsters.

Her long dark hair, highlighted green, covered her shoulders, and her lips were colored a deep green to match the uniform. All this was designed to attract the eye away from her face, the right side of which was often covered by the lustrous hair. While she didn't hide the scars around her eye, she didn't want them to dominate her features. Quite the opposite. Every inch of her appearance was calculated to indicate strength, power, and sexuality.

She strode to center stage where the overhead lights cast stark shadows, lending drama to her entrance.

"You may call me Madame Hydra," she said. There was a trace of a European accent evident to anyone with discerning ears, but she doubted anyone in the room was that sophisticated. These were drones, soldiers paid to do her bidding, not do anything difficult.

Like thinking.

Thanks to a microphone at the edge of the stage, her amplified voice was loud as it echoed across the vast chamber.

"Hail Hydra! Immortal Hydra! We shall never be destroyed. Cut off a limb and two more shall take its place!" Several hundred voices cried in unison.

"Hail Hydra!"

It sounded strong, powerful, and convincing. She spoke again, and the audience fell silent.

"For decades, HYDRA has been building its forces, growing a network of operations the likes of which the world has never seen, and like the mythical beast for which we are named, our tendrils reach into every civilized country on this planet.

"Our location, here in the world's greatest city, lends us a pivotal role in achieving the goals of our organization, and under my leadership you will stand at the forefront of the blitzkrieg. We will launch the first great strike in the final campaign.

"The Supreme Hydra says that the time has come to act."

At the invocation of their leader's name, there was a collective gasp.

Behind her, a thirty-foot-high screen snapped to life, momentarily displaying the tentacled skull that was their logo before switching to a camera's-eye view of Madame Hydra herself. In this way, all would see her as she took the reins of power.

"Our reach is global, and our goal is world domination, so that we may correct the ills perpetrated by greedy leaders, incompetent despots, and those who think themselves better than the rest," she said. There was a roar of approval, yet she herself didn't follow the party line. No, her physical and mental scars ran deep, and she was more interested in violence for its own sake. HYDRA currently offered her the best opportunity to achieve that goal. None in the room needed to know how much the hunger for wanton destruction fueled her every waking moment.

On the screen, the image switched from her figure to that of a map of the world, and narrowed its focus to the Northern Hemisphere, then the East Coast, and finally the island of Manhattan. The satellite imagery was sharper than anything these agents had seen before, and there was murmuring in the ranks.

"Baron Wolfgang von Strucker was a loyal soldier in the Third Reich's ill-fated attempt to conquer the world. He incurred Adolf Hitler's wrath and fled Germany rather than face execution. He built a power base in the Far East, and discovered a Japanese faction forming a secret society likewise bent on world domination," she continued. "Wisely, he co-opted them and became their tactician. His raids on factories and warehouses provided matériel they needed to arm themselves, while instilling fear in their opponents. When they achieved nominal strength, he assassinated the

Japanese warlord who stood in his way, and established himself as the Supreme Hydra."

What no one in the room realized was that she followed his template to the letter, in a way that even Strucker had never recognized. One of the first women granted a position of power within HYDRA, she had allowed Strucker—then the Supreme Hydra—to use her as he saw fit while she rose through the ranks. When ready, she would eliminate the leadership, hidden on the so-called Hydra Island, establishing herself as the new Supreme Leader.

But for now, she needed them to believe in her authority and her commitment to HYDRA's ideals.

"HYDRA has spent years establishing secret holdings in every major city, every country, and every government on the planet. There have been skirmishes, to be sure, even defeats, but we have emerged stronger, because . . ."

She paused to see how rapt their attention was. Then her voice rose.

"Cut off a limb, and two more shall take its place!"

Instantly everyone in the room stood, thrusting their fists into the air.

"Cut off a limb and two more shall take its place!" they thundered.

She smiled coldly with approval.

"Baron Strucker has lived well beyond the limits of human aging, through means we are not meant to understand," she continued. "He has been a great leader, and his tactics have served us well, but it is time to move forward." How he managed to live as a vital man well into his ninetieth year baffled her, but she had never learned his secret.

No matter, for she knew his weakness. . . .

"Now we exist in the era of rapidly changing technology, and that, too, shall help us achieve our goals. Soon those who manufacture such weapons shall fall under our control." The transistor was the last thing Strucker had understood completely, she knew, and that was something she could exploit. Soon there would be no one to question her authority.

"We here in the field know who stands to oppose us," she said, altering her tone to sound conspiratorial. Across the room as far as she could see, heads nodded in agreement. "Here in America, there are the FBI, the CIA, the NSA, and branches of local law enforcement. Our brethren around the world must contend with the likes of Interpol, Britain's MI6, the Russian FSB, China's Ministry of State Security, the Mossad, ABIN, and many others.

"And now there is a new international threat."

The screen behind her altered on cue, and displayed a circle containing the stylized shape of an eagle. At the center of the eagle was a classically shaped shield, a horizontal blue stripe at the top containing three stars, and seven vertical stripes below alternating red and white.

The eagle's claws were splayed, while the wings and tail stretched out to the edge of the circle, not unlike the tentacles in the HYDRA coat of arms.

How fitting, she mused.

"They call themselves S.H.I.E.L.D., an amusing acronym for Supreme Headquarters, International Espionage, Law Enforcement Division. Founded only months ago, they represent the countries of the free world, but are not beholden to NATO or even the United Nations."

She glanced to her left. A waiting attendant walked onto the stage and handed her a manila folder. Madame Hydra nodded curtly and then turned, hefting the thin folder in the air as the screen once again went live. The image zoomed in close to show her green-clad hand and the S.H.I.E.L.D. logo affixed to the front of the file.

"Upon learning of their existence, we sought them out, and learned. We then sent one of our members to cut off their head. Their operation has been crippled with his death, and the time is right to strike a lethal blow."

With her free hand she reached into a pocket on her

wide leather belt, withdrawing a cigarette lighter, the stage lights making it glow like a religious icon. Her thumb opened the top and then rolled the strike wheel so that the lighter flared to life.

"This is what we do to our vanquished enemies," she cried, and she lit the folder. Hungrily, the flame consumed it, along with its contents. It was a showy bit of ritual, but it was what was expected, and she had to perform flawlessly.

As the charred remains fell to the stage floor, a spontaneous cheer resounded from the still-standing agents.

"HYDRA must crush this new agency before it can gain a toehold on the world stage," she cried out, her magnified voice drowning out the cheers. Within moments, the shouting ended and silence returned. Only her voice was heard.

"In the process, we will do everything possible to damage America's own resources, undermining the world's confidence and assaulting the U.S. economy.

"Already our sister cells have struck successfully throughout Europe. We must do no less in New York City, the center of the global financial marketplace. Here is where we will deliver the pivotal blow, to add to the sense of global chaos.

"In assuming command of this operation, I have assessed our resources and come to a pivotal conclusion. We are well manned, but poorly outfitted. This must be rectified immediately so we can launch a devastating assault, regardless of S.H.I.E.L.D. or any other force that may oppose us. Our immediate goal shall be to acquire everything we need—by any means necessary—in preparation for the final conflict.

"Now go. Return to your places within the ranks of our enemies, and ready yourselves for your assignments. And remember, we serve none but the Supreme Hydra, as the world shall soon serve us."

She paused again, and then delivered the final stroke.

"Hail Hydra! Immortal Hydra. We shall never be destroyed. Cut off a limb and two more shall take its place."

With that she strode from the stage, leaving only thunderous applause in her wake.

The woman's voice was muffled from behind the mask she wore. A mask of solid metal.

A mask of solid gold.

She was seated at a simple desk in a small office space leased by a dummy corporation in a Midtown Manhattan high-rise. Few knew what went on behind the office doors, and management was paid promptly every month, so they had no reason to snoop.

The desk, furnishings, and other trappings all came from an office catalogue. They had been installed a decade earlier, and were worn here and there—a chip out of the desk, a stain on the carpet. To anyone from the cleaning staff or to a delivery person, this was the workplace of a part-time financial advisor. Yet, like the woman, the office hid its secrets.

The gleaming camera and video screen were normally secreted within the desk when not in operation. On the screen appeared the visage of a distinguished European aristocrat. His hair, gray at the temples, was worn long and brushed back, revealing a high forehead marked with lines. He wore a monocle that seemed to be more for effect than necessity, and an expression hinting at the rage that lay beneath.

This was Count Luchino Nefaria, whose ancestral holdings spoke of great wealth, and served as a front for the criminal enterprise known as the Maggia. Similar to the Cosa Nostra, the Maggia was a century-old secret society that boasted activities from drug trafficking to slavery, all maintained via a loosely organized hierarchy of "families." Their activities had simple goals: money and influence.

As the leader of an Italian branch of the organization,

Nefaria had earned the traditional title of "the Big M," though he found the title vulgar, and used it only when he didn't want to involve his own name in a transaction.

The woman addressing him was aptly known as Madame Masque, though he also knew her as Giulietta—his daughter. For the moment, though, no family connection was to be acknowledged, lest others might hear.

The conversation was not going well.

"How can this be?" he demanded, and the question was filled with anger. But she was determined to maintain her composure—something the mask made much easier.

"Competition," she replied coolly. "There are now mobs from Russia and Colombia challenging us for the drug trade. Enforcement at the borders is up, and with the new administration in power, the war on drugs is running at full tilt. It was bound to cut into our profits."

"Changes in government mean nothing," he countered. "Everyone has their price or their weakness—all you have to do is find it."

Before she could respond, he continued, his voice hard.

"And rivals are simply targets," he asserted. "If they challenge your authority, you eliminate them!"

Easier said than done, she mused silently. *Even with Yaponchik gone, the Russians still have Brighton Beach fortified, and the Colombians have signed a treaty with Fisk.*

But rather than antagonize her father, she decided to try another angle.

"Even if we manage to knock off one mob, another will just move in to take their place," she said. "It's always been that way in America, especially here in New York. It's not like it is in Greece, or Symkaria, where our local branches don't have to kowtow to the Kingpin." She hesitated, and then added archly, "Of course, if the Colombians can arrive at an understanding with Wilson Fisk, you might come and try for something similar. He would never deal with a mere subordinate, though."

That gave him pause, she noted with some satisfaction. Nefaria rarely left his fortress home in Italy, and delegated global operations to regional chieftains—his daughter among them. He didn't answer for a long moment. His face, though, grew red in frustration.

"Increase profits or we face extinction," he barked, sounding most unfatherlike. She suspected that he had some mad scheme in the works, and needed the money to complete it. His desire was palpable, and it rather frightened her.

His claims of doom were hyperbolic, but not all that far from the truth, either. The Maggia was quickly being eclipsed on the world stage—a situation the other criminal families had to contend with, as well. The world was changing, and they had to evolve.

She would have to find an answer. There was no alternative.

"It can't just be drugs, gambling, or prostitution," she said, her tone confident again. "There's too much competition. And we'll need to stay beneath the radar of the local authorities as much as we can." District Attorney Blake Tower was making it increasingly difficult for every criminal enterprise, and he seemed untouchable. As charismatic as he was successful, she suspected he hoped to follow in the footsteps of Rudolph Giuliani, who had also been a DA, to become the next candidate for mayor.

"So the other mobs are scrambling, as well," Nefaria said. "Didn't you just note that a vacuum is easily filled? Why not by us, then?"

"That would be the ideal in the long term," she acknowledged. "But if you need cash flow now, we need to find a more immediate solution. But you're right," she continued. "We will need to change with the times."

"Or face extinction." His voice had softened, the reality of the situation finally sinking in. But the change was fleeting.

"However you do it, just do it quickly," he said sharply. Then he added, "Or I will be forced to find someone who can."

"Understood," she said in a steady tone.

Without warning he cut the connection. The screen on her desk went dark, and she let out a deep breath. The sound was hollow beneath her golden mask. With a steady hand, she activated the control that dropped the technological marvel back into the desk.

Sitting back in the chair, she reviewed her options. She had been considering the problem even before her father delivered his ultimatum, and her network of informants told her of high-placed buyers who were seeking military technology, and didn't care where it came from.

It was time to see if they would put their cash where their mouths were. But this wasn't something that could be achieved by brute force. No, she would need to take a personal hand in this operation, and approach it with finesse.

And in so doing, she would reaffirm her position within the family hierarchy, making it impossible for Nefaria to simply cast her aside. Father though he might be, no one treated her like chattel.

Indeed, she would make herself indispensable. Then she would walk away from the Maggia and everything it represented, once and for all.

iii.

The rush of air was something he could never totally screen out. But then again, he didn't work hard at the fix, either. It was almost indiscernible—as was the whine of the jets—but he was aware of everything that touched his senses in this intimately closed environment. And that was as it should be.

Truth be told, Tony Stark liked the sound of air zipping past him as he reached speeds nearing Mach .5. It reminded him of the amazing thing he was doing, flying high over the Long Island Sound in a suit of armor he had created with his own two hands.

He had always had an intuitive feel for engineering, and he wasn't blowing smoke when he told the board how much he liked working in research and development. His inventiveness led to many of the breakthroughs that kept Stark Industries miles ahead of the competition.

It also preserved his life on a daily basis.

Without the armor chestplate, tiny pieces of shrapnel would slice into his heart and kill him in an instant. Instead, powerful magnets kept the fragments—remains of an explosive device—away from the cardiac muscle and let him live.

From that lifesaving device had grown the rest of the armor, which he found himself endlessly refining. What Stark wore this cool fall day was Model 4—his most sophisticated to date—and he was already thinking of new modifications he could craft to upgrade its systems.

It was an involuntary process, really, one he could no

more quit than breathing. He mentally kept a running list of things he would execute whenever time permitted.

Time. That was the one thing he could not conquer.

Since he had become Iron Man, he'd come to realize how much society needed his armored counterpart, as various threats appeared around the world. While there seemed to be more than enough superhumans on the domestic scene—with more arriving on what appeared to be an hourly basis—it was the increasing number of international criminals that had him most concerned. From Russia's Crimson Dynamo to China's Radioactive Man, every country seemed to be experiencing an explosion of new dangers. Hell, even Latveria's current ruler was what everyone in the free world would consider a terrorist, in the grand tradition of Muammar al-Gadaffi.

Then again, that's why he was an engineer, and not a politician.

Still, the threats continued to mount, but as the physicists taught, for every action there was an equal and opposite reaction. A villain arrived on the scene and a hero seemed to rise up to oppose him and preserve the public good.

And vice versa . . .

Stark considered his technology and how it could be misused by countries that changed regimes with frightening regularity. Instead, he preferred using his skills and inventions himself, entrusting only a few pieces to others lest things spiral out of control. The new S.H.I.E.L.D. operation looked promising, and if things worked out well, he'd be happy to develop new things for them. But first, he wanted to take the measure of their leadership. Something about their Executive Council worried him, so the field leader became even more important in his estimation.

Something bumped him out of his reverie. He turned his attention to a construction site near the Throg's Neck Bridge. A crane towered fifteen stories above a group of men, and something seemed off to him.

"Magnify by ten," he said softly but clearly.

Instantly, the heads-up display in his peripheral vision gave him a close-up view, and once the enlarged image came into focus he saw that support bolts on the crane had loosened. The man operating the crane was waving his arms frantically, trying to signal his coworkers that they had to scatter. But they didn't seem to hear him.

"Increase boot propulsion fifteen percent," Stark said, and instantly the sound of rushing increased perceptibly—at least to his ears—and he pointed his gauntleted hands downward, directing the airflow. He cut through the sky, all the while continuing to analyze the crane's precarious situation. A brisk verbal command brought up schematics showing the machine's design, with highlights noting its weak points and others designating structural strengths which he could exploit.

If it fell, he would have to catch it *and* the operator while keeping track of other debris that might fall onto the site below.

"Uni-beam to 1370 degrees," he commanded. He rarely let the armor go that high given the energy consumption and heat distribution, but he had little choice right now.

He saw the circular lens in his chestplate begin to glow. The air around it began to waver from the heat. A display light clicked green next to his left eye, and he knew the beam was ready.

"Loudspeaker," he said. Another green light blinked.

"This is Iron Man, clear the area below." His voice, mechanized and sounding nothing like Tony Stark, rang out, and he noted with satisfaction that people were looking into the sky and pointing.

Good. I've got their attention.

He imagined them wondering if he was a bird or a plane, but dismissed the thought and focused on the rapidly approaching crane, which continued to tilt alarmingly.

Quickly he swooped once around the entire machine to

fully assess the situation, and then let loose a tightly focused beam. It tapered to a thin point as it arrived at the crane's base, and the intense heat began to melt the metal, fusing the cab to the girders on which it sat. Waves of heat blurred the scene, but the instrumentation confirmed what he thought he was watching.

"Hover mode, one hundred percent stability."

Iron Man seemed to float in the air as he concentrated on making certain the beam didn't shift from its target until the crane was secure to the tower's skeletal structure. Too much heat and the molten metal wouldn't support the weight. Too little and the weld wouldn't be secure.

Meanwhile, he was running late for his appointment.

As the cab heated up, the man inside appeared to panic, so while he worked Stark used the loudspeaker to calm him down. Once the crane was secure, he moved in. His internal sensors let him know his energy reserves were down to 83 percent, which would be fine for the rest of the day unless a giant lizard breathing atomic fire decided to rise from Long Island Sound and challenge him to a few rounds.

He maneuvered his jets to bring him closer to the crane's cab, then reached inside and eased out the overweight man. He was slick with sweat. Stark carefully held him away from the still-cooling circular emitter in the middle of his chest.

"I owe you a beer," the man said, and then he let out a gasp as they dipped suddenly. Iron Man's boot jets automatically compensated for the increased load.

"Make it Johnny Walker Blue and you have a deal, friend," the armored hero replied.

"Whatever you want, Shellhead," the man agreed enthusiastically. "And call me Mike."

Stark cringed within his helmet. How he hated that nickname—"Shellhead"—but the Hulk had blurted it out some time back, and it had stuck. Like football players and movie stars, he was a bona fide celebrity, and nicknames came with the territory. To some it was a badge of honor, but Stark would have preferred to have his marketing people come up with something more flattering, and then leak it to the press.

Well, you can't always get what you want. That was a lesson his mother had taught him, long before Mick Jagger co-opted it, and times like this he was reminded of how true it was.

The unlikely pair lowered to the ground and the boots shut off. They stood for a moment, then Mike held out a beefy hand. Being careful to disengage the hydraulics, Iron Man shook Mike's hand as the others cheered around them. EMTs had arrived by then, and they took the worker away to check him over while the foreman approached.

"Thanks for takin' care of my guy," he said, then he peered up at the crane. "Gonna have to dismantle the crane, though—way you've got it welded, it's pretty much scrap metal."

"Good luck with that," Stark replied as he glanced at the chronometer display in his helmet. "Well, I'd love to stay and chat, but I'm late for a meeting."

With that, his boots whined softly and he rose into the air, slowly at first, then increased his speed with each passing second. In well under a minute the ground had disappeared below, and he was rising into the darkening clouds.

As the Golden Avenger emerged atop the clouds, he saw the location of his appointment in the distance. It was an impressive sight, and one he didn't think he would ever tire of seeing.

The S.H.I.E.L.D. headquarters was mammoth, and shaped roughly like an aircraft carrier. But rather than floating on the surface of the ocean, it hovered above the earth, and thus had been dubbed the "helicarrier." It sported four giant turbo props and engine pods that not only kept it afloat but allowed it to maneuver.

When Stark Industries had first been approached by the newly minted clandestine operation, S.H.I.E.L.D. wanted something designed that would remain on land—something large and imposing, to act as a symbol of security. But unlike the years following World War II, when the United Nations building was constructed in New York City, the nations that had signed the treaty forming S.H.I.E.L.D. couldn't agree on the location. The one thing they *could* agree upon was that no one wanted both the UN and S.H.I.E.L.D. headquartered in the United States.

The endless squabbling frustrated the apolitical Stark, until he finally suggested something mobile. An amendment was proposed and S.H.I.E.L.D. was granted unlimited access to the signatories' airspace, thus preventing the organization from being beholden to any one nation.

With that settled, it came time to actually build and launch the damned thing. For once, Stark knew he lacked the detailed knowledge necessary to do it alone. Instead, he reached out to another great engineering mind—Reed Richards, a member of the illustrious Fantastic Four. But Richards' forte was theoretical engineering, and there were some issues he couldn't easily resolve. So he, in turn, had suggested that they contact a man they knew only by the name of Forge.

Stark was inherently suspicious of an individual with Forge's enshrouded background, but he trusted Richards implicitly.

Stark prided himself on being difficult to impress, but when it took Forge two cups of coffee and ninety minutes to address the issues that had stumped the other geniuses, well, he was impressed. Once they had arrived at the carrier-like configuration, he had recommended a curvature that would all but eliminate the issue of wind resistance, and other modifications had improved the overall function of the helicarrier.

When asked, Forge made it clear he wasn't interested in joining SI, but they made sure S.H.I.E.L.D. paid the man for his time.

The Directorate's main headquarters was quietly tested in Egypt's deserts, and, thanks to the latest in stealth technology, rose unseen into the sky. Then word arrived that the temporary S.H.I.E.L.D. operations in Atlanta had been destroyed along with Stoner.

Now the helicarrier was airborne and, to all intents and purposes, rudderless.

Iron Man radioed ahead, was given clearance to land, and was directed to a spot on the landing pad atop the vessel. He touched down and allowed powerful magnets to hold him in place as the thin air rushed by at a speed that would have blown a normal man over the edge.

A door fitted into one of the protrusions atop the helicarrier slid open, and he entered. As it closed, and oxygen was pumped in, the Plexiglas shields at his nose and mouth snapped open with a barely audible *click*.

He was scanned from head to toe, and could feel the entire cabin move downward. A transponder built into his epaulette spoke with the helicarrier's computers, confirming his identity and authorizing access to the vessel. The transponder worked only when the armor was inhabited, and only then after confirming that the wearer was Stark. The biometrics were something new he added the last time he had upgraded his armor—one more item he had crossed off his mental checklist.

The cabin slowed, then it gently came to a stop and the door opened once more. Standing before him wearing an off-the-rack suit, red tie askew, was an African American man with a military-grade crew cut.

"Welcome, Iron Man. My name is Gabe Jones, and I'll act as your liaison," the man said in a voice that betrayed his age. He looked thirty, perhaps thirty-five, but sounded older—perhaps as much as a decade more. They shook hands, and Jones gestured the way down a gleaming corridor.

The lighting was fully on and reflected off his crimson-and-yellow armor, casting odd reflections on the walls. Periodically there were panels with communications and computing gear, much of which he had designed himself. Several of the panels were open, and people in blue coveralls worked on the wiring. There was a sense of urgency in their actions.

The helicarrier may have launched, Stark mused, but it wasn't operational. The timetable had been moved up in direct response to the Atlanta bombing.

Stoner's death bothered him, and he felt a pang of guilt. He had met the man only a couple of times, but the major had been a good man, and something in the back of Stark's mind said, *You should have been there*. Since donning the armor, he had been forced to adjust to the painful reality that he couldn't be everywhere at once. So he quelled the voice.

Mostly.

Iron Man paused as he watched one woman connect a diagnostic tool to an exposed bundle of wiring. He looked at the readout and hesitated. She felt his presence, and held up the device so he could take a closer look.

"Too much power is pulsing for the fiber," he said. "Go with a wider cable, rated 7G or better."

"Yes, sir, thank you, sir," she said and started to raise a hand in salute. She stopped and gave him a sheepish grin.

"You'll find it in IT, deck sixteen," Jones told her. She nodded and this time snapped off a salute.

"You military?" Iron Man asked as they began walking again.

"Long time ago," Jones answered. "Some things don't seem to change."

"What do you mean?"

"We fought to end war, to make the world a safer

place . . . but it didn't do the trick," he replied without
looking at his companion. "There's always someone to
fight. Someone always wants more, and they have to be
smacked down." Though his expression was stoic, something in his voice betrayed the strain everyone in
S.H.I.E.L.D. was experiencing.

"Well, Stark Industries built you quite the flyswatter,"
Iron Man remarked.

"That you did."

They turned and seemed to be heading toward the center
of the large vessel—something his internal sensors confirmed
at a glance. There were fewer people scurrying about, and
things looked more finished. Everything was gleaming, and
he could detect the smell of polish through his mask.

"Wish you didn't need to, though," Jones added.

"To be honest, soldier, me either."

The two men arrived at a large metallic door. It had no
nameplate, but a uniformed agent stood guard. He gaped
a bit at the sight of Iron Man, but regained his composure
and examined the ID tag that hung from Jones's lapel. For
a moment the man's eyes sought a similar tag on Stark's armor, then came to the conclusion that the avenger needed
no identification.

He placed his thumb over a sensor panel, which glowed
as it scanned the print. There was a pause as the data was
processed, and then the door spiraled open.

Jones led him into the room, while the agent remained
on the other side of the door.

The large, circular room was lit from below. The walls
were absolutely smooth, without rivet or seam. A large,
crimson chair sat atop a yellow dais, and there was room
around the chair for maybe six others to stand before
claustrophobia set in. Eight feet up from the floor, though,
the metal gave way to translucent panels, which flickered
to life.

A dozen silhouettes appeared, ghostly images surrounding

them in a circle, and a male voice came from a hidden speaker.

"Thank you for coming, Iron Man."

S.H.I.E.L.D.'s Executive Council liked its privacy, he knew. He had been offered the opportunity to join their ranks, which at the moment could truly be considered an "inner circle," he mused wryly.

He had declined the offer.

"Sorry I was late," he said.

A different voice replied, this one a woman.

"Not a problem. We've had delays of our own. But the urgency of our situation remains."

"What's the status, then?"

A third voice answered.

"The helicarrier is within days of being fully functional. We're just under three-quarters fully staffed, but we lost too many at our temporary quarters. A new round of recruits are being vetted on a rush basis."

"Do you know who did this?" Stark asked. That very question had dogged him ever since word of the assassination had reached SI.

Those who had died had done so anonymously. He hadn't been able to attend Stoner's funeral, because, to all intents and purposes, S.H.I.E.L.D. didn't exist. For a public figure like Tony Stark to attend would have drawn the wrong sort of attention.

He had seen to it, though, that the family's immediate debts were covered, hoping to ease their pain in the long term.

"We haven't been able to confirm it," replied the man who had spoken first, "but it appears to have been the organization that led to the founding of S.H.I.E.L.D. It seems to have fired the opening salvo."

"Does it have a name?" Stark pressed.

There was a pause.

"It's HYDRA."

iv.

There it was. A new war had been declared.

Jones was right—there was always a new enemy. Not that Stark had doubted him. HYDRA had killed Stoner, and they already had made an attempt on his successor. Stark had been there, and owed his life to the man.

They had met only that once, and while it had been one of the most memorable conferences of his career, it had left as many questions as it had answers. The security of the free world was to rest on the shoulders of one man, and Stark wanted to make certain he was the *right* man.

"We're going to need some additional materials from Stark Industries," the third said, cutting in, and he began reciting items from a list. But Iron Man had his own agenda.

"I want to talk with Fury," he said flatly.

"The colonel is occupied elsewhere," the first voice replied. "If you have any questions or concerns, we would prefer that you address them with us."

"Now, as I was saying," the third voice continued, undeterred. "Your updated navigational gyros, developed under contract with NASA, would be invaluable in our fleet of vehicles, and you've developed a new generation of fragmentary grenades. . . ."

Enough, Iron Man thought to himself. He was being treated like a clerk, and given a shopping list.

"Nothing is going to be done," he said brusquely, "until I talk with Fury."

While he knew—and for the most part trusted—the members of the Executive Council, he wasn't taking them at their word. Nor did he like their persistent focus on acquiring more and more SI military materials.

Finally the first person spoke up. His voice was calm, showing no signs of the antagonistic element that had entered the discussion.

"Very well, if it will help to expedite our requests, I see no reason to object. Jones, bring him in."

"Yes, sir."

With that, he spun on his heel and pressed a stud set in the doorframe. When the door opened, he exited and it shut behind him. Once again the chamber was sealed.

Iron Man stood in place, savoring his small victory. It was the little things in life, he considered. While he idly wondered if Mike was still at the bar, he doubted the helicarrier was anywhere near Long Island by now. It would forever remain a moving target.

"May we continue?" the third voice asked through the speaker, a hint of irritation now evident in his words. But Iron Man wasn't impressed.

"Put the list through standard channels for review—you can skip the RFP process," he responded. "Mark it expedited, and copy Pepper Potts."

He smiled within the mask. No matter who these shadowy figures might be, they would *not* dictate to him.

The silent stalemate lasted another few minutes, and Stark busied himself with a review of the materials currently on order from S.H.I.E.L.D. As he suspected, more than 60 percent were military in nature, and he made a mental note to keep better track of what was supplied.

The door finally reopened, and Jones walked back in, followed by a second man.

The newcomer was broader, and even fitter, than Jones. He wore an expensive suit but it, too, was off-the-rack and fit him better. His shoes were polished, and the watch he wore was an antique, and in good shape. There was a tobacco smell—not cigarettes, but a freshly smoked cigar. A display noted that it had been a Sol Cubano Maduro, or "Cuban Sun," actually manufactured in Nicaragua. Not an overly expensive brand, but decent quality.

As he had before with Jones, Stark tried to gauge the man's age, but found he couldn't. Mid-forties maybe, but the gray in his brown hair seemed more pronounced. His face was lined with character, and dominated by a simple eye patch over the left eye, which actually made his handsome features even more arresting, despite the five o'clock shadow.

"Shellhead," he announced in a deep voice, and held out a hand.

"Good to see you, Fury," Iron Man replied, and they shook.

"You know, there's something I've always wondered," the military man replied. "What's an asset like you doing in a tin can?"

Inside his helmet, Stark grinned as Fury tugged at the tie as if it were a garrote.

"That's top secret information," he replied.

"As the new director of S.H.I.E.L.D., he will have access to all information, no matter the classification level," one of the voices chimed in, sounding needlessly imperious.

"Then why don't you join us in person," Iron Man countered, earning him a grin from the new man.

When no response came, it was all he could do not to chuckle aloud. That would just rub salt in it, he knew. So, instead, he gestured to the door and spoke.

"Well then, we're finished here. . . ." He turned to leave. "Colonel Fury and I are going to continue the conversation in private now."

"We weren't done," one of the voices said—the one with the laundry list.

"As I told you, simply submit your requests. Pepper will

see to it that they're addressed immediately." Without waiting for a reply, he walked out, followed by Fury and Jones.

Stark suspected that his actions hadn't earned him any favors. But he gave them his best equipment at below market prices, and he invested an inordinate amount of his own time in their efforts. There would be no questioning his loyalties.

He'd have to carefully consider the munitions, though.

The three walked a short distance to a set of double doors, which were flanked by two of the jumpsuited agents, the S.H.I.E.L.D. symbol evident on their biceps.

Entering the director's office, Stark was intrigued to see that on a credenza sat a framed picture of Major Stoner and his family. Once more, his fractured heart went out to the woman and her two children.

Fury hadn't yet taken the time to personalize the office in any way. Along with the credenza, it boasted a desk, coffee table, bookshelves, a sofa, and a couple of chairs for guests. The colonel carelessly gestured toward the seats by the couch, then walked over to the far credenza and opened up the top. Reaching in, he withdrew three highball glasses and then a bottle of amber liquor.

Returning to Jones and Iron Man, Fury set the glasses on a small coffee table, poured drinks, and lowered himself into the couch.

"You do drink, don't ya, Stark." It wasn't a question.

Iron Man nodded and then reached up, depressing hidden biometric studs that allowed the two main portions of his helmet to separate. Carefully, he eased the golden faceplate off and set it atop the small table. He then lifted the glass and waved it under his nose. A fine scotch, he concluded, although he couldn't identify the label.

He tipped the glass in Fury's direction.

"Glad to see you settling in, Fury. Congratulations again on your appointment."

"Cheers, Colonel," Jones added.

The quick burn of the alcohol felt good as Stark took a sip. He let it linger on the back of his tongue before swallowing. This was the good stuff, and he wanted to savor it.

"So, tell me, how did a stubborn sonuvabitch like you ever make colonel?"

"Long story, but I was a sergeant for a while, and then they moved me into intelligence." Fury sounded as if he'd told this story many times before, and couldn't care less. "Knocked around the alphabet agencies for a while, and suddenly I'm getting grilled on a weekly schedule. I think they know everything about me but my mother's bra size."

"Oh, we have that, too, Nick," Jones chuckled. "But it's classified."

Fury grunted.

"Apparently, they found a report I wrote a bunch of years back, around the time of that Hate-Monger incident, suggesting that we needed an autonomous international intelligence agency."

"Then why weren't you the first pick for director?" Stark asked. Clearly there was more to Fury than showed on the surface. If he'd had the foresight to suggest an operation of this sort, long before HYDRA or any of the other terrorist groups had emerged as a creditable threat, then he was a visionary. That he could rise through the ranks and somehow stay free of the Pentagon's quagmired bureaucracy also served as a testament to the man.

"You can ask the dirty dozen back there," the colonel said, not at all sounding as if his ego had been bruised. "I was happy to be the runner-up."

"Did you know Stoner?"

"Never met him, but he sounded like a good man," Fury said, looking over at the framed picture. Silently, he pointed the glass in that direction, and was followed by the others as they drank in salute.

"So how'd they finally come to their senses?" Stark asked.

"You'd have to ask them," Fury said. "One day I'm chasing spooks, the next I'm whisked up here, made to stand before some scanner doohickey, then brought before the council. Some of the most famous Joes from every nation in the world were sitting on high, but I still didn't get it. I'd forgotten all about the report, truth to tell."

"Someone was smart enough to remember," Jones added.

"True enough," Fury admitted. "I sat in the chair and talked to these people and first heard about HYDRA. Then they told me about Stoner and asked me to replace him. Now, I'm just a bare-knuckles kinda guy. A barroom brawler. Where did I come off leadin' a hot-shot outfit like this? I figured I'd fall flat on my ugly pan."

"Well, some of us were taking bets," Jones said with a grin.

"See what I have to work with?" Fury asked, finishing off his glass.

"What changed your mind?" inquired Stark.

"As they sat there extolling my virtues, something felt wrong beneath my shoe, and sure enough, it was a trip wire, setting off a timer."

"Sabotage aboard the helicarrier?" Stark was shocked, having never heard that his coinvention had been infiltrated and threatened. This was making the fight more personal by the moment.

"Yeah," Fury acknowledged. "It was pure reflex, but I ripped the chair from the pedestal, ran out of the room into the corridor, and found a porthole. I shoved the thing through your strengthened glass, risking early detonation, but got it outside before the explosion."

Stark had edged toward the end of his chair, captivated by the tale, wondering how this had been kept from him.

"I spun around and began barking orders. It was pure adrenaline and instinct, but that's when it became apparent they needed me."

"Who planted the bomb?"

"Some lowly technician bribed and blackmailed by HYDRA, as it turned out," Fury said in disgust.

"Nice job," Stark said, more than a little impressed with the colonel by now.

"You don't like the Executive Council much, do you?" Fury asked Stark.

"They're all fine people," he replied. Then his face screwed up in annoyance before he continued. "It's just that they're so insulated, and sometimes I think they forget that we're all in this together."

"Ahhh, they just like feeling in control," Fury said. "Look, as soon as the plan was approved, they got S.H.I.E.L.D. built from scratch in what has to be record time. They recognized a threat and acted—so I say, good for them.

"But now me, Gabe, and the others are ready to get started, and at that point they fade into the background."

It'll be a cold day in hell before they give up that *much control,* Stark mused. He drained his glass and set it down.

Fury, the good host, immediately refilled it.

"I'm all in favor of that," Stark admitted aloud. "The last thing you need is to be running S.H.I.E.L.D. by committee."

"Here's the thing, though: We can't do this without you and your toys," Fury continued.

"Well, you won't get me," Stark countered. "I'm already committed to the Avengers."

"You can keep them," Fury said as he waved his hand in the air and settled back in the couch. The man was comfortable in his own skin, Stark observed. He wished he could feel so at ease these days. Then the colonel continued.

"You guys keep the streets safe from the other costumed nut jobs out there. We're not designed to go after the Masters of Evil—gotta love the name, though. No, we're after the ones who've dug in for the long haul, and are out there determined to make us all march to their tune. From the

Unabomber to HYDRA, and now we've learned that their tech division branched off, calling themselves . . ."

He seemed lost for a moment, and Jones smoothly filled in.

"Advanced Idea Mechanics," he said. "They shorten it to AIM." Stark noticed that the two were incredibly at ease with each other, and wondered if they had served together in the army. He made a note to check into it.

"Yeah, everyone's gotta have a cute acronym these days," Fury added.

"As for my toys," Stark said, "that could be tricky. I'm trying to evolve SI away from munitions. But there are plenty of others who can fill your needs."

"They're nice, sure," Fury said, "but none of them have an egghead like Tony Stark behind 'em. We want the stuff the others haven't even *thought* of yet."

Suddenly the door slid open. All three of them paused and looked up. Walking in, wearing his dress uniform, was a tall, rugged-looking African American man. Upon seeing Stark, he broke into a broad grin, his eyes lighting up. Then he saw Fury, snapped to attention, and fired off a salute.

"At ease, Lieutenant," Fury said, gesturing. "Come have a drink."

James Rhodes joined the trio, pausing to help himself to a fresh glass, into which Fury poured some scotch. He took a seat next to Iron Man, and continued grinning in his direction.

"Good to see you, Rhodey," Stark said. Back when he built his very first rudimentary suit of armor, he'd been in the hands of Southeast Asian terrorists. This was the Marine Corps pilot who'd helped him escape. From that, a friendship had been born. He'd offered Rhodes a place within Stark Industries, guaranteed for life, but the lieutenant had deferred until the day when his military service came to an end.

"I have to admit, though," Stark continued, "this isn't

exactly where I would have expected to find you. What are you doing here?"

"I'm the Corps' liaison to S.H.I.E.L.D.," Rhodes said.

"That's great news—congratulations!"

"I heard you were on board and requested a chance to see you," his friend said, ever the soldier. "The colonel invited me down."

"Glad to have you," Fury said, lighting up a fresh cigar before continuing.

"Before long, we'll all be up to our armpits in terrorists, and we're gonna need a score card to keep track of 'em. . . ."

"You know there's no smoking on the helicarrier," Jones chided his friend.

"Check my contract," Fury said with a snort. "This room is the exception, and thanks to the best in Stark technology"—he nodded in Stark's direction—"secondhand smoke isn't an issue.

"So, anyway," he continued, "along with HYDRA, AIM is well on its way to becoming a threat. There are all the usual suspects in the Middle East and Indonesia, and the Hand out of Japan is massing its forces—they could be an issue down the road."

"The Hand?" Rhodes asked.

"Think Yakuza, but deadlier," Jones explained.

"Yeah, it's outfits like these that give S.H.I.E.L.D. a reason to exist," Fury said. "To fight the good fight, we need to be ready. Personnel *and* matériel. Stark, we need to know that you're on board."

"I'm here, aren't I?"

"Yes, but I saw the kind of grief you gave 'em when they were asking for more equipment," Fury said, his tone sober. "We can't afford to have that happen every time we come begging."

"That was their attitude, not my unwillingness," Stark replied.

"That's good to know, 'cause you're the best at what

you do—and I'm not just blowing smoke up your skirt to get you to build us a bunch of new toys." As if on cue, he turned his head and launched a pungent cloud of smoke into the air.

"Good thing, because I'm not wearing a skirt," Stark said. "Nick, I give you my personal guarantee that S.H.I.E.L.D. can count on our support."

"Fair enough," Fury replied. "We've got to be prepared, or someday one of these jokers will gain the upper hand. Meanwhile, anything they can do, we've got to do it better."

Stark drained his second glass and decided it was enough for now. After all, he had to make certain he could navigate his way back home. On a whim he checked his satellite positioning system, to estimate how far the helicarrier's drift had carried them.

It was going to be a long trip home.

"You'll be prepared, Colonel," he said.

Walking away from Fury's office, Iron Man and James Rhodes caught up for the first time in months. As they did so, Stark's mind drifted back to the circumstances that had caused their paths to cross.

He had been touring Southeast Asia, and was trekking well off the beaten path when he stepped on a landmine— one of many the residents in that part of the world dealt with on a daily basis. Red-hot pieces of metal tore through skin and muscle, narrowly missing his heart and leaving him helpless when found by the forces of a local warlord named Wong-Chu. His fame preceded him, and he was recognized.

As a result, his battered body was placed in the same cell as Professor Ho Yinsen, a world-famous physicist whose work Stark had studied while attending MIT. Wong-Chu instructed the two men to use their expertise to construct weapons that would render his Sin-Cong forces unstoppable.

But Stark had his own agenda. The shrapnel lodged close to his heart threatened to kill him at any moment, so while he and Yinsen pretended to build weapons they fashioned a bulky gray chestplate with a magnetic field generator that kept the metal fragments at bay. Accessory after accessory was added, including some crude weaponry, and before long Iron Man 1.0 was complete.

Yet without power, the armor would be little more than a metal coffin.

As the batteries charged, Wong-Chu discovered their perfidy, and Yinsen sacrificed his life to distract the terrorists and buy Stark the time he needed to live.

Iron Man avenged his friend and fellow scientist by destroying the base camp, and then he fled into the jungle. It was a selfless act Stark would never forget, and frequently relived in those moments before he woke up each day.

He expended most of his power to destroy Wong-Chu's base camp, and fled until his armor ran out of energy. By then, he had found Rhodes, who was unsuccessfully attempting to repair a fallen helicopter. Stark offered to repair the craft in exchange for a ride, and together they escaped under heavy fire.

"So, when are you going to take me up on my offer, Rhodey?" Stark asked with a wry grin, though it was once again hidden beneath the iron mask.

"Same as usual, T—Iron Man. When I'm done."

"Well, remember that when Fury offers you a post in Slorenia," Stark countered. "I hear the winters are delightful." He was feeling comfortable, and pleased. Fury wasn't what he had expected—in fact, he was better. He was a man's man, someone who could think for himself and wouldn't be beholden to the powers that be. S.H.I.E.L.D. was his baby now, and it sounded as if he knew what he was doing.

Stark's boots were quietly clacking against the flooring

as they headed for the nearest elevator that would take him back to the flight deck.

"Fury's got nothing to say about it," Rhodes replied. "I'm a U.S. Marine officer, first and foremost. I'm not into being a spy, what with an exploding wristwatch and all that bull."

"Just checking," Iron Man said as they stood before the elevator door. "And I'm glad to hear it. After all, you're too good a pilot to lose to this outfit."

The door slid open and they stepped into the small cabin. Rhodes waved his ID in front of a sensor, allowing him to direct the lift. He then punched in the destination, and with a soft sigh the cabin moved upward.

"What do you think of the director?" Stark asked.

Rhodes thought for a moment, then smiled.

"Seems like the right guy for the job," he offered. "No stick up his ass like Stoner."

"You knew Stoner?"

"Guy was good, but wound too tight, if you ask me," Rhodes said. "Could be he was too busy writing the rule book for S.H.I.E.L.D. to live by. Might have been too much for any one man to handle."

"Can Fury handle it?"

"He came up with the idea in the first place, and he's stepping in when it's mostly a reality," Rhodes said. "He'll make it his own, but the book's been written now."

"Fury will rewrite it," Stark predicted. "You'll see."

"He might at that," Rhodes agreed, then he gestured around them. "This place is amazing, Tony. In addition to the helicarrier, they've built facilities in every nation that signed the treaty. Stuff that was hidden within other military budgets so no one would know what's going on. The training is being handled on every continent, mixing up the nationalities and making everyone think globally. It takes the UN peacekeepers to the next level."

"It *is* impressive," Stark admitted. "But you have to

wonder, without UN oversight, who will make certain S.H.I.E.L.D. fights the good fight?"

"You mean, who watches the watchmen?"

"Something like that." The lift slowed to a stop, and the doors opened to a small, narrow corridor. At the end was the frame for a door, and beyond that, air and clouds.

"Fury, I guess," Rhodes said. He paused and looked at his friend. "You got something on your mind?"

There was a silence as Stark considered the question.

"This is an awful lot of firepower for any one person to manage, even someone as good as Fury seems to be," he finally replied.

"You're just a worrywart."

"Maybe so, but this is coming uncomfortably close to absolute power. . . ."

"Not even close," Rhodes said. "He isn't the one in a high-tech suit of armor, or carrying a magic hammer, or turning green when he's pissed off."

"Point taken. But no one should have this kind of power without proper checks and balances."

Maybe not even the Avengers, he mused silently.

With that they shook hands, and Iron Man headed for the airlock while Rhodes retreated back to the elevator. As the doors in front of him opened, Iron Man heard the muffled roar of the winds that would unceasingly buffet the incredible craft for as long as it remained aloft.

V.

The sun shone brightly in the cloudless sky as Tony Stark entered the general administration building of what had grown into the SI campus. In the months since he had returned from Southeast Asia, Stark Industries had experienced unprecedented growth, and there were now two dozen buildings of various sizes where things got done.

The campus sat on the shore of Long Island Sound, and set back from the water's edge was the building where he maintained an office. He tended to avoid it, however, preferring to walk the campus and inevitably wind up in the gleaming cluster of buildings where much of the research and development was handled.

Below the main R & D building, sub-cellar five rested one level below anything that showed up on the architectural drawings. There Stark maintained a private lab and wholly automated manufacturing center where he could revise and manufacture new suits of armor.

Much as that subterranean complex called to him, though, Stark ignored it today as he strolled through the glass doors into the marble and chrome foyer of general administration. The eight-story building was new, with a far better design than what had been there before. In fact, SI had been forced to rebuild large portions of the campus following a recent incident that had left some of the structures in ruins.

Striding across the spacious lobby, the sun streaming through the two-story floor-to-ceiling windows, he peered at the video screens that displayed welcome notices to

visiting executives from other outfits. He hoped that one
of the notices might spark a memory, because try as he
might, he couldn't recall what his schedule called for this
morning. It was, after all, constantly revised to accommo-
date his armored obligations.

As he strolled past the security desk, he hefted his leather
briefcase in greeting. Frank, the beefy ex-jock who headed
up the day detail, waved in return, then looked back down
at the morning *Daily Bugle*. Without being obvious, he
also depressed a hidden button that unlocked the doors
leading to the executive elevator bank.

A singular elevator door opened, and Stark briskly
stepped into the car.

The Muzak that was playing was an instrumental version of Madonna's most recent hit, and Stark let his mind
wander as the elevator took no more than thirty seconds
to whisk him to the top level. While the floor included the
main conference room and the offices of his department
heads, his own office could be accessed only via this lift.

At least, that was the only *known* access.

The doors parted and Stark stepped into the brightly lit
anteroom. Hanging on the paneled walls were various ex-
amples of SI's brand advertising, there to give the shareholders the impression that he cared about increasing their
egos, and their wallets. He could smell the freshly cut flowers that were displayed in vases set atop pedestals spaced
every few feet. The florist had carefully arranged the colors
to match the arrival of fall, beginning with bright golds by
the elevator, gradually giving way to darker hues as the
visitor approached the reception desk.

Pepper Potts sat behind the sizeable desk, which
boasted stacks of files and paperwork that looked messy,
but he knew from experience that everything was precisely organized. She was wearing a headset, and was in
the process of scribbling a note when she spotted her boss.
She shot him a smile, which Stark returned. Just the sight

of her reassured him, giving him the sense that everything was under control.

Her red hair was hanging loose today, ending just above her shoulders, and she was wearing a navy two-piece suit with a peach blouse that revealed a golden necklace. She was the very model of the executive assistant, and not for the first time he felt blessed that she had found her way into his life.

Before he reached her, she hung up her call and gathered a stack of folders, mail, and a steaming mug of coffee. The smell of freshly brewed Kona coffee was better than anything Chanel could muster up, he realized.

"Morning, boss," she said brightly.

"Morning, Pepper," Stark replied, accepting the mug and taking a deep sip. Together they entered his private office, which most people would consider big enough to be an apartment. To the left through the door sat his desk, a heavy wooden leftover from his father's days as president. On the return sat a computer monitor, while a second screen sat on the credenza behind the desk. The surface was highly polished and devoid of paper. The in-box had been relegated to the credenza, and was infrequently used as Stark insisted that more and more of their communications be executed by email and through collaborative software.

To the right of the door was a meeting space with a tall round table and five padded chairs surrounding it. Just past that was a sunken conversation pit with matching couches and chairs and giant windows that overlooked the sound. The walls were adorned with framed pictures that included his father, Howard, his mother, Maria, and his grandfather, Howard Sr., along with images of the various buildings that had housed the growing company. The office was both a workspace and a shrine to the family's industriousness.

Walking to his desk chair, he settled in and took another sip as he extended his right hand to accept whatever Pepper had brought with her.

"Where do we begin today?"

She glanced at her ever-present to-do pad and reviewed his schedule of meetings with various department heads and outside vendors. To his constant irritation, she resisted adopting an electronic pad, and stubbornly relied on paper and pen.

"Senator Byrd's office has been calling hourly," she said, and he winced.

"What does he want now? Is it campaign season again?"

"No, but they're very insistent, and say that it has something to do with internal security."

"In other words, he wants to draft Iron Man to do some dirty work for him. Got it." He would call the senator back in his own good time. "What else have we got?"

"Singh called from fabrication, and he says they're having a problem with the new OS."

"He's always having problems with the operating system," Stark said, sipping more coffee and glancing at the email on his screen.

"Don't I know it," she said, letting her demeanor slip for a moment. "But I've already had IT over there three times this week, and it doesn't seem to do any good."

"Well, I don't make house calls," Stark said. "Besides, I'm an engineer, not a programmer. Call Redmond and have the OS project lead come out and fix it."

"I doubt that he makes house calls, either," Pepper noted. "Not at his pay grade."

"He will if we make a donation somewhere significant," Stark responded. "The new OS is supposed to be used by everyone here, and if it's balky then Singh won't be the only one who's whining. Chances are, they never field-tested on an operation this demanding, and that's their problem. But I don't care—we paid to get results. Do whatever you need to do to get this fixed, and use my name if you have to."

"I'm on it," she replied, which meant he'd never have to

worry about the issue again. Then she continued, and
there was an amused lilt to her voice.

"Your date wants to know what you're wearing to the
LLS dance."

Stark paused. First, he tried to remember what LLS
stood for, then he tried to recall when the dance was. Finally, he struggled to figure out which woman was to be
his date for the night.

As if reading his mind, she crisply filled in the gaps.

"It's Ashley Bancroft you're taking to the Leukemia and
Lymphoma Society Charity Dinner Dance tonight. She'll
be wearing a turquoise Vera Wang."

"Ah, Ashley . . . of course," Stark said, his mind filling
with an image of the curvaceous news anchor. She had her
own cable talk show, and they had begun dating—on and
off—after she had interviewed him some six months back.

"So, will it be the Canali suit, with the Eton shirt and
matching tie?" Pepper asked, and he knew full well that it
wasn't really a question. As soon as she left, she would be
making a call to the house staff to ensure that the ensemble
was waiting for him whenever he managed to get back and
change.

"Without a doubt," he answered, then asked, "What else
do we have?"

"You wanted me to find you a free afternoon to go
spend time with the aeronautics division. That looks to be
today."

"Terrific," Stark said, and he was genuinely pleased. He'd
been looking forward to spending some time with the people who were designing equipment for the next generation
of space vehicles, to replace the space shuttle one day and
even return man to the moon. If he was to cut back on the
munitions, he needed to focus the company's energies on
something far more altruistic.

And profitable. Truth was, he *did* care about revenues.
After all, a lot of people worked for him, and he was re-

sponsible for their lives. Thus, he had to remain conscious of the bottom line.

"Cunningham will be pleased to see you," she said. Theresa had been with the aeronautics division ever since Stark had redirected it from aircraft to spacecraft. Stark genuinely enjoyed being around her, and in a purely professional capacity—a rarity for him, and something that seemed to amuse Pepper.

"But before you can play, you have the quarterly Digital R & D report to review," she said in a tone that yanked him back to earth.

"That's Burstein's group, right?"

"As it has been for the last three years," she said without missing a beat. "He'll be here at ten, and he's bringing along his new number two. You'll like her, she's cute."

Stark lowered his coffee mug and raised an eyebrow at his assistant.

She merely grinned, spun on her heels, and headed back to her desk.

The way she understood him—*tolerated* him—bordered on saintly, and he often wondered why she didn't go run some corporation herself, with the title she deserved. *Best not to think about it . . .*

Stark quickly called up the digital department's last report to refresh his memory, rather than have Burstein do it. The man was a dedicated professional, but he tended to belabor points that had already been covered.

That done, he continued reading through the growing volume of email, including notes from Senator Byrd's chief of staff, queries from Baldridge, Howard Meachum from Rand-Meachum, a reporter from *Forbes,* and many more.

Everyone wanted something.

But these were the messages that got past Pepper, meaning they were to be considered significant. Without her, his digital in-box would be filled tenfold.

An instant message popped up on his screen. *Burstein is here.*

Moments later his doors swung open once again, and Pepper led a pair of people into the room—one of them a striking brunette, he noticed.

Pepper was carrying a fresh mug of coffee for him, and she hesitated, waiting for him to indicate where he wanted to conduct the meeting. Stark caught the questioning look and gestured toward the table and chairs.

"Michael, it's good to see you," Stark said enthusiastically as he rose. Rounding the desk, he accepted the new mug in his left hand while shaking Burstein's hand with the right.

"Good to see you, too, sir," Burstein said in a soft voice. He was in his mid-thirties, slightly overweight, and prematurely balding, and he wore a colorful yarmulke pinned to his thinning hair. His clothes never seemed to fit right, nor did he ever wear a tie—an affectation Stark allowed. After all, comfortable people were productive people.

Burstein turned and waggled his right hand in the direction of his companion. "Cute"—Stark heard the echo in his head, and wondered at his assistant's tendency toward understatement.

Instead, the woman was gorgeous, with tan skin, and long black hair neatly tied behind her back. Extraordinarily fit, she wore a deep red dress with gold thread embroidery and a skirt that ended a hair too much above the knee to really be appropriate for the office. Stark decided he'd let it go for now, since the shapely legs revealed by the hemline were well worth a look.

"Mr. Stark, this is Gabriella Marquez, whom we added to staff only recently," he said. "She's our new operations manager, here to track all our programs and make sure the trains run on time." He beamed as if he was introducing his own daughter.

"Welcome to Stark Industries, Ms. Marquez," Stark said, offering her his hand. He tried to keep his tone purely professional, but a look from Pepper indicated that he'd failed. She shook the hand with a single pump, her grip firm.

"Thank you, Mr. Stark," she replied, and then she walked over to the table and selected a chair, one angled to avoid looking out the windows. She carried in her hand a thick binder with the SI logo branded in white against its green cover.

"Would you like some coffee or water, Ms. Marquez? . . . Michael?" he asked.

"No thank you, sir," Burstein replied, and Marquez shook her head in agreement.

"Well then, let's get down to business," Stark continued. "I can't believe it's been a quarter gone by already." He joined her at the table. Burstein followed and took the chair between them, earning him a dark look that only Pepper noticed, causing her to stifle a giggle as she left the office.

Stark sat back and listened intently to the report. Though he had scanned it already, he wanted to hear what Burstein had to say. With every passing day, computers and data processing were becoming increasingly important to Stark Industries. As it was in the 1960s, many of their advancements evolved in the context of the space program, and the breakthroughs Stark made in enhancing his armor put the company light-years ahead of the competition—if they could even be considered competitive.

Burstein's group, therefore, was highly valued, and he needed the very best for his team. The man had graduated from Harvard, held a doctorate from MIT, and had helped grow the division to where it stood today. Not quite Microsoft or Apple, since SI wasn't focused entirely on computer technology, but certainly formidable.

Once they got past the overlong review of the division's revenues for the previous quarter, and where the numbers stood currently, Stark was intrigued to watch as the department head turned the rest of the discussion over to Marquez. What impressed him immediately was the way she attacked the information, placing it all in context, making certain she compared their progress against Sun Microsystems, Data General, Lucent, and other competitors. She not only knew her stuff, but she knew *their* stuff, and made certain the data was clear and concise.

When technological terms were brought up, she never paused to see if her employers were keeping up. She assumed they knew what she was talking about, or that they would interrupt if the need arose—which it never did.

Within twenty minutes she had covered everything, whereas Burstein had taken closer to an hour.

As Marquez spoke, he studied her. She had gray eyes that seemed hard, even cold. Still, someone that attractive wasn't likely to be all business, he supposed. He idly wondered at the fact that her hiring had gone entirely unnoticed, but then again, with the exception of his department heads, most employees came and went without his involvement.

Even when he interrupted with a comment or witticism, Marquez simply nodded and continued. Never cracked a smile, never varied from her pace. He wished he had more like her, and yet . . .

She intrigued him, and he found himself wondering if she ever let loose.

I really shouldn't go there.

Once the business was done, the conversation became more relaxed. Obsessed as he was with his work, Stark frequently had to remember that his employees were people, with lives away from SI's massive campus.

Burstein went on about his wife's knitting, while Marquez had to be coaxed into sharing anything about her daily life, and even then it was brief. If she hoped to keep him at arm's length, she was having the opposite effect.

She was a mystery, and one he intended to solve.

The rest of the day proved quietly productive, an all-too-rare occurrence these days, he mused. Stark managed to keep to his schedule, which Pepper set up in such a way that he had time to attack the mountain of email and return the most vital of calls. The only ones he dodged were from the senator, and those only because they threatened to derail the rest of his day—or week. He knew that, when the time was right, Pepper would clear a few hours and he would be able to devote himself to the political side of the business.

He managed to make it to the aerospace division on time, where a delighted Cunningham walked him through the latest developments, including the area where they were trying out some new gyroscopes for a satellite project. The hope was that they could be adapted to the next generation of spacecraft, as well.

He was suitably impressed, and lingered with the engineers, talking shop.

Even so, he had some time to kill before going home to change for the charity event. Taking the monorail from aerospace over to the computer sciences development building, he watched as the sun hung large and red, brightly filling the lower portion of the sky, a reminder of impending winter. The light show was dramatic, and he let his mind wander during the brief ride. Once the monorail slid to a stop at the station, he felt relaxed and in high spirits.

He nodded a greeting to employees he didn't recognize, and said hello to the ones he knew—the ones who had been there in his early days, and remained as the company grew. Some dated back to his father's tenure, but those were few and far between these days.

Of course, they all knew him, not only as their employer

but also as a celebrity, a titan of commerce, and a hero. It made him uncomfortable when they addressed him freely, while he didn't even know their names.

A quick check of the building's electronic interface told him where Marquez's office was located, and he wasn't at all surprised to find that she was still busy at work, although Burstein was already packing up to go home.

She sat at a computer terminal, headset in place, and seemed focused on a task that was requiring every ounce of concentration. Her knit brow actually made her even more attractive, and he wondered if he was drawn as much to the work ethic as he was to her undeniable beauty. The desk lamp threw light off her cheekbones, which seemed shiny, and he imagined that she probably didn't put a lot of thought into makeup, or she'd have made better use of the pancake.

"Something good?" he asked loudly enough to be heard as he nonchalantly stood against the frame of her door. If he had startled her, she didn't show it, and she replied without even looking up.

"An interesting bit of code we're trying to smooth over, to allow faster functions from the mainframe," she replied. "I'm doing some comparisons to see if anyone else is running into the same problem."

No pleasantries, no deference. Totally caught up in the work.

"Find anything?" He stepped into the room and stood before the desk, trying not to peek and offer suggestions. While he was a quick study, he most certainly wasn't a programmer.

"Maybe tomorrow, sir," she said, and she finally looked up. She removed the headset, which she hadn't actually been using, and which must have been left in place long after the need for it had passed.

Too distracted to put it down. Stark identified with that,

since he did much the same thing when he tinkered in the lab.

"Well, I just wanted to stop by and welcome you to Stark Industries," he offered.

"You did that this morning, sir," she said, coolly meeting his gaze.

"That I did. But I wanted to add that your presentation this morning was very well done. I wish more reports went that smoothly."

"Thank you, sir," she replied.

He paused, letting the silence fill to see if that prompted her to say something else, something at all pleasant or personal. She didn't rise to the bait, and seemed perfectly content to wait him out, meeting his gaze and showing no inclination to return to the data on her screen.

"Well," he said, finally breaking the silence, "I'd like to celebrate with a drink. Would you care to join me?"

"That is very gracious of you, Mr. Stark," she replied evenly, without revealing whether or not she meant it.

"Please, it's Tony," he said with a grin.

"That is very gracious of you . . . Tony," she repeated. "I'll be done here shortly. Is there some place we can meet?"

"I have a wonderfully stocked bar in my office," he said. "Perhaps you could stop by on your way out." He wanted to start off with the home field advantage, before shifting to neutral territory.

She paused for a moment before responding.

"Very well," she said, still not indicating her level of interest. Stark found it disconcerting—by this time, most women would have signaled something, *anything*, and not being able to read her was perplexing.

The phone rang, and Marquez looked at the digital display.

"It's Ms. Potts," she said.

"Must be for me," Tony said, and he reached for the handset. "There's no escaping her." Somehow Pepper always knew where he was, and since he was pretty sure he would know it if she had him bugged, he figured the only alternative was ESP.

Marquez activated the call, unplugging her headset.

"Tony, your police scanner just went off," Pepper said, sounding unusually breathless. *"There's an attack at the Port Newark docks. Police think it's a terrorist incident."*

HYDRA . . .

"I'm on my way," Stark said, and he hung up.

Marquez merely shot him a quizzical look—the first time he'd seen a crack in her veneer.

"Unfortunately, the demands on my time don't seem to adhere to a nine-to-five schedule, and occasionally something comes up that forces me to drop everything."

"And something just did," she said declaratively. To his disappointment, she didn't seem terribly concerned.

"Yep, it's the sort of thing you have to get used to with me," he replied. "The price of being the boss." He turned to go, paused, and added, "I have to run, but I owe you a rain check—and I always pay my debts."

The industrialist hurried from the office before she could reply.

vi.

The R & D building was close to Digital, so he dashed across campus, rather than waste time with the monorail.

He entered the lobby, breathing hard, and was recognized and waved through. He approached an elevator that showed no call button.

"Open."

The door slid silently aside, and he entered. It shut just as silently. He began to remove his shirt and tie.

"Down, sub-basement five."

Just as silently, the car dropped, and he continued to strip down. Within moments he was in his private lab.

Standing in his chest plate, boxers, and socks, Stark eased into the golden metallic mesh arms and legs, then the boots and gloves. Finally, he placed the scarlet cowl portion of the helmet over his ears, listening to it click into place within his collar. The golden faceplate was then magnetically sealed to the cowl.

Within moments, powerful electromagnets had fixed the armor around its wearer—first the arms, then the legs, then the gauntlets and boots, and finally the helmet. Clasps snapped into place.

"Activate." The darkness within the helmet vanished, and was replaced by digital displays feeding him internal diagnostics and external data. A computer link gave him an instant view from a security camera at the Port Newark docks. Another provided him a detailed schematic of the facility.

"Open exit." A panel slid back in the ceiling, revealing a

long dark tube. A tiny light appeared in the distance, indicating that a similar panel had opened at the other end.

"Jets, twenty-five percent." Instantly he felt a vibration that rumbled up through his entire body. He rose slowly, entering the tube without touching the sides, and exiting into the glow of the setting sun.

"Jets, seventy-five percent."

Within seconds, he was high above the plant and adjusting his trajectory to take him past Manhattan and across the river to New Jersey. He commanded his radio gear to tap into the New Jersey police band. A hiss of static hurt his ears, and he told the volume to lower itself.

As he waited for useful information, he checked a feed from a weather satellite and determined that it was to be a dry night, 47 percent humidity with a current temperature of 48 degrees. *Nice bit of symmetry,* he noted, then focused as he heard calls for backup and medical teams.

Good thing he hadn't had that drink or two—he would need to stay sharp-witted if he was wading into battle.

Focusing on the security camera again, he found it of little use. Smoke obscured much of the image, and when he switched to a different camera, it showed the same. Shadowy figures flitted in and out of sight, and there was the occasional flash of small-arms fire.

As he flew, Stark reviewed the data: Port Newark-Elizabeth Marine Terminal was the principal container ship facility for goods entering and leaving the northeastern quadrant of North America, and included docks exclusive to Stark Industries. That HYDRA was attacking probably meant they wanted something within one or more of the containers—perhaps his. By waiting until twilight to attack, they made certain the union workers on the day shift would have left, and the small night crew was on hand.

For a moment, Iron Man considered seeing where the S.H.I.E.L.D. helicarrier might be, and if he, too, could request backup from Fury's men. For the first time in his career he had a growing number of allies he could call upon when needed.

But the logistics of dealing with others could be as counterproductive as it was helpful, and besides, he had grown accustomed to fighting his own fights, regardless of the opponent.

If this really was just a bunch of HYDRA agents, they weren't likely to cause him much trouble.

A yellow beam of light pierced the sky, directing Iron Man's attention to a ship at the docks. It seemed to be the center of the action, and that was fine by him—it would be much easier to localize the carnage.

He altered his course, aiming for the ship and angling downward. With magnified vision, he saw that the ship was overrun with green-suited HYDRA agents, their uniforms making them difficult to spot in the twilight. Judging from the design, he wagered that the goggles gave them night vision, as well. Each agent was carrying a high-tech pistol that no doubt packed more firepower than a mere police-issue Glock .45. The design was unfamiliar to his trained eye, so he gave it a mental shrug.

Security teams and local police swarmed the dock, and there were police boats and a Coast Guard craft in the water, but the terrorists maintained the high ground, and the good guys couldn't make any headway. So he aimed himself at the greatest concentration of agents, who were ringed around an open portal from which the containers would emerge.

One advantage he had was that they were making so much noise and concentrating on one another, so that no one noticed his approach. All too rarely did the armored Avenger enjoy the element of surprise, and he smiled at the notion.

"Repulsors, energize. Standby mode."

He was looking forward to meeting HYDRA in person.

Slowing his speed, Iron Man clenched his hands into fists and plowed into a half-dozen agents as they swarmed around one edge of the hold. They scattered like lawn gnomes and his momentum carried him clear across the gaping opening and into another half-dozen green-clad enemies of the state.

They also fell every which way, and he zipped past them and angled up, once again cutting jet power to remain in the area.

A number of the combatants recovered from his unexpected arrival, and took aim with their weapons. Several red beams of energy—probably high-intensity lasers, he surmised—lanced through the gloom and hit him from head to toe. The beams reflected off the protective coating he had developed for his armor, dissipating harmlessly in the darkening air. He shrugged off the assault, and lowered himself to the deck.

Some of the beams cut off, then returned an instant later. They must have increased the intensity, because this time his internal sensors showed spots where his armor was heating up, nevertheless remaining well within its tolerance levels. After all, he had built this suit to withstand the intense friction of atmospheric entry.

Rather than stand still and run the risk that they might find some way to do damage, he waded into the still-standing agents, picking them up two at a time and tossing them overboard. The nearly one-hundred-foot drop into Newark Bay would startle but not seriously harm them—as long as they knew how to swim. Besides, the authorities were waiting to pick them up. In quick order, six agents were overboard, but before he could pick up numbers seven and eight a fresh barrage of fire managed to stagger him. This time there were some impact weapons, as well, causing him to reach out and grab a piece of the vessel's hull to hold on to.

His grip tightened, and he felt the metal bend under the pressure.

He quickly scanned with both audio and video sensors, to see if he could identify who was in charge, but no one appeared to be giving orders. Perhaps they were being directed from a distance, or they were just independent thinkers.

Dismissing the latter assumption, Iron Man resumed taking down the agents in ones and twos, figuring that the diminishing resources would cause the others to flee out of sheer self-preservation.

For a moment he wondered if they were part of an organization that would execute its agents rather than let them be interrogated. He didn't want to cause anyone—not even HYDRA agents—to die. But it was a question for Fury and for another time, so he shoved it out of his mind, reached out, and crushed one of the high-tech weapons while it was still in an enemy's hand.

"Radioactivity detected."

The warning took him by surprise. For a brief moment he wondered if the pistol he had crushed had been nuclear powered, but a quick check indicated that it had not.

With a command, he shifted his field of vision, using sensor input to scan for the source of the atomic material. Toward the ship's stern there was a blocky case that was shimmering in waves of green on the scanner. Something had been activated, and now it threatened to irradiate everyone in the vicinity, from the sea life below the surface to the police on the docks.

A more detailed scan revealed that the object was a dirty bomb, an explosive that when detonated would spread radioactive waste, exposing everyone in the vicinity to potentially lethal levels of radioactivity and rendering the docks and surrounding area uninhabitable. Worse, the waste would be carried by the winds, out over the inhabited areas of Newark.

The armor would protect its human wearer, but only for so long, since he was a man of iron—not lead. The dirty bomb had to be contained, and he carried nothing that would be adequate for such an emergency.

The HYDRA agents—those who were still standing—continued to fire on him, so he activated his rocket jets and lifted into the air. In a matter of moments he was out of range.

He accessed the Stark Industries inventory database, entering specific keywords. Quickly he found what he was looking for, and headed for the nearest warehouse that displayed a large red circle with the SI corporate logo painted on the wall. He sent a signal that caused the door to open on his approach, then another that commanded a specific container to open.

Inside was a bulky piece of equipment that had a harness and padded shoulders that would slip over his head. Despite the weight, he hefted it as though it were a toy, and without a moment's hesitation he took to the air again.

Returning to the ship, he noted that the HYDRA agents had all scattered away from the case, which continued to emit increasing doses of radioactive material. He moved in close, and located the explosive portion of the device. He kept an eye on a readout in his helmet, but for the moment his armor's shields were blocking the radiation.

A quick examination identified a standard, even pedestrian design, and within seconds he had disabled it. Then he launched himself into the air again. Gloved fingers flicked several switches on the harness he wore, and the device lit up with red and orange light.

Falling back to a distance of about ten feet from the boxy bomb, he locked his jets in hover mode, and then opened a nozzle that spewed forth a viscous gray substance. It shot with great force across the distance and began coating the bomb. Once a thin layer had been applied, Iron Man allowed himself to move in closer, and continued to coat the bomb until all that was visible was a misshapen lump of wet, gray goo.

Stark Industries had developed the liquid lead foam and delivery system for just such emergencies, and had outfitted ports all along the eastern seaboard with these safety devices. They had been installed using a federal grant he had wheedled out of Senator Byrd.

Best wheedle he'd ever performed.

With the majority of the radiation now blocked, Iron Man gingerly scooped up the messy bomb and slowly took to the air. Once above the ship, he radioed the Nuclear Regulatory Commission for instructions as to the best place to drop it off.

There was no sign of the HYDRA agents. Those who hadn't been taken into custody had simply vanished.

Keeping the frequency open for instructions, he ordered his onboard computer to access the Port Authority's records systems and download the ship's identity and registered manifest, which he would study once he discharged his immediate obligation.

"Iron Man?" A voice came over the live connection.

"Here."

"Your best bet is to bring the bomb to Indian Point Energy Center, north of Peekskill, just twenty-four miles north of Manhattan. We've got containment facilities there, and we'll be able to decontaminate you, as well. What's the status of the explosive package?"

"Dead as a doornail," he responded.

"Perfect—we should be able to handle it from here, then. See you shortly."

Stark concluded that he would be able to get there, be scrubbed clean, and get back home before he had to pick up . . .

His date for the night . . .

Ashley!

As he flew, he studied the downloaded manifest, trying

to guess the object of HYDRA's desire. His brow wrinkled in a frown when he discovered that the ship had been transporting Stark Industries communications equipment. Nothing overtly aggressive, but tech that would give its owner a distinct advantage.

He had a feeling this was only the beginning of something far more sinister.

While jetting back from Indian Point, Stark checked in with Pepper Potts, reviewing calls received since he had left the plant. He knew full well he was bothering her at home, but also knew she expected the call and was mad when he didn't let her know he was safe.

He and Pepper had a complex relationship, which had been evolving since she first came to work for him, only weeks after he came back from Southeast Asia. They had become closer than most brothers and sisters, but unlike siblings, there smoldered feelings between the two of them that neither dared act upon, given their professional connection.

And then there was Happy.

Happy Hogan had rescued Stark from a racing car accident, and it was a grateful industrialist who hired the former boxer as his chauffeur. Much as with Rhodey, it was a heartfelt job offer that stood for life. Together Pepper and Happy had become his support system from that day forward, and they were among the first to make the connection between SI's resident hero and their employer.

In a sense, they were his surrogate family.

It just happened that Happy had fallen head over heels in love with Pepper, practically from the first moment he had seen her, and he made no attempt to hide it. She, in turn, showed him no more overt encouragement than she showed Stark, thus leaving both of them firmly in the dark.

Who could really tell what was going on in her heart? He wasn't even convinced that she knew herself.

"All's well, Ms. Potts," Stark said by satellite connection.

"So I heard," she replied. "We've received the usual media inquiries, but I pawned them all off on Pithins."

"Good girl," he said. Artemis Pithins had never imagined that handling SI's public relations would also mean handling a superhero's press. Still, he was a good man for the work, and was given extra staff to handle the demand.

"Is Happy at the house?"

"He'll be there after his dinner break, ready to whisk you to the event."

"Excellent. Say, it's been a good day. We got through the entire agenda for once, our stock was up two and a half points, and I just saved New Jersey. We should celebrate.

"Want to join me for the gala tonight?"

There was a hesitation, and at first he thought their connection had somehow been cut, but then realized she had been caught by surprise.

Of course, he was already committed to bringing . . . damn, what was her name?

But Pepper was certain to be a better companion, and in this case three would *definitely* be better than two.

"Thanks for the awfully nice offer, Mr. Stark, but you have Ashley . . ."

Ashley!

". . . waiting to be picked up, and you know what they say."

He had a feeling he did.

"Three's a crowd?" he offered.

"Three's most definitely a crowd."

Well, that sealed it. But he thought he detected something in her voice, a hesitation perhaps.

He would just have to make the most of it with . . . Ashley.

Ashley Bancroft.

He repeated the name a few times, then flew home, still in the dark.

*   *   *

Baron Strucker treated all HYDRA agents as interchangeable cogs in his engine for global domination. As a rule, he never referred to them by name. Everyone was assigned a number, and that's how they were summoned.

He had adopted this methodology while serving in the Führer's Reich, and Madame Hydra considered it a most effective way to manage—almost corporate in its simplicity. As a result, she knew nothing about the agents who were standing in the small room she used as an office, other than the fact that they had survived a brutal training regimen, and had sworn undying devotion to the cause.

That didn't make them competent.

The office was kept dim, so much so that it was hard to tell exactly what shade of gray the carpet was, and it had a strange series of patterns that were impossible to make out. Her desk was utilitarian and had a basic computer and phone installation. She spent little time here, but it was the perfect location for a private conversation.

The man before her was smoke damaged, his breathing ragged, and he needed medical attention. But he was loyal first, and had come immediately to report.

Not that it would do him any good. Mercy was for the weak.

Two other men stood behind him, nodding when he spoke. They were equally disheveled, their green uniforms more blackened, the yellow trim covered in a layer of grime.

"The cargo ship was sitting there, unguarded," she said in a tone intended to strike fear. "You had a full contingent of personnel, and the latest weaponry. Explain how Iron Man stopped you."

"We planned . . . poorly," he said, and those few words sent him into a paroxysm of coughing. After a few moments he regained control. "We needed a full schematic of the ship, beyond just a container number. As a result, we lost precious time in searching, and that allowed the authorities to arrive . . . followed by the Avenger."

The two men nodded in unison. She shifted her glare to them, and they tried to disappear into the shadows.

Then she returned to the man who stood forward—the man who had been in charge of the operation.

"I provided you with the assignment," she replied without moving. Her voice sounded calm but low, forcing them to strain to catch every word. "If you determined that additional information was required, then you should have made use of the computers at your disposal. Do not seek to deflect the responsibility . . . on me, or on any of your fellow agents.

"Any failure is entirely yours to own."

Without warning, her left hand whipped across her lithe body, yanked her pistol from its holster at her hip, and fired off one shot. The entry wound was tiny, a blackened spot in the center of the hooded forehead, which snapped back as the body crashed to the floor.

The exit wound was something else entirely, as hood, skull, blood, and brains exploded outward, covering the two men who were in the direct path of the gore. One cried out, and they both flinched as pieces of their colleague spattered them.

They struggled to regain their composure, and one wiped a bit of bloody flesh from his lower lip.

"Field leaders need to do a better job preparing for a mission," Madame Hydra said to the two of them. "Since we failed to acquire the item we sought, a replacement will be required." She paused before continuing, setting the pistol on her desk within easy reach.

"A direct encounter with Iron Man establishes an unfortunate precedent, as well, and no doubt we will see more of him. Agent 145 . . ." She pointed at one of the two men, and his face went pale in the dimness. "Report for a new mission briefing in the morning. Now go—both of you!"

With palpable relief, they saluted, mumbled "Hail Hydra," and left the office, stepping carefully around the body of their former superior.

Once the door was closed, she put the pistol back in its holster and debated calling someone in to clean up the mess. Instead, she decided to see if either of the men would actually think to have it done. Constant testing was necessary, to identify initiative and leadership abilities, but all too often the agents under her command came up short.

Cut off a limb and two more shall take its place.

That was all well and good, but she knew it was hyperbole. And even if twice as many turned up, were they all as ill-equipped to execute her commands, the problem would be compounded—not solved. The answer would be even more intense training, and repeated reminders of the price of failure. Only the strong would have a place in the coming order.

The technology she sought would continue to keep HYDRA on the cutting edge. With AIM now a splintered group and, in many ways, the competition, she had to fend for herself. While much could be acquired from existing suppliers, some goods weren't yet available on the open market, and they would need to be taken by other means.

As she shut down her computer for the night, she noted that it—and much of the equipment she felt was necessary—came from Stark Industries. She had researched Tony Stark, the engineer and owner who was considered by many to be charming and charismatic. He was a celebrity; a hard-drinking ladies' man who just also happened to be a genius and a hero.

The Iron Man technology alone would make HYDRA unbeatable. She let her mind wander and imagined the skies over Manhattan as they grew dark with swarms of green-and-yellow versions of that armor.

Yet Stark guarded his secrets jealously, and she knew she could not obtain the armor outright. But beneath the suit there was only a man—and stripping SI clean of its prototype weaponry, its technological advancements, would cause the crippled company to implode, creating untold damage. How many lives would be ruined.

The prospect made her smile. Desperate people became excellent tools.

En route from the hidden HYDRA base to her private apartments elsewhere in Manhattan, Madame Hydra continued to toy with the notion of stripping Stark Industries bare and laying waste to the husk. If she could sink Stark, the impact on Wall Street would ruin the financial center of the universe. The ripples would then extend down the coast and engulf Washington, D.C. She imagined tipping over the dominoes that could bring down the greatest nation in the world.

And it all would start with Tony Stark.

She couldn't send a squadron of agents after the billionaire. No, he had already shown what happened when he was faced by the threat of brute force.

Sometimes a more personal approach was called for.

vii.

Heads turned as the limo came to a halt, and a figure in white emerged.

She stood elegantly tall, and the white gown draped itself alluringly over each curve, leaving one shoulder entirely bare. Her green-tinted hair, hanging mysteriously over one eye, lent a dramatic touch—as did the expensive jewels she wore around her long neck and on her hands.

The horde of photographers lining the red velvet ropes elbowed one another and tried to figure out who she was. None knew of a green-tressed celebrity. Maybe she was foreign or royalty. Regardless, their cameras jostled for the best angle and flashes exploded for nearly a full minute as she slowly walked down to the wide red carpet toward the building's entrance.

Many shouted out questions, inquiring as to who she was, why she was there, and whether or not she had a date.

The woman said nothing, nor did she even acknowledge hearing the questions. Instead, she strode without pause and let her swaying body language speak volumes for her.

A blue uniformed doorman held the door and let her in without question. His look was one of utter delight. Some people just loved their jobs.

Once inside, she gave a name to the harried-looking woman in the wool blazer and turtleneck who carried the beaten clipboard with the guest list. The name was found, a felt pen marked it off, and the woman in white was granted access to the elevator that would take her to the top floor, where the party was being held.

Emerging into a wave of music, Madame Hydra walked out and went straight for the bar, ignoring the waiters carrying trays of champagne flutes. The music was from a live band she did not recognize, but she suspected they were popular on the radio, something she never indulged in.

She arrived at the bar, ordered a gimlet, and as the bartender quickly poured, her eyes slowly scanned the room, absorbing, cataloguing, and filing everything, including the exits, should something go amiss.

The expansive room was filled with the power elite of New York City, captains of industry all, most of whom were being fawned over by models, actresses, actors, politicians, musicians, and others who considered themselves superior. People mingled, the buzz of conversation loud enough to compete with the throbbing music, but the room was large, spacious, and acoustically designed not to overwhelm the moment.

She accepted the drink, nodded to the bartender, then gave him a look at her bare back as she studied the people.

Spotting a familiar face, she launched herself forward and made a direct line for Kyle Richmond, CEO of Richmond Enterprises. The younger man possessed classically handsome features, with brown hair parted to the side. He also exhibited an easygoing personality as someone who was accustomed to wealth. Madame Hydra assumed she would not be allowed to immediately approach Stark, or he'd become suspicious, so she decided to work the room, starting here.

Clinging to Richmond's arm was a wafer-thin model, her blond hair slickly styled. She had been poured into a dress that left very little to the imagination, and as such she was the perfect decoration for a millionaire.

Despite his accoutrement, he noticed her immediately.

"Hi, I'm Kyle Richmond," he said happily, thrusting out a hand. "And you might be . . . ?"

"Bored," she said, not at all hiding her European accent.

That got her an interested look from the man and a scowl from the woman. After a moment he seemed to remember that the blonde was there.

"This is Trish Starr," Richmond said. "She's a model." He seemed to have already enjoyed the open bar, or he was just naturally oblivious. Starr, a blandly attractive woman, nodded in chilly welcome.

"That's a Hungarian accent, isn't it?" she asked.

Such a discerning ear from such a vapid woman surprised Madame Hydra—and she was rarely surprised.

"Yes," she replied. "I was born there."

"That's interesting," the model said without a hint of sincerity. "And what brings you here?"

"A good cause," Madame Hydra replied, getting an approving nod from Richmond.

She was beginning to think that enough time had been spent with the couple, who clearly had nothing to offer her. During their brief talk she had already located Stark, and the woman he was squiring seemed far more interesting in appearance. She approved of his apparently discerning eye, which had been the reason for the dress she was wearing.

Richmond spoke up again, interrupting her observations.

"Trish here was just telling me about a flute piece she's been practicing—"

"No doubt she is very accomplished with her mouth," Madame Hydra said, cutting him off and earning her an angry look from the woman. "I'm terribly sorry, Mr. Richmond—"

"Kyle," he responded.

"Ah, yes, Kyle, but I see someone with whom I must speak." Without another word, she headed off in the direction of Drexel Cord.

With each step she was coming closer to her prey.

Cord was older than Stark, with thinning gray hair and

a severe look to his face, which was well lined. Through Cord Industries, he controlled technology and design firms under a variety of brands, and he was known as a ruthless negotiator. She suspected HYDRA would benefit from raiding his facilities, as well, and she made a mental note to further investigate this option.

"Drexel, nice to see you away from that castle you reconstructed," she said with a believable laugh in her voice and a false twinkle in her eye. She recalled that Cord, in a showy display as part of his long-simmering rivalry with Stark Industries, had a European castle reconstructed on the coast, stone for stone.

He gaped at her without a hint of recognition. The look of uncertainty told her that he might be a tiger in the boardroom, but he wouldn't do well at the poker table. Of course, the man had also suffered from at least one nervous breakdown, not good for the pressure cooker of a card game. She gave him a peck on the cheek and added a flourish, all in plain sight of Stark.

To her satisfaction, she thought she had attracted a glance.

"So nice to see you again," Cord said without adding a name since—after all—he had no clue who she was.

"Indeed it is," Madame Hydra continued. "How is Janice?"

The mention of his daughter changed the look in his eye, and he began to perform as if on cue. As he babbled about how well she was growing up, Madame Hydra made certain to catch Stark's eye again, and surreptitiously kept watching as he snuck looks her way despite the attractive woman at his side.

The woman was also scanning the room, no doubt for her own reasons.

Finally, success. The couple came their way and Stark shot her a look that caused a warm feeling to flare in her stomach. As quickly as it appeared, however, it vanished. Never once would she allow a soft emotion to share space with the hatred that she harbored.

"Drex, you old dog," Stark said jovially.

"Stark," Cord acknowledged without the cordial tone. In an instant she read the hostility the older man felt for the smarter man. They were rivals, and she suspected the enmity between them was the result of jealousy on Cord's part.

"Tony Stark," she said. He tipped his wine glass in her direction, then introduced Ashley Bancroft.

The woman was wearing a red wrap dress with shoulder pads that even Madame Hydra knew were of yesterday's fashion. While expensive, the clothing showed some wear, indicating that she was not among the idle rich who filled the room. Her lustrous black hair was well coiffed, and her makeup expertly arranged, but she wasn't a classic beauty.

"I thought I knew everyone in the room," Bancroft said. "After all, most of them have been on my show."

That revealed her as a television personality, since she would have been wasted on radio.

"I'm sorry, but I don't think I've seen it," Madame Hydra replied.

Bancroft gave her an appraising look, trying to determine if she should be offended or not. The HYDRA leader enjoyed watching the woman's wheels turn.

"Sometimes I think you're not missing all that much," she said with a laugh, and then took a healthy drink from her glass.

"She's actually grilled me harder than Rather or Brokaw," Stark admitted. "Does her homework every time."

Bancroft kissed him on the cheek, and Madame Hydra wanted to snap her neck. Instead, she smiled.

"If that's the case, then why do it?"

"I think he just likes the fringe benefits," Bancroft said

with a giggle. "Seriously, I like probing these men deeply, to find out what makes them tick."

"And Stark?"

"He's a cool exec," the reporter replied. "With a heart of steel."

Stark blanched at the description, and took a quick drink to hide his reaction, but not fast enough to escape Madame Hydra's notice.

"Perhaps he just needs the right question to pierce that armor," she said.

They all laughed, and she laughed with them. Cord, she noted, was staring daggers at Stark, while Bancroft seemed more interested in her drink than her man.

Seeing an opportunity, Madame Hydra sidled over to Stark and asked softly, "Buy a girl a drink."

"Absolutely," Stark said, placing his wine glass—mostly finished—on a nearby tall table. Bancroft looked confused, and perhaps angry at being abandoned, but Cord, predator that he was, began chatting her up. She had enough of a newshound's sense to keep him talking.

The last thing Madame Hydra heard as they moved away was Bancroft asking him about a merger involving Cord's chemical division.

The man needed a shave, and certainly a bath, but Madame Masque endured it because he was a necessary evil.

In fact, he was the Maggia's best fence in New York, and he knew it. Francois was oily, and he trafficked in secrets as much as in "found" property. This afforded him many advantages when the time came to move something that was best kept unseen.

To protect herself, Madame Masque had chosen Washington Square Park, which was already filled with drug dealers wearing hoodie sweatshirts and harassing people who were trying to walk through the lower Manhattan green space. Because the temperature had dropped, the park was relatively empty of pushers, buyers, and lovers.

She was wearing a belted overcoat and had a scarf entirely around her head, allowing her to abandon the golden mask for the moment, while still covering her features.

"Do you understand what this is, Francois?" she asked, walking at his side.

"*Oui,* Madame, it is a hard disc containing vital plans for a new vertical takeoff and landing aircraft that Stark intends to deliver to the Marines," the man replied. He was heavily bundled against the chill, although his clothes didn't manage to contain the smell.

"Excellent," she said. "Then you understand its value."

They walked a bit farther, waving off a young Latino youth who offered to sell them a dime bag. Once he was gone, Francois looked directly into her eyes.

Suddenly conscious of the absence of her mask, she struggled not to look away.

"Of course I do, Madame," he said. "This would give certain countries military parities that they would not otherwise enjoy. Some would pay millions to have plans this detailed."

"Then you understand the need for me to *receive* those millions, and nothing less," she said, trying to keep the tension from her voice. She had to deliver, and dared not disappoint her father. The millions would go far toward whatever Nefaria was crafting, yet she also knew it would not be enough.

Would it ever be enough to satisfy his voracious needs?

Or for her to receive his approval?

They passed a lone vendor and he bought a heated pretzel the size of his hat. Francois broke off a piece and offered it to Madame Masque, who declined with a wave of her hand. He shrugged and took a bite. They walked to a corner of the park, passed a row of chess tables, turned, and traced the perimeter as people hurried by in the direction of the subway station.

"Don't worry," he said curtly. "Four Middle Eastern countries want this, as does Madripoor."

"How quickly can you make a sale?"

"Do you want a fast return, or the *highest* return?"

"Can't I have both?"

"No."

"Then the highest."

"Give me a week, ten days tops. I have the wire information, and will phone you when I have completed a transaction. Don't call me until then," he instructed.

"Don't fail me, Francois."

"Never, Madame. But do trust me."

He tipped his hat at her, took a bite of the pretzel, and walked off carrying the hard drive that contained the stolen materials. She watched him vanish belowground, heading for a subway, and his walk was so confident, so knowing, that she also knew no one would dare try to bother him.

Straightening her shoulders and attempting to match that gait, she left the park and thought of other ways to bring in money for the Maggia.

It promised to be a long night.

"You don't think she was being a little too pishy . . . pushy," Ashley Bancroft asked in a slurred voice.

"What, asking me for a drink?" Stark said innocently, his hand tracing a path up her exposed thigh. She was fine with that, despite knowing that the driver could probably see everything in the rearview mirror.

They had left the party twenty minutes earlier, and she couldn't seem to stop speculating about who the green-haired woman was. With the hair, that figure, and the dress, everyone had watched her, but no one seemed to know her. And yet, she seemed to know them.

Bancroft's reporter's instincts were working in overdrive,

but were also slowed by the liquor she had continued to pour into her system.

Stark suspected he could bring her to his home—either the apartment he kept in Manhattan, separate from Avengers Mansion, or the house out on Long Island—and they could enjoy each other's company for several hours more. She certainly seemed receptive, and she was most attractive.

He handled his liquor better than she did, and appraised her with a keen eye. She would be a fine catch, a wonderful woman with whom to spend time and get to know intimately.

The press had already presumed that she was another notch in the proverbial bedpost, and were no doubt writing it up for the morning gossip columns. He wondered if her ratings would go up because of their connection.

But no one knew the truth.

"Ash," he said softly.

She looked at him, blinked, and looked again, trying to focus.

"Ash, I'm not feeling all that well. I'm going to ask Happy to drop you at home."

"Home?" she said. "*My* home?"

"Yes, dear, your home. Your bed."

"Mmmm, bed," she said dreamily. "You and me. Bed."

"No, not quite. Your bed and you. Me and my bed. I just don't feel well."

"Is it your heart?" He was known to have a heart condition, though few knew the source. Had the truth come out, it would reveal an Achilles' heel—one that, eventually, someone would successfully exploit.

He hated when the conversation took this turn. He disliked the chestplate that kept him alive, and he hated using it as a crutch.

Truth be told, he'd love to take her home and ravish her. But once they got there, and began undressing each other, she'd find the chestplate, and things would stop. The cold

metal would be an impenetrable barrier between them. He
learned that lesson very early on, after returning from Asia
and trying to resume his playboy ways.

No matter who the woman, no matter how intelligent or
understanding, they'd stop, run their hands over it, and that
would be that. Time and again, the chestplate proved a
barrier—or, as one woman put it, a "buzzkill."

There had been one time when he had loved a woman
enough to risk taking off the chestplate. Joanna Nivena
had been his fiancée at the time, and he had fooled himself
into thinking that an hour or two without it might be
worth taking the chance.

Instantly, without the magnets working, he'd felt intense
pain in the center of his chest, radiating out. It had been so
crippling that he almost hadn't got the chestplate back on.

He never tried that again. She understood, and stood by
him as he wallowed in despair and liquor. Stood by him as
long as she had been able.

There were times when he wondered if he might be able
to rig something up that would allow him to make love with
a woman, like a normal man. While notions rattled around
in his brain, it was something he never got around to tinkering with in the lab.

Truth be told, he'd admit to himself on particularly
gloomy nights, he had grown accustomed to being physically and emotionally walled off.

"Happy, take us to Ms. Bancroft's home, please," Stark
said loudly.

"Yes, sir," Hogan replied.

"Oh pooh," Ashley added.

Hogan dropped him at the front door of the family mansion and after confirming a morning pickup time, he drove
off, seemingly oblivious to the personal pain Stark was
feeling, which no amount of alcohol could mask.

But despite what he had said, Stark didn't go to bed.

Instead, he went to the personal work lab he had installed in the lower level of the town house. This had initially been his summer boyhood home—the real home was a mansion in Manhattan—but he had turned that over to the Avengers and relocated to the Long Island building. He suspected Maria would have approved of the decision.

Though smaller, Howard Stark's former tinkering space was otherwise a near-identical match to the lab on sub-level five at the corporate campus. Every upgrade had been replicated here, so the equipment remained state-of-the-art and gave Stark the flexibility to work whenever and wherever he pleased. Additionally, the duplicate space was devoid of the project *du jour* he had at the other site, meaning he could work fresh.

The house staff had retired, and Stark wouldn't have troubled them at this hour, which was why he'd had a coffeepot installed in the lab. The smell of brewing coffee—this time a Sumatran blend—brought him a measure of comfort and would begin to counteract whatever alcohol remained in his system.

He picked up a sonic screwdriver and began applying it to a partially constructed object, filled with miniaturized motors and nascent cooling systems. The circuits were exposed, and not yet connected to anything. This was how he worked when there was no goal—pure blue sky. He'd tinker with this and that, and see what the results might be.

This object might become a mining tool, a drill perhaps—something compact for tight spaces. He wasn't sure if it could generate enough speed, though, and began to work on the power supply.

Filling his first mug of the night, he drank it black and studied the item that fit in the palm of his right hand. It had a reasonable heft, and he tried to estimate its finished weight, calculating that it was likely to be too heavy for the stabilizers he had crafted.

As he considered ways to reduce the weight, he shrugged

off his jacket and in so doing noticed a piece of paper sticking out of the inside pocket. Intrigued, he took it out, and saw it was folded over just once.

There on the paper, in elegant green script, was a phone number.

viii.

Sometime after midnight Tony Stark stopped looking at the digital clock that hung on the wall by the near-empty coffeepot.

He was entirely focused on increasing the speed of the proto-drill, testing it on stray pieces of wood and metal. The mug by his elbow had grown cold, and he was so consumed with the project that he didn't pay attention to the frequency of his yawns, either.

What finally caused him to pause from his work was the shrill beeping sound. At first he couldn't recognize the tone, but he knew it had to be urgent—otherwise he wouldn't have designed it to be so annoying.

Glancing about the lab, he focused on a blinking light seen through a clutter of discarded projects. The light came from a panel set into the far wall.

It was a security alert from SI Long Island.

He quickly crossed the lab, and already was tugging at his tie in case he needed to don the armor. The digital readout told him that it was an internal alert, and that it involved the computer systems.

He doubted his top man in the engineering division, Abe Zimmer, was still around, since it was, after all, 3:23 in the morning. Same with Garrison Quint, his head of security. He couldn't recall the name of his night-shift security chief, but *who* it was didn't matter as much as what they did.

He considered calling in, but decided not to run the risk of distracting his team at a critical moment. No doubt his phone would be ringing any moment.

From his own terminal, Stark quickly accessed the internal-security diagnostics and discovered that someone was attempting to hack the system. While a prodigy at many things, he was at best only mildly talented at a keyboard. Nevertheless, he tried to locate the source of the breach, and therefore to discern the intruder's identity.

A series of IP addresses flashed on the screen, and then it went blank. Fingers flew across the keyboard, and a map came up. His trace seemed to point toward Kansas, which made little sense.

Then again, a hacker can be anywhere. . . .

Again, the screen went blank.

At 3:29, when the phone still hadn't rung, Stark was becoming annoyed. Rather than wait any further, and perhaps let things get out of control, he dialed the plant.

The call could not be completed.

He tried a second time, with the same result, and he knew something was wrong.

The buttons tore as he ripped off his shirt. He reached for his briefcase, which contained the armor and would open only for him. So flexible was his armor that it could be folded like cloth—until he activated the magnetic field that made it as hard as titanium steel.

He had the armor on within two minutes, and was heading for the stairs.

Once on the deserted street, he practically leapt into the air, arms over his head, as the boots engaged and thrust was applied. The internal sensors warned him that the outside temperature was 38.6 degrees, and he engaged the heating circuits, which were preprogrammed to keep the suit comfortable.

He arced high in the night sky, ignoring the beauty of the stars twinkling above him, and instead activated his comm system, which tapped into the phone connections. Again he tried the security office, and again there was no connection. The silence was deafening.

Another check of the computer link proved equally futile.

Someone had cut all communications with Stark LI.

Frustrated, he instructed both systems to continue trying to open a connection, and to alert him should either succeed.

Pressing his speed to nearly maximum, he crossed the distance in under four minutes—but it was still too long to suit Stark. It was eons in computing time—more than enough for serious damage to be done.

Everything seemed quiet. They still had power, so there were lights illuminating the monorail, the main road, each building entrance, and key walkways. There were flashing red lights atop each building to warn off aircraft or—these days—flying super folk.

The mainframes that were under cyber attack were located in the basement of the administration building, so Iron Man circled it once, scanning for break-in points. Nothing obvious was visible, nor were any of the night security detail evident.

With a heavy impact that cracked the macadam, the Golden Avenger landed and transmitted a signal that automatically unlocked the doors.

In the lobby he found a small group of security officers, one of them giving instructions to the rest. All eyes turned to Iron Man as he approached.

Keefer . . . that was the name.

"Well, Mr. Keefer—what the hell's going on?" he demanded. "Why haven't I been able to raise you for"—he checked his chronometer—"more than eight minutes?"

The man answered with a deep voice.

"All communications have been down, Mr. Stark, with the exception of a couple of individual cell phones," he said. "We're trying to trace a computer breach."

"Any clue what happened?" Stark responded irritably.

"Uh, no, sir, no, we don't," Keefer admitted. "We got the alert, then nothing. No computer link of any sort. We've called in Mr. Zimmer to see what he can determine, and we were about to head down to the mainframe room."

Smart, they went for the right person before bothering the boss. That made him feel better, but the sense of violation still nagged at him. Whoever had accessed the system was smart, as well.

"Well then, let's get going."

He moved quickly to the emergency stairs, Keefer and two of the men in tow, and descended as quickly as he could without causing damage to his own property. He attempted a thermal scan, but it yielded nothing, given the reinforced concrete, metal, and tile work that lay between him and the mainframe.

Reaching the basement and racing down the dimly lit corridor, he headed straight for the clean room where the mainframes were stored, neat rows of powerful computers kept in a strictly controlled environment. Reaching the clean room, he motioned for the men to wait, and stepped inside.

Pressurized jets removed all particulate matter from his armor, and the High Efficiency Particulate Air filters captured the offending dust. Simultaneously he used his computer interface to gain access to the SI security grid. Nothing appeared untoward, and a visual scan showed no sign of forced entry or anything to indicate that the facilities had been breached.

The forced-air jets shut off, a door opened, and he stepped into the mainframe room, standing just within the doorway and letting it slide closed behind him with a gentle *shush* sound. The room hummed quietly, with immense power running from one end to the next.

In many ways, this was his greatest asset, and his greatest weapon. Information.

To his left stood a small table and a desktop computer terminal, with everything looking to be in standby mode. Taking manual control of the computer link, he sent out a signal, and to his surprise he gained access to the system.

Again, he traced the access pathways targeted by the security alert, and again he discovered nothing—nothing at all.

The door shushed open again, and the security contingent entered. Lost in thought, he didn't acknowledge them.

Whoever had accessed the system was smart, all right. Whatever had been copied remained unknown for the moment, but he suspected Zimmer would come up with information.

That thought did little to ease the growing sense of disquiet that lurked in the back of his mind.

Stark managed four and a half hours of sleep before his mind summoned him instantly awake.

He remained preoccupied as he went through the motions of washing up, getting dressed, and eating without really being conscious of what he was doing.

Hogan was waiting in front of the house, and must have seen the look on his face, because he didn't try to engage in idle chitchat.

Questions plagued Stark during the entire drive onto the Long Island Expressway and out to the SI campus. The events of the recent past converged as he tried to figure out if there might be a connection between HYDRA's raid on the ship and then—just hours later—an attack on his data storage.

He called Pepper and asked her to locate Abe Zimmer and have him ready with a report of what he had discovered.

As soon as he arrived, she handed him a mug of coffee and with a wave of her hand indicated that the computer whiz was waiting within his office.

"Abe, what happened?" Stark asked without preamble.

Seated in a chair by the desk, Zimmer was balding, with a ring of gray hair, and wore wire-framed glasses on his lined face, which had a worried expression. He was lean, and covered his dress shirt and tie with a white lab coat embroidered with the SI and computer-division logos, and his name.

Zimmer was in his early sixties, and had come to SI after earning his reputation for the pioneering work he did on artificial intelligence during the 1970s, alongside Professor Marvin Minsky at MIT. After running his own company for a time, he was personally recruited to head up Stark Industries' data processing and computer groups.

"We have an entire computer bank that was wiped clean of memory," Zimmer said without standing up in the presence of his superior.

"What? How?" Stark put down his mug, stunned by the extent of the attack.

"They got a communications network we were designing for the DOD."

Damn. If this involved the Department of Defense, he would have to contact Senator Byrd. There would be no more dodging the man.

"And?" He prayed there would be some *good* news.

"And I don't know yet," Zimmer replied. "We're still trying to recover something from our backup systems, but the files may have been wiped there, too."

"You. Don't. Know?"

Zimmer winced.

"Yet."

"Yet."

Stark paused to digest what he had been told. If Abe Zimmer had had a few hours to dig for facts, and he was still stumped, then it had to be bad.

Damn.

"Coordinate with Burstein, and get me an update by

lunchtime," Stark said brusquely. "Figure this out, Abe."

"No kidding. I'm real curious who did this, because I want to have them put away, or I want to hire them," Zimmer said as he rose and headed for the door. "I'll let you know which it's gonna be."

As he left, the door didn't even have the chance to shut.

Garrison Quint walked right in, his face set in stone. Stark knew that look. He took very personally anything that affected their security.

"Mr. Stark," he said, and he stood practically at attention.

"Garrison," the industrialist responded, and he extended his hand. They shook with a single pump, and then Stark gestured at him to sit.

"Looks like we got caught with our pants down," the industrialist said, careful not to make his voice sound accusing. "What can we do about it?"

"What needs to be done, sir," Quint replied. "We're calling in the troops, and will be doing a full inventory."

"Gar, that'll take weeks," Stark said. "We'll never find our man that way."

"We don't really have a choice," Quint said. "This inventory will be part of a full security review to determine that all locks work, that all key cards are accounted for. We'll do a sweep of all personnel and run through channels to determine that no one has run into any trouble recently.

"Sir, at this point we have no clues, so we can't dismiss any possibilities," he continued. "It's the only way we can figure out how this happened, and for that matter, if it happened more than once."

At that, Stark's eyes widened in surprise.

That had never even occurred to him.

"Get on it, then," he agreed.

"We've already started, and Ms. Potts authorized the

overtime," he said with a tight smile. "We'll start with my own team, then spread out."

"Perfect," Stark replied. "Gar, you guys are the best—they were just a little better, this time. Don't let this eat you up."

"I'll rest when this is settled."

They shook hands again, and the man practically marched out of the office. *Military experience just never fades away*, Stark mused.

He walked to his desk and slumped into the chair. He was physically tired, yet his mind was racing through what he knew . . . and what he didn't know.

Pepper walked in, wearing a forest-green dress and black shoes, and handed him the usual stack of papers, plus his second mug of coffee for the day.

"I have Senator Byrd's office on the line," she said.

Of course she did.

"No sense putting it off, eh?"

"Not at all," she agreed. "Let him yell, so you can move on to the next thing."

"Which would be?"

"Oh, I'm sure something interesting will turn up."

"You and the Chinese love to use that word," Stark said as he grabbed the phone, activating the line. "Interesting."

Yeah, he thought, *this is going to be interesting.*

He got through to the senator's office, and was put on hold. But it didn't last long.

"Senator?" he said into the phone. "Tony Stark."

"It's about damned time, Stark!" came the gravelly voice. What the senator lacked in protocol he made up for in volume. "Why have you been ducking my calls?"

"Well, I wouldn't exactly call it 'ducking,' Senator," he replied. *No, dodging would probably be more accurate.* "I'm sure you heard about the incident in New Jersey. But that's not why I called. Are you sitting down?"

"It's that bad?"

"Potentially."

"Then shoot."

Here goes . . .

"It's the SI 912 project, the communications network we're developing for DOD. The computers with the data on our development, well, they've been wiped clean."

"Christ on a crutch. How on earth did you let that happen?"

"We're still figuring it out, but this was sabotage, plain and simple. Skillful and effective, so we're still piecing together the 'how'—but the 'why' should be obvious."

"At least you must have had the data backed up."

"Actually . . ."

"Oh, crap." There was a momentary silence. "Foreign or corporate?"

"My gut says corporate," Stark answered, but he knew he was lying. His gut still was trying to decide if it was foreign, corporate, or HYDRA.

"The Army's going to be pissed off if that technology makes it out of the country," Byrd pressed. "That's a contract I brought to you, Stark, and it's one New York State needed."

And thus the political wrangling began. . . .

"Steele Industries was outbid, but if they get wind of this, they'll be back in the game, and that would mean thousands of jobs for Pennsylvania. It's not what I want in an election year.

"You know, Stark, this isn't the first time something's happened to your operation since you came out of the shell."

Stark had to give him that. The presence of his armored alter ego seemed to attract as many nutjobs as it deterred. His security force was the largest of any corporation on Long Island, as was his insurance premium.

"Senator, we're going to get to the bottom of this," Stark

said, trying to curtail the diatribe. Byrd was both an ally and watchdog—a mixed combination, since his involvement could help or hamper, depending on the situation. "I'll keep your office apprised of any breakthroughs."

"You do that," Byrd replied, beginning to calm down at last. "Tony, I don't have to tell you that with increased Republican control, it's getting harder to get things done here in the Capitol." He paused for a moment. "You have friends on both sides of the aisle, and in the Oval Office, but even so, if it looks like you're losing control, people are going to start asking questions.

"When the DOD hears about this one, they're going to blow a gasket. Don't be surprised if Appropriations or some other committee doesn't haul your ass down here."

"Always a joy," Stark said.

"They're going to be asking why Iron Man is out saving the city, when people are running off with your proprietary tech. Hell's bells, this is going to cost you, and maybe long term. You need to focus, and stop running off in that metal suit of yours."

"I do that, sir, and the city doesn't get saved."

"That's why we've got the Avengers. Or S.H.I.E.L.D., for that matter—oh, god, this could cost us *their* contracts, too."

Cost us? When did we become us?

Somehow Byrd always acted as if he had a personal stake in SI business—and in a sense, he did. What was good for SI was good for the state, and it had an impact on the national economy, as well.

And he wasn't entirely off base with his implications. After all, the growing number of superheroes might mean that he would be able to step back.

Could he really just take a breather, and focus on SI?

"Listen, Tony," Byrd said, cutting into his thoughts. "I'll do what I can to minimize the damage down here, and you make sure your people come up with results." He paused once more, then added, "The alternative won't be pretty."

"I can appreciate that, Senator," Stark said. "I'll make sure we keep you posted."

"See that you do. Good-bye, Stark."

"Good-bye, Senator."

He brooded in silence for a time, ignoring the growing list of email on his computer screen, and the mail Pepper had handed him some time earlier—what seemed like an eternity ago.

Finishing his coffee, he plunked the mug down and turned to his second screen. He accessed a private set of files that were fingerprint protected, and began studying the ship's manifest once more.

Most of the cargo containers had been filled with security-related items, but all of them common. Nothing unique to one manufacturer or country. One container was SI-owned, and contained mining equipment they had developed for a client in New South Wales.

He doubted HYDRA intended to go mining.

So they must have been after something in one of the other containers. Yet a more detailed scan of the manifest showed nothing of interest. The only thing that was even vaguely high-tech was the mining equipment.

That took him back to the line of thought he'd been stuck on during the drive from the city.

What connection could there be between mining equipment and DOD communications technology?

That seemed easy.

None.

Pepper cleared her throat.

She had that look that said she had been standing there for a while. He winced.

"You know how I thought something interesting would turn up?" she asked.

Stark nodded, eyebrows pulled into a questioning frown.

"Well, Gabe Jones and Kenn Hoekstra from S.H.I.E.L.D. wish to speak with you."

"Great—I can guess what they're here for," he said. "News travels fast, doesn't it?"

She nodded, and then hesitated a moment.

"Speaking of which, who is she?"

Stark was confused, but then he smiled broadly for the first time that day.

"Oh, you mean Ashley. Ha! I'll wager you thought I'd already forgotten."

"No, not her," Pepper said. "The one with the green hair."

That took him by surprise. *How did she . . . ?*

"I'm not sure I caught her name," he said, earning him a smirk. "But how'd you hear about it?"

"You haven't seen the *Bugle* today, have you? Miriam Birchwood wrote about it, and there's a picture. They don't usually run color in that section, but it seems as if they thought it was justified."

"I'm sure they did," Stark said, not at all happy. He needed to call Ashley, make sure she was okay, but keep things cool, too.

"Well, as entertaining as my social life seems to be, I'm pretty sure that's not what Mr. Jones and Mr. Hoekstra are here to discuss," he said. "Better face the music. Send them in, please."

"Will do."

Jones wore a dark brown suit and Hoekstra, younger, shorter, was dressed in the dark blue duty uniform with the logo on the sleeve. They walked into the office. Stark gestured for them to sit at the desk, rather than move to another portion of the spacious office.

This was going to be all business, he suspected. And Jones confirmed it.

"Tony, what happened?"

He gave Jones a quick recap of the events of the previous night, and even broached his idea that it might have been connected with the incident at the docks. At the mention of the dirty bomb, Jones made a face.

"What's wrong?" Stark asked quickly. It wasn't the reaction he had expected.

Jones sat back and said, "Nuclear is new for HYDRA."

"How can we be certain," Stark countered. "Just how much do we know about them right now?"

"It's why I brought Kenn along," Jones explained. "When we heard about the assault on the container ship, we figured we ought to bring you up to speed. He's our expert."

Hoekstra straightened in his chair and addressed Stark directly in a firm voice. He gave a capsule history, complete with the suspected links between HYDRA and the Neo-Nazis. He identified the various nations in which terrorist activities could be traced to the organization, and noted the suspected connection between HYDRA and AIM.

Stark found that particularly interesting because of AIM's technological focus.

The worst part was the fact that they had made no progress in identifying HYDRA's command structure, or locating any of its key operational centers. The terrorists seemed to be able to engage law enforcement, no matter where their activities took place, then disappear without a trace.

When Hoekstra finished, Jones turned his attention to the computer break-in, comparing notes to see if there was a connection.

"I can't honestly say that there is one," Stark admitted. "It just seems strange that two such radically different assaults could occur, so close in time, yet with no apparent connection."

"I've never been a big believer in coincidence," Jones agreed.

Stark rang Pepper and asked her to have Zimmer join them. As he did, he thought about the ship, the theft, and—for no reason he could explain—the phone number he had found in his pocket.

Mysteries all.

ix.

Francois did not look happy.

Here on a street corner in the Alphabet City portion of Manhattan, the day was gray and bleak, and he disliked seeing his breath form steam in the air. It was still October, too early for it to be so cold during the day.

"I told you I needed a week," he grumbled as she walked up.

She was wearing the mask this time. Her hat and scarf kept it from being too obvious, and this was the East Village, after all. Very little looked out of place here.

Even so, some passersby noticed, and moved on quickly.

"I have more business for you, and I thought that made it worth interrupting your routine," she said. Her gloved hands were wrapped around a large Styrofoam cup of coffee.

Hearing there was fresh profit to be made, he allowed his stern look to soften, but still offered no pleasantries.

"What do you have now?" he demanded.

"Something everyone wants these days."

"Truth, justice, and the American way?" he asked scoffingly. "Peace on earth, goodwill toward men?"

"Not quite," she said, and the mask hid her expression. "A state-of-the-art communications network."

"There are plenty of mobile phones on the market, with more coming each day," he said dismissively. "Most everyone can get what they need at the local Radio Shack."

"Not like this," she said, and she removed a set of floppy disks wrapped with a rubber band. He never ceased to be impressed by how much information could be compressed onto smaller and smaller media. It made his job easier with every passing year.

"State-of-the-art, the full range of military applications," she explained, handing him a specs sheet. "Ahead of anything out there, and likely to continue to be for months—if not years—to come."

He scanned the sheet, and whistled in spite of himself. Then he recovered his composure.

"I think we can find a buyer," he said. "Usual terms?"

"Of course."

He nodded, and she did the same, then turned to her right and headed into a clothing store. He watched her form, noting that she was shapely even under the outerwear.

Then he stuffed the disks into the leather satchel he had slung over one shoulder, and walked in the opposite direction, mentally calculating what he thought he could get for this latest morsel, and what his take would be.

He and Madame Masque had been doing business for some time now, but two deals in a week was a first, and he wondered what had prompted the move. He knew she fronted for the Maggia, and knew not to cross them, but still he detected an urgency in her, and would not be at all surprised if she turned up with something else before too much longer.

Boot heels clacking on cement, Madame Hydra strolled through the warehouse near Manhattan's lower docks. The exterior was as nondescript as every other warehouse in the area, which was fine by her.

Within, however, the entire left side of the building was stacked floor-to-ceiling with cargo containers from boats and trains. Many of them bore the Stark Industries logo. Countless HYDRA agents were busily opening, uncrating, and inventorying their contents.

To her right, metal tables were lined one after the other,

each filled with various mechanical and electronic components. More agents struggled with manuals or instruction sheets, attempting to assemble the devices.

Directly before her, at the end of the structure, were racks containing the objects that had been completed. Slowly but surely, enough matériel was being assembled to supply an army.

Her army.

She preferred keeping the warehouse unheated, to motivate the men to work and get out. Goosebumps rose on her exposed flesh, but she ignored the sensation, maintaining her stride. As she approached the racks, an agent in charge handed over a clipboard and marker, then stood rigidly at attention.

"Is it all here?"

"Every bit of it, ma'am."

"What do we hear from New Jersey?"

The agent glanced over his shoulder, looking to another agent. They really did all look alike to her, and she wondered how they could tell one from the other. Nevertheless, the second agent stepped forward and nodded in affirmation.

"Last night's operation was far more successful. All three cargo containers were taken."

"Excellent. And the construction?"

The first agent waved his right arm like a ringmaster, as if suggesting that nothing more need be said.

She stared at him coldly.

"Work is proceeding on schedule," he said quickly. "Without the shipments from AIM, we're struggling a bit, but are managing. We should have everything here completed within the week."

"And if I asked that it be done sooner?"

"Then it would be done sooner, Madame Hydra."

"Good," she said, and she strode off to examine the completed machinery that promised to be her future.

The papers in her hand were like an adult's Christmas list, boasting various munitions, ammunition, tools, and other matériel. This would rebuild their stores, and allow them to prepare for the coming engagement. It was the best equipment available from America's brightest corporations, and it would be sorely missed by the military and law-enforcement agencies for whom it had been intended.

But the operation she had planned would need some very specific resources—ones that wouldn't be available on any market, legal or otherwise, nor were likely to be transported anytime soon.

Those, she would need to procure herself.

"Look at her," one man said under his breath as he took an armload of ATN Night Shadow night-vision binoculars from a container and transferred them to the shelving. "Acts like this was all done by magic."

"You know what these things cost?" another asked as he hefted a pair of the binoculars. "A grand a piece, easy. And these we *bought*. She must think we have cash to burn. Why didn't we just take them?"

"She has us buying some of this crap and stealing the rest," the first man replied. "I sure don't get it."

"Me neither. And why are we stuck with the scut work? There's gotta be some sort of support crew we can get to haul this crap."

"What, you getting lazy?"

"No, but this isn't what I signed up for," the second man declared, "and I didn't go through all that shit in training camp just to haul a bunch of crates for a crazy bitch with green hair."

"If we're gonna end up on top when the time comes, then we're gonna need all the muscle we can get."

"Yeah, but with what we paid for this stuff, we could

have bought half of New York and blown it up anytime we wanted."

"An intriguing notion," a voice purred in his ear, and he froze, a fully loaded crate balanced on his shoulder.

Crap, I hope she didn't hear. . . .

"Perhaps you should transfer to logistics," Madame Hydra continued.

"There are times," she said, louder now, "when buying things through dummy companies makes sense. It's less risky, and the authorities have a harder time seeing a pattern in what we're doing."

She laid a hand on his biceps, and he tensed.

"Does that not make sense?"

"V-very much so," he said, the crate beginning to sway slightly.

"But this work is so menial, and you joined our ranks to be a conqueror, not a dockworker," she said. Her hand gripped his arm and tightened, her nails digging into the muscle, making the man wince. Sweat began to drip from beneath his goggles.

"Nevertheless, before we can conquer, we must cripple," she continued. "And to cripple, we must prepare, and we must make certain we have the resources we need. Do you understand?"

Holding the man tightly, she let the words sink in, and all he could manage was an affirmative nod. The arm holding the crate was beginning to cramp, and it hurt like hell.

"Good." She released his arm and walked away. He shifted to set down the load.

Thank god. She must not've . . .

Suddenly she spun on him.

"You will work the next three eight-hour shifts," she said sharply, then she turned to the group foreman. "He is to have no food or water, nor any breaks at all. If he fails to accomplish his duties successfully, deal with him, then take his place for the remainder of the time."

"Yes, Madame Hydra," the foreman said crisply. With that, she turned back to the man with the box.

"If you question me even one more time, you will never again have to worry about hauling crates for a crazy bitch with green hair."

X.

As he flew over the city of Boston, its skyline brightly lit in the night, Iron Man realized that he hadn't been there in some time. He liked the city, its mix of old and new architecture, and the seats of learning at Harvard and MIT. He just never seemed to have time to come for a visit.

The Seaport Hotel was a beautiful facility overlooking the Inner Harbor. Just beyond the hotel were docks where ferries carried people to and from neighboring areas, including Provincetown or Logan Airport. The hotel also had about 180,000 square feet of convention space, and was hosting the Advanced Aerodynamics Association's military trade show. Stark Industries was exhibiting at AAA, and as much as he wanted to see what Lockheed, Ferris, Boeing, and the others had on display, he had more pressing concerns.

In back of the hotel, the four loading docks were all ablaze, lighting up the night sky in yellows and oranges that echoed the just-ending fall foliage. The air was filled with the shrill sirens from the fire department, the police, and the emergency medical teams, all converging on the scene and each pitched differently, so that the result was raucous and chaotic.

Just ahead of the arriving emergency responders, green-clad HYDRA agents were spilling from the fiery docking stations, arms laden with crates as they scattered to avoid capture. Iron Man's lenses magnified the images, and he saw that many of the items they carried, while vaguely identifiable, were largely unfamiliar to him. These were the latest in advancements being demonstrated to the trade.

"Boot propulsion to sixty percent."

He swooped down, charging his weapons systems.

"Disengage night lenses." As the scene in front of him took on natural detail, he targeted the trio of agents closest to him. He came in low and fast, allowing himself to become a blunt object, knocking them to the ground, sending their stolen goods scattering.

Fists of steel knocked another two men on their asses. He activated the propulsion units in his gloves to right himself, then landed.

A sudden impact staggered him, and a glow surrounded him as charged-particle weapons were fired. He staggered a bit with each impact, but all the weapons would do was make him angrier.

He was already angry because another drink he had planned with Marquez had been put on hold. That it was HYDRA made it even more of a thorn in his side, since he had yet to figure out what they wanted in New Jersey, Long Island, and, as of tonight, Boston.

Stark was an engineer, trained to solve problems in a neat and orderly fashion, and yet there seemed to be no logic to the thefts. They weren't simple weapons thefts, which would have made sense. The fact that he had yet to figure this one out was wearing on him.

And he was also tired. He hadn't gone a day without putting on the armor for a week now. He had a business to run, Byrd wanted him in Washington for hearings, and now this.

As a result, he wasn't being particularly careful with the men or the stolen objects. Allowing the high-tech pistol fire to continue, he waded into the agents and tossed them around like sacks of flour. Each man sailed through the air and landed with a dull thud on the concrete.

He did make certain none landed near the tongues of flame that were spreading from within the convention space.

Grabbing one terrorist by the back of the neck, he hefted

the body, then noticed the telltale curves. A female HYDRA agent. He'd seen very few of them, but she wore the uniform, so he tossed her, too. But he aimed so she'd land on someone soft, rather than the hard ground.

First-response vehicles began to arrive, with the fire department in the lead. There were sporadic bursts of gunfire, and several agents were retreating into the darkness without firing, so he took to the air, keeping low and following them.

"Engage night lenses."

The escaping agents were heading for a sleek-looking, low-slung aircraft that was of a design he did not recognize. He did see the exhausts glow red as the vehicle powered up.

A loud *whoomp* from behind reminded him that the burning hotel and its contents were of a higher priority than HYDRA's agents. So he turned back.

More fire trucks were arriving and black-coated men and women were scrambling to get their hoses and ladders set up. The fire, meantime, was spreading faster than the sprinkler systems could address. Steam was mixing with smoke, filling the air and obscuring the scene.

Iron Man landed and grabbed the first hose he saw by one end. The firefighter's knee-jerk reaction was to become irate.

"What do you think you're doing?"

"Getting started," Iron Man replied, and the fighter got the picture.

"Yeah, you'll have better luck than we would," he acknowledged. "Take position, and we'll have the water on in a moment," he added with a wink, and then he waved to those behind him.

Iron Man tested the slack, then took to the air. As he flew, he felt the pressure fill the hose. As the water emerged with a rush, he aimed it in an arc, wetting down the entire dock area. That the unconscious HYDRA personnel were soaked as a result was just topping on the cake. The cold water began to revive some of them, and whenever one tried to stand, he used the high-pressure spray to knock him back to the pavement.

The fire began to diminish, and he flew the hose into the building. Unlike the firefighters, his internal-environment systems prevented the flames from doing him any damage, and he was able to extinguish the last of the flames. As he did, Iron Man juggled ideas in his mind—ways he might be able to adapt aspects of the protective suit for use by emergency personnel.

Before the fire chief could thank him, the Golden Avenger returned to the spot where the HYDRA craft had been, but there was no sign of it, nor was there a way to trace it. A quick check of records from Logan Airport revealed that it had been thoroughly cloaked as it had departed Boston airspace.

Annoyed at all the time he had lost, Iron Man returned to the skies and arced toward Long Island.

As he flew, he called up information from the AAA and studied the list of exhibitors, then narrowed in on what had been displayed. He cross-referenced the list with the Jersey manifest, but no obvious connection offered itself, and most likely nothing would.

But he'd be damned if he'd let it lie.

The trip home would have been a nice chance to actually unwind and enjoy the view. The fall night was clear and the stars twinkled merrily above him as sea traffic moved below. Instead, he brooded.

Passing over Long Island, he returned to the mansion, shucking off the armor and placing it in the cleaning unit, where scrubbers cleaned off the debris and washed the smoky smell away. Dressed in a sport shirt and woolen pants, a barefoot Stark entered the den and headed for the bar. He poured himself three fingers of scotch and slumped into an easy chair.

He was still juggling the various lists in his head, trying to figure out what HYDRA was preparing. Nothing added up, no matter how many different ways he looked at it.

Perhaps if he had someone to bounce ideas off of . . .

But surrounded though he might be by people, Stark was also very isolated. Ever since he had become Iron Man, he had allowed a lot of his personal friendships to lapse. Something, after all, had had to give.

There was always a bevy of women, but few his intellectual equal. He couldn't just call one of them up and start chatting about terrorists and shipping manifests. . . .

Rhodey was no doubt aboard the helicarrier. Happy Hogan might be around, but he was no puzzle solver.

Pepper Potts, though, was. She somehow managed to take all the bits and pieces of SI and made them run smoothly for him, more CEO than executive assistant. His attractive aide would certainly see something he was missing.

Decision made, he drained the glass and walked over to the desk and phone. By the phone was a piece of paper with the handwritten phone number he had been surreptitiously given a few days before.

He paused.

It's too late to call Pepper, he thought to himself. *It's not fair of me to ask her to give up her down time.*

He picked up the slip.

No, perhaps a diversion will serve to clear my mind.

The following morning, a tired Stark arrived at the two-square-mile campus, and his expression seemed to match the cloudy skies.

He had come close to calling the number the night before, but common sense had taken hold, and he had opted for sleep. But when the alarm clock had awakened him, while his body might have been somewhat refreshed, the same couldn't be said for his mood.

When he walked off the elevator and saw S.H.I.E.L.D.

agents by Pepper's desk, he knew the storm was going to be inside, too.

Nick Fury sat in his office, sipping a cup of coffee, two days' growth on his cheeks. He looked as tired as Stark.

"Fury."

"Stark."

"So glad you know each other," Pepper said archly. She overtly avoided looking at the invader in her employer's sanctum, and handed Stark only his mug of coffee, retaining the mail in her other hand.

"I've cleared your morning for the colonel."

"Thanks, Pepper," he replied without looking at her. Instead, he took a seat on the couch and heard the soft click of the doors closing.

"What the hell is going on?" Fury asked.

"With HYDRA?"

"No, with the Islanders. They just lost four in a row."

Stark was genuinely confused, and sipped at the hot liquid to cover it.

"Of course I mean HYDRA. . . ." Fury sounded more irritated than Stark had expected. In fact, it sounded personal to him, too.

Interesting.

"They hit Jersey, now they go to Boston," he continued. "And from what we're hearing, there have been other heists that have their fingerprints on them. But it's not just firearms—in fact, that seems to be less than half of it. What do they want?"

"What does any super-secret criminal organization want?" Stark challenged.

"To take over the world—I get that. It's how they're going about it that I don't get. You told Gabe you think the smash-and-grab was part of something bigger, but did your visit to Beantown give you any more of a clue?"

"Not at all," Stark admitted. At least Fury wasn't blaming him for what had been happening. Unlike the senator.

"I have to level with you, Stark," the colonel said. "They just installed me to run this thing, and I still have most of my men training. We're still gearing up. The blast in Atlanta means we've lost time and personnel, but the Council doesn't give a damn, and still has us rushing everything. I'm going double-time, but I still have to make certain we're not being sloppy, and leaving ourselves exposed.

"I can task men to a scene, and have others do the interrogation, but right now I need some clues before I start throwing the agency's resources at something."

"Or some*one*—I get it," Stark agreed.

That Fury had admitted all this meant he wasn't afraid of asking for help. Everything Stark had read in his file convinced him that the colonel should have been the Council's first choice. Stoner was a good man, but Fury had conceived this notion decades ago, and clearly had a sense of where such an operation should be taken.

"What about the HYDRA flunkies grabbed at the New Jersey dock, or in Boston?" Stark asked.

"Those yahoos you left us had nothing to say," Fury replied. "Either they're completely in the dark, or they're good at dodging our questions. We may need to use some special procedures on 'em, and luckily, the current administration seems to look the other way."

"I'm not sure how I feel about that," Stark responded. "Wouldn't it be lovely to have mind readers? It'd save you the trouble."

Fury nodded and drank his coffee.

"Yeah, it don't sit well with me, either."

Stark, though, was thinking about some reading he had done, about improved ways to detect a person's physical reactions to questions. Basically a souped-up version of the lie detector, which was no longer admissible in court.

One more item for his to-do list.

"What will you do with the men in the meantime?"

"Good question. Our international charter didn't quite

outline where we'd house long-term prisoners. Essentially, the commonwealth of Massachusetts wants them prosecuted for the arson last night. On the one hand, it takes them off my hands," the colonel said. "On the other, if HYDRA wants them back, then I'm risking the lives of everyone in the prison."

Stark nodded in silent agreement, his mind racing, listing and discarding options.

"Of course," Fury continued, "they're just field soldiers. None of them probably knows too much. HYDRA has existed for decades this way. Everything decentralized and compartmentalized."

"Decades? Why on earth are they becoming so active now?" Stark said. From what Fury was describing, it seemed as if HYDRA treated its men as if they were on the manifest. All part of a machine, huge and elusive.

"Yeah, HYDRA's been laying low for years, and they took their time building so they didn't show up on any radar," Fury explained. "In a way, I envy them—I don't have the luxury."

At that moment, Stark's desktop computer chimed and his office door opened. Pepper and the S.H.I.E.L.D. agents spilled into the room.

"Someone's attacking the R & D labs," she said in a rush.

Fury was already out of his seat, hand reaching for a sidearm.

Stark was also up. He looked at the director, then his assistant.

"Pepper, show Fury the way."

As soon as they had left, he ran to his desk, grabbed his briefcase, and continued to a corner of the office, where he depressed a hidden stud that opened up a passageway. Once the door slid shut, he was already going through the change from suit to armor.

Stark owed thanks to the Mole Man. The SI facilities

had originally been built long before there was an Iron
Man. When the grotesque criminal had destroyed portions
of the main buildings and they had needed to be reconstructed, he'd had the designers work in a series of access
ways that allowed him to get from point to point faster
than would have been possible before.

He calculated that he could be at the lab minutes ahead
of S.H.I.E.L.D., even with time for changing.

The suit in place, he powered up, and what had seemed
like form-fitting fabric went rigid, conforming perfectly to
his body. Every joint and seal were engineered to offer absolutely no resistance, so his freedom of movement was
never in any way hampered.

Iron Man reached a passage that had been designed
specifically for horizontal movement. While he could fly,
anyone else would have been forced to crawl. It was pitch-
black, as well.

He used his boot jets at quarter speed—no sense in taking unnecessary risks—and engaged his night lenses. As he
flew, branches of the tunnel curved away gently, minimiz-
ing the risk of impact. Security barriers opened and closed
as directed by remote signals.

He was becoming angrier by the moment. A physical assault on the SI campus was akin to hitting him directly in
the face.

Iron Man accessed the security communications channel, and learned that the intruders had used gas to over-
come any resistance.

"Engage seals, activate internal environment."

Sensors directed him to the appropriate branch, and he
remotely opened the access panel that would admit him to
the basement of the R & D building. As the panel slid open,
a yellowish gas was instantly evident. Even as he moved
to the upper floors, he captured a sample and began an
analysis.

"Fury, it's Iron Man," he said. "Something toxic is in the air here. Stay out until I deal with it."

"*Acknowledged.*"

With that he emerged into the research lab, and his thermal sensors led him through the haze to collapsed bodies of several employees. He didn't recognize them, but it still felt as if his own family had been attacked.

He could see that they were breathing. *Good, that means the mixture isn't lethal. That opens up more options.*

Hefting two into his arms, he walked to the nearest floor-to-ceiling window and commanded the circular emitter on his chestplate to send out a single burst of energy. The glass shattered and the gas swirled into the fall air.

Iron Man then gently activated his boot jets and floated through the shattered window, carrying the two outside to where security personnel were gathered and emergency medical vehicles were already arriving, followed by Pepper. Fury and his men were already there, too.

As he re-entered the building to help more, he found that someone had sealed the main door, and cracked it open so others could rush to safety. Back in the lab, he spotted the supine form of Gabriella Marquez lying next to a desk, picked her up, and flew her out to the waiting medical staff.

One of the emergency medical technicians approached.

"Any idea what it is?"

"My internal sensors can't identify it, so it's not a common toxin, but it's not immediately deadly. Everyone who's come into contact with it is sick or unconscious, but no one looks to be dead.

"I've captured a sample of it," he added, and he pulled a small vial from the cuff of his gauntlet, handing it to the EMT.

With that, he flew back into the building. He paused in front of the control panel for the HVAC system and manually activated the exhaust pumps. Then he headed back to the lab.

By the time he landed the haze had dissipated, so Stark was able to do a better survey of the damage. The lab was part of Burstein's department, and this particular space had been assigned to design the next generation of satellite technology for telecommunications.

There was a station dedicated to a prototype they had been developing, and from what he could see, they had made substantial progress in building it.

As Fury rushed into the room, pistol leading the way, Iron Man was hunched over a terminal and was assessing the latest reports.

"What happened?"

"I'm hoping your team can do a forensics sweep and figure out how the gas was delivered. I don't see anything obvious."

"What are you doing then?"

"Checking the daily log reports to figure out what's here, and what may be gone."

"Did you see any sign of HYDRA?"

"No, but someone attacked this one lab, and most likely wanted something from this room," Iron Man replied icily. Again he felt the stab of anger that someone would put his people at risk.

Fury directed his men to begin studying the room as Iron Man continued working the computer.

"What's been going on in here?" he asked. "Why do you think this was their target?"

"We've been designing a satellite—but for commercial applications, not military use," Iron Man said.

"Does it have any connection with what had already been taken?"

"It's not unlike the communications network we were building for the DOD, but since the applications are different, that means the standards are different, as well."

"So no," Fury said.

"Not yet," Iron Man said, but he was still determined to *make* this make sense.

They both were silent for a few minutes, until they heard someone approach. Iron Man looked up from the computer and saw a shaky-looking Marquez enter the lab.

"I'm not certain you should be here, Ms. Marquez," he said. "How are you feeling?"

"I feel pretty ill, if you must know," she answered, and her voice sounded weak, but she didn't make any move to leave. She remained in the doorway and observed the S.H.I.E.L.D. agents at work. When it became clear that she intended to remain, he introduced her to Fury.

"Can you tell if anything is missing?" the colonel asked.

Her eyes scanned the room and focused on the large black table where the partially completed satellite sat. They then went wide, and Iron Man felt a sinking feeling in the pit of his stomach.

"The gyroscopes," she said. "They were entirely new in design, and they're not here."

"Well, now we know what they wanted," Fury noted.

"I was just checking those out three days ago," Iron Man said hotly, and he turned his attention back to the computer.

"Thank god," he said. "The schematics are still here so they can be rebuilt."

"Michael Burstein told me that they took a month for the tooling," Marquez said. "That'll put us far behind schedule." She coughed roughly.

"We can deal with that," Iron Man said defiantly. "It gives me time for some upgrades I had been thinking about. Better now than later." Fury drifted over to where his men were studying the scene, and Iron Man faced her directly.

"You need to get out of here, head back to the grounds and fresher air. We don't know what this stuff is, and I'd rather you were cleared by the medics."

"We should have secured the hardware at the first sign of the gas," Marquez replied without moving an inch.

"No, safety first," Iron Man said firmly. "And given the level of sophistication this operation seems to have boasted, I doubt you would have had the chance—they seem to have covered all the bases, and disappeared without a trace."

Fury approached the two with a grim look on his face.

"The delivery seems to have come from the ventilation system—some doohickey attached with a timer."

Iron Man nodded. "Any idea how they got in and out?"

"One thing at a time," the S.H.I.E.L.D. director said. "We'll finish here, and reconvene at your office to decide what we do next."

"That gives me some time, then," Iron Man said to Marquez. "Why don't you and Burstein meet me at the executive dining room at one o'clock. We can discuss the upgrades over lunch." She nodded, and turned to leave.

As she did so, Fury commented under his breath, "You hire your staff from modeling agencies? Every dame I see here is beautiful."

"Just lucky, I suppose," Iron Man replied.

"Luck my eye," Fury said.

Watching Burstein and Marquez talk over the meal made Stark feel better. She seemed hale and healthy, no more cough tingeing her voice.

Sipping from his scotch, he let his mind review the morning, and added it to what he already knew. HYDRA was operating on several fronts, so more and more pieces of the puzzle were emerging, and he needed to begin fitting those pieces together. But the connections eluded him.

Perhaps Fury would find something the industrialist was missing, once he had studied the results of his own investigation. He seemed like a sharp, dedicated man—not at all polished like the politicians with whom they both had to deal. In many ways, the colonel was a breath of fresh air.

Two attacks on different parts of SI.

"Standard" robberies in New Jersey and Boston, and an extraordinary assault on his own home ground.

What could they be building?

Marquez gazed his way. She had pale gray eyes that seemed to promise great dimension, and he stared back, fascinated.

After a time, she broke the silent exchange, gave him a brief smile, and returned to her salad.

Stark gulped down the rest of his drink.

As they were getting ready to leave, the tone sounded on his cell phone.

"Hi, Pepper," he said a bit too loudly for the restaurant. "On my way back."

"The sooner, the better," she said, and her voice sounded odd.

"Why?" he asked. "What's up?"

"We've had a fatality, Mr. Stark."

xi.

Back at his office, he waited for Fury. He ignored his emails and paced the office.

How could this have happened?

It had been Drum, a lab technician who had been with the company for more than ten years. He had been fine—wasn't even one of those who lost consciousness. He had been checked out at the on-site medical clinic, and was getting ready to leave when he collapsed.

"They said it was a seizure of some sort," Pepper had explained. "Something specific to his body chemistry."

Drum had become an unintentional casualty of whatever it was that HYDRA was planning. Unintentional, but no less dead.

It gnawed at Stark, and prevented him from getting productive work done in either of his identities.

Wisely, Pepper kept everyone away from the office, and he could hear her sending away messengers, department heads, and even the woman who normally came by to water the plants.

Finally, she tapped lightly on the door frame and peeked around, interrupting his pacing.

"I really hate to disturb you—" she began.

"No, you don't," Stark said, forcing a smile on his face. "You're making sure I'm not in here drinking myself into a stupor."

"Well, I'm concerned for your well-being. I can tell when you're overtired, and that's not good for when you're needed."

"Is it an armored situation?" His brows knit with concern.

"No, it's not for Iron Man," she answered. "Senator Byrd called, and you're to be in Washington tomorrow morning. Hearings begin at ten.

"Should I call Felix?" she added.

Stark shook his head, finally stopped pacing, and sat in his chair. He then gestured for Pepper to also sit, and he admired how gracefully she settled into the seat.

"You know when my family founded the company, and you know what it means to me," he began. There was no need to remind her of SI's history, since she knew it almost as well as he did, usually using it to begin grilling prospective employees.

"To have it attacked twice in a week, with no rhyme or reason, no clue as to who did it and why . . . it's maddening," he said. "And then to lose a good man, whose only crime was to be in the wrong place at the wrong time, and to trust me to keep him safe . . ."

She remained silent, but nodded in agreement.

"We've got to stop them before it happens again," Stark said darkly. "What is it I'm missing? What connection could there be between a communications network and gyros for a satellite?"

"Nothing that occurs to me, but of course, my degree was in English—not technobabble," she said.

Stark flashed back to the first time he had seen her, a bright-eyed twenty-something in the secretarial pool. His father was still running the show, she had just been hired to assist him, and the bright red hair and shapely figure couldn't have been missed. *Certainly* not by Tony Stark.

For weeks he heard from Howard Stark just how efficient she was, so that when his father had . . . passed away, there was little question who would come work for him when he inherited the company.

By the time that happened, she had taken evening business

courses and seemed to have an uncanny sense for how things ran. He was the technician, but she made certain he had the tools to work with, and that the trains always ran smoothly.

"Maybe it's like when my car was last in the shop," she began. He stared at her, uncertain of where this was going.

"One summer, I'd find a pool of water underneath the engine. Not always, but sometimes. Nothing was wrong, and the car ran fine. I took it in for a look, but Eddie the mechanic couldn't locate the problem.

"Then came the day I found a bigger puddle, and took it in for service. This time Eddie said it was the water pump, and he fixed it in an afternoon. The problem had to get worse before it could be identified."

"So, what you're saying is, I'll have to suffer another attack before figuring out what's going on here?"

"Maybe," Pepper agreed. "As much as it pains me to say it."

"Not as much as it pains me. And *definitely* not as much as it will pain the one responsible for what happened here today."

"You're certain it's HYDRA?"

"Who else could it be?" he shot back, and instantly he knew he had been too harsh.

Pepper sat in silence, letting her boss cool off, and Stark appreciated it.

This was really getting to him, and the idea of wasting a day in D.C., kissing political ass, was aggravating beyond measure.

He dismissed her for the night, called Hogan to arrange a pickup time, and determined to work things out at home.

Once Mr. Stark had left for the night, Pepper was still at her desk. He didn't question that she had stayed, since she often kept flexible hours. He pretty much gave her free rein to do as she desired.

She thought back to the beginning, when she had ap-

plied for the secretarial job at Stark Industries and met
Howard Stark for the first time. The young Pepper had
been in awe of him, and it was his example that sent her to
night classes to learn more about business. She wanted to be
a valuable asset, not just an interchangeable cog in the SI
machine.

All too soon, though, Howard had died and his son,
Tony—just out of his teens and a certifiable genius—had
uneasily moved from the lab to the boardroom. He was
handsome—so much so that she had trouble keeping her
eyes off him, even though he seemed to have eyes only for
starlets, models, and flashy women. She, on the other hand,
had loud freckles, and tended to dress conservatively, preferring comfort over style.

He had finally noticed her when she had been reviewing
a contract and caught a major accounting error that would
have cost the company a lot of money. Mr. Stark had been
even more impressed by the fact that, though he had made
the error himself, she hadn't hesitated to bring it to his attention. From that day forward he hadn't questioned her
judgment.

Weeks had gone by, though, and he never seemed to notice her beyond her efficiency, so she decided to spend a
long weekend undergoing a makeover. She changed her
hairstyle, tried new makeup, and upgraded her wardrobe
to something befitting the right hand of America's most
eligible bachelor.

She was pretty sure he noticed immediately. Still, business always came before pleasure.

Then he became Iron Man.

She hadn't known at first that it was Mr. Stark in the armor. He had claimed to have added Iron Man to the staff
both as state-of-the-art security and a corporate represen-
tation of just what Stark Industries could produce.

At the same time, Mr. Stark had become prone to unex-
plained absences, and Pepper had assumed that he was

either locked in his lab or in the arms of some *Sports Illustrated* model or hotel heiress—getting over the breakup with his fiancée. She found herself with increased responsibilities as he relied more and more on her innate business acumen, promoting her to executive assistant and letting her make more of the day-to-day decisions for the company.

Which was why she had no trouble accessing the company's human-resources files, as she began doing a little puzzle solving on her own.

Drexel Cord sat in the conference room of Cord Chemical, a division of Cord Industries based in Pennsylvania, signing an agreement. Madame Hydra strolled into the room.

He was a business tycoon who happened to do some of his business with the underworld, and he had become a necessary tool. She knew there'd be grumbling from her underlings that she had flown west, spent money, and come back with something they could so easily have stolen.

She didn't care—they were shortsighted idiots. Already, S.H.I.E.L.D. was investigating Boston, and the less of a trail she left, the better.

"Ah, my dear," he said in a dry voice, rising to meet her. "How wonderful it is to see you again—you bring a ray of sunshine into an old man's day." His handshake was firm, she noted, and again she realized that he was not to be underestimated.

"And you, Drexel," she answered with a slightly breathy voice. "Do you have the soil-sampling tools my company ordered?"

"Packed and ready to ship," he said, nodding his bald head. "Of course, you need to sign the agreement . . . and give us the payment."

She read the document carefully, certain that someone

like Cord would try to cheat them somehow. In truth, she had come to enjoy the old man, perhaps because he carried an air of death about him, and she would have been somewhat disappointed had she been forced to kill him.

Instead, she was pleased to see that everything was in order. In exchange for the devices, she would pay $10,000 now, and another $10,000 upon delivery.

He handed her a Mont Blanc pen, keeping the cap for himself. She hastily scrawled a name, one that matched the credentials under which she did business.

She blew gently on the black ink and handed the document over. As he admired the name, a communications device on her hip emitted a beep. The signal came from her apartment's phone line, relayed through untraceable satellites to the communicator. This way, her civilian guise would appear to be in New York at all times.

Raising a green-gloved finger in the air, she turned, withdrew the device, and activated the circuit.

It was Stark.

"The last transaction only brought in fifty thousand dollars," he snapped. "It's nowhere near enough."

"What would you have me do, flood the market?" Masque shouted back, her voice ringing from the vibrations against the metallic mask that was affixed to her face. "Then the prices will go down—and what will you do then?

"Besides, Francois isn't done with the big-ticket items I just passed along to him." His impatience infuriated her. "I need more time!"

"Give them sexier acquisitions," he demanded. "Things they can't live without."

"Such as?" she countered. In truth, she was almost afraid to learn what he would consider "sexier." The fact that he was her father didn't make it any better.

She didn't actually expect him to give her a straight

answer, regardless, but he must have anticipated the question. He rattled off a litany of exotic items—all high-tech pieces of equipment, culled from Osborn Enterprises, Rand-Meachum, Stane, Cord, and Stark.

Each and every one of them, one of a kind. He had done his research. An email appeared in her in-box, with the list attached.

"Bring me the working models or their plans—it matters not which—and then our coffers will be full, and we may resume full operations," he said. "With the right weapon in my hands, none will stand in my way as I reassert my authority."

"It would be easier to just storm the gangs and kill every last one of them. The amount of blood shed would be the same."

"You don't mean that," he said.

"Oh, but I do, dear Papa," she said, her voice tight and ironic. "To access all these companies, to bypass their security, to grab these things, and get back out—trust me, there will be blood."

Mine, she added silently. *Not that it would matter to him.*

"Do you have a better idea?"

There was tense silence as neither moved. Neither was willing to give an inch.

"Very well, pick one company and concentrate your efforts there," he finally said, breaking the stalemate. "Choose the most advanced—start with Stark. This device that he is developing for law enforcement, it is unlike anything his competitors have on the drawing board. It will fetch a huge sum."

She shook her head.

"I will not make an overt move against Stark Enterprises and expose myself to Iron Man," she said. "He is too formidable."

"I do not care if he is formidable," Nefaria said, his

voice surprisingly calm. "I have faced America's superhumans, and they have failed to crush me.

"Yet you appear to be in over your head," he added. "Clearly, I must consider a different approach."

The screen went blank before she could shout a protest.

She slumped back in her chair. Robbed of the open conflict, she found herself utterly deflated.

Opening the email attachment, she printed out the list of items, and focused on the ones under the heading of "Stark Industries." Settling in her chair, she did a quick risk assessment for each one.

Some would be impossible. Others would simply be . . . difficult. Not that it mattered.

Arguing with her father was one thing, but disappointing him was something else entirely. Few survived the experience, and she was pretty certain family blood flowed as easily as any.

The Subcommittee on Strategic Forces was filled with eleven unhappy-looking senators, including the white-haired Harlan Byrd. In meeting room SD-342, they sat behind their wooden table, metallic nameplates facing the gallery, nine men in identical dark suits and solid-colored ties, the two women in similarly dark attire.

Normally, their meetings were quiet affairs, but today the press was in attendance, and they had come in droves. After all, it wasn't every day that a famous personality such as Anthony Stark appeared to give testimony. Genius, playboy, and Avenger, all rolled into one photogenic package.

It was a hastily convened session, but every member of the committee had made it a point to be there, to have their moment on C-SPAN or perhaps the network news. Camera crews and photographers jockeyed for position along the sides of the room, and other members of Congress along with their aides—many of them female—took every available seat.

Clicking shutters and a whispered undercurrent filled the air.

At five minutes before ten, the doors opened. A hush fell over the crowd, displaced by disappointed murmurs when the black-suited figure of Happy Hogan walked through the room, his features showing the results of his former career as a boxer, his laminated access badge bright against his outfit. He smiled shyly in the glare, but the crowd craned to see beyond him.

He stepped to the side, and in through the doors walked Stark. Instantly the room was filled with the visual staccato of camera flashes.

He really hated this, the time wasted, the nonsense of the investigation, but it was all a necessary evil. Knowing the proceedings would be recorded, he had seen to it that he was freshly shaven and was wearing a brand-new, Ermenegildo Zegna gray pinstriped suit with a pale yellow shirt and a dark blue-striped tie. His shoes reflected the light thrust his way, and his briefcase seemed recently polished.

He was pretty sure few could see the shadows around his eyes, or could read the tension he was feeling as he flashed his white teeth for a moment.

Rather than wink and flirt with the women, as he tended to do when the cameras were not present, Stark stared ahead at the subcommittee, nodded at Byrd, and took his seat behind the table that was facing the group. The only things on the tabletop were a microphone, a glass, and a pitcher of water.

Stark placed his briefcase by his feet and settled into the chair.

At precisely ten, the subcommittee chairman—Randall Birskovich, the Republican from Minnesota—gaveled the meeting to order. After the preliminaries, he had Stark identify himself for the secretary.

Then the grilling began.

"Mr. Stark, were you present when the incident at your plant took place?"

"Yes, Senator, I was in my office." *Meeting with the director of an agency that's still so secret, you've probably never heard of it.*

"Mr. Stark, how is it that the intruders managed to slip by your security without a trace?"

"We're still investigating that aspect of the intrusion." *They probably clicked together their ruby slippers, and went back to Kansas.*

"Concerning the earlier breach in your security, are you always in the habit of leaving your computer security exposed?"

"No, Madam Senator, that's not usually the case." *We just thought we'd try it once, to see what it felt like.*

"How far along was the project that was stolen, and is any of it recoverable?"

"Yes, we have backup files, and this incident will cause us to re-examine it for further improvements in the technology." *Or we could all just visit the nearest bar, and enjoy a good shot of Stolichnaya.*

"When will the communications network be ready for use by the Department of Defense?"

And the questions went on, so that he barely had a chance to answer one question before the next arrived. While some of the senators employed a reasonable approach, others clearly thought of him as a dilettante, and offered him no mercy. Stark tried to sound confident and professional, refusing to rise to the bait regardless of how often it was offered.

As the questions began to repeat themselves, he felt confidence begin to give way to anger. He sipped at the water, wishing it were something stronger.

He knew it was an election cycle, and everyone wanted to look their best for the cameras, to be on the record as being tough on the superhero. He had infuriated many of them a few years back when he refused to let them manufacture his armor for the troops. He readily designed, built, and sold them the finest technology.

Everything except the armor.

That was where he drew the line. It was his and his alone, never to be duplicated. Any country's army, encased in the armor, would have a strategic advantage that—under the wrong commander in chief—would unnecessarily and irrevocably alter the balance of power.

At least it would be irrevocable until someone *else* got their hands on the secrets. Then the stakes would simply escalate. No, he wasn't going to allow that Pandora's box to open.

Already, Russia had built the Crimson Dynamo and Titanium Man in response to what they declared to be American aggression. The Chinese would have done the same had they not seen the rise of the Mandarin, a powerful—and power-mad—warlord whose activities seemed to keep the Communist government occupied.

Few other countries had the resources or skill to even attempt to duplicate the armor, which was fine by Stark.

They'd asked in the past. In fact, badgered him to the point where he'd collapsed, and the world saw him exposed, his chestplate captured by a dozen cameras.

He'd refused to turn over the armor then, and he vowed that he would never change his mind.

While one senator wound up a long discourse on the safety of American troops around the globe, and the need for the communications network, Stark allowed himself to relax a bit, and this enabled his mind to multitask, bringing his attention back to HYDRA.

They had attacked S.H.I.E.L.D. even before they were fully operational, and only Nick Fury's quick reflexes and combat-honed instincts had foiled the attempt. Could they be planning to build something to take down the helicarrier?

No, the technology didn't seem to be aerial in nature. Were the field offices around the world in trouble, before people even knew they were there? How many lives would HYDRA be willing to risk, and willing to sacrifice? Their philosophy seemed to be that individual human lives— even their own—were infinitely replaceable.

That's probably what they thought about Shel Drum, he thought darkly. *Irrelevant, and inconsequential.* While he hadn't been able to attend Stoner's funeral, he would be certain not to miss Drum's.

Finally, an hour and forty-five minutes after he had first walked into the room, the chair adjourned the hearing. Nothing had been decided, nothing had been said that made Stark feel any better or worse than he already felt.

Of course, it would take a great deal for the senators— or anyone—to beat him up any more than he was doing to himself.

xii.

"Overall, you didn't embarrass yourself," Byrd said, pushing away his empty plate. "Not too much."

Stark managed to eat only some of the steak and potatoes before losing his appetite. After that he sat, sipping at his martini, ignoring the stares from the wait staff and other power players filling the restaurant just a few blocks from the Capitol.

"So nice to hear," he replied, the irritation plain in his voice.

"Look, don't get smart with me—I may be your only ally on the committee," the senator replied. "My advice, knock the price down and meet the schedule if at all possible. That'll buy you some goodwill."

"What, saving America every now and then doesn't buy me a break or two?"

Byrd just stared for a moment before replying.

"You're the one who told me that what you do in the armor shouldn't be counted against what you do in the factory," he said. "Either you mean that, or you don't."

Stark didn't respond. He sipped the last of the martini, feeling the warm glow mix with the anger that refused to go away, and practically slammed the glass atop the linen tablecloth.

"Damn it, Senator, I've got to find the bastard who's doing this to me," he said, more to himself than his dining companion. "They've targeted me, and I've got to find out *why*."

"Are you sure it's personal?" Byrd asked. "Could it be

coming from overseas?" Byrd was always looking for a foreign enemy to blame, Stark knew, since it played better in the media.

"No, we've got some of the perpetrators in custody, and they aren't affiliated with any one country," he answered, signaling for another drink. "We know who the overarching enemy is, but for them to be carrying out the sort of attacks we've been dealing with, there has to be involvement by someone closer to home. And that *does* make it personal—especially when people die."

"I heard about that," Byrd said. "You have my condolences." And to Stark's surprise, he sounded as if he meant it.

As the lunch wound down, he made a beeline for the limo and—regardless of Happy Hogan's well-intentioned attempts—he never sunk to the level of banal conversation. Instead, he brooded in the backseat, and then on the flight north.

By the time he reached SI, it was after five p.m. He needed to shake off the funk.

Stark breezed into his office, and asked Pepper if anything was pressing. She shook her head no, then confirmed that S.H.I.E.L.D. still had not been in touch.

That was all he needed. He tossed her a sleepy wink that he knew wouldn't fool her, and headed right back out.

He stood in the doorway of Gabriella Marquez's office. Much of her department had left for the day, but she was still there, writing a report. He cleared his throat; she looked up, and a strange expression flitted across her face. She blinked once in recognition, then gave him a tight smile—professional at best.

She was definitely going to be a challenge.

"Another late night?" he asked, leaning against the door frame.

"Yes, Mr. St—uh, Tony," she said.

"Mr. Tony," he repeated, and laughed. "There was a bootblack who used to visit the offices when I first started out. Guy was named Joachim, and it seemed to me that he was ancient, though he was probably about fifty. Always called me Mr. Tony in a thick accent that I loved to hear. Gave a great shine, too."

She nodded once. Her eyes lingered over his face, then moved down and stopped. She met his gaze again.

"Sir, if I may," she said. "You look terrible."

Again, he laughed, and it felt good to let some of the weariness be evident.

"Yeah, I'm feeling somewhat beat and beaten up."

"The hearing didn't go well, then?"

"Figured word had gotten around," he replied. "You don't listen to the news, though, do you?"

"Not during business hours. It would be too much of a distraction, and that's not what I'm paid for."

"A distraction. I like that," he said as he finally entered the small office and began studying the few knickknacks that personalized it. He always figured it was those touches that told him something he wouldn't find in the personnel files.

There was a box of tissues in a decorative holder, and atop her filing cabinet was a New York Knicks flag. There was a photo on her desk, but he couldn't see it from his angle.

Nothing else.

"Well, today's distraction was pretty much what I expected, so I took my lumps like a good boy. Now we have to re-create the network. Did your team locate the backups?"

"Of course," she replied, and she gestured to reels of magnetic tape at the corner of her tidy desk. "We lost maybe five hours of work, but Mr. Burstein tells me it's easily replicated. We won't miss the schedule."

Stark thought about that for the moment.

"But someone else has the tech now, and they don't have to play catch-up," he said.

Was he barking up the wrong tree? Could this have just been a matter of industrial espionage? *Cord? Osborn?*

"And if it's one of our competitors, they don't have the R & D costs we've put into it," he mused. "They could undersell us, and still make a tidy profit." Then he yawned. He tried not to do that in front of others, preferring to maintain his image, but the days seemed to be catching up to him.

"Are you really worried about being undersold?"

"Not really, Gabriella," he said. "Actually, I'm more concerned that the frequencies we identified will be grabbed, rendering the network useless."

"We checked them today and they're clean as a whistle," she said, her tone reassuring for a change. "You just need to make certain the FCC grants the DOD guaranteed access, and the network will be fine."

"My guys are on it," he said, feeling somewhat better. He moved away from the door, and stumbled slightly.

"Please, sit," she said. "I don't want you falling down in here. Explaining it to security would be rather embarrassing."

They both smiled at the thought, though he was reasonably certain the image it conjured in his mind was different from what she might be imagining. *Better not go there,* he thought, so he spoke up.

"Truth to tell, I was hoping to coax you to join me for dinner."

To his surprise, she smiled, a broad, warm smile that lightened the all-professional demeanor she normally wore. *I must be making more progress than I thought.*

"Thank you, Tony, but I suspect you'd be a poor dinner partner tonight."

Oh.

"What you need is an early night for a change," she said. "Why don't we plan something for the weekend, instead?"

Yes! Score one for the old Stark charm.

"A brilliant notion," he agreed. "Early to bed tonight, and dinner on Friday to kick off the weekend."

She nodded, and smiled again. Rather than sensing the shrapnel near his heart, he felt a lightening and grinned.

"Until Friday, then," he said and tossed off a salute, turning and heading out of the office.

Gabriella Marquez resumed her work even before his footsteps had faded away, though she watched the door out of the corner of her eye, in case he decided to return.

That would be inconvenient.

She reached into her top-left drawer, withdrew a blank swipe card, and inserted it into a magnetic recorder she kept on the credenza behind her. Making a duplicate of an office key was step one.

With Stark gone and not likely to return, she could move on to step two.

While Stark had hoped for distracting companionship, he realized, as soon as Marquez said it, that what he really needed was a night off.

No HYDRA.

No Avengers.

No crises.

A quiet dinner, a drink or two, and some sleep.

Hogan called ahead to alert the house staff that his boss was coming home and to prepare a meal. The chauffer-slash-bodyguard again tried small talk, and this time Stark made appreciative noises in response.

He said something about a movie called *The Legend of Bagger Vance*, and the industrialist wondered when was the last time that he had actually gone to the movies. Of course, he could always call Redford and have a copy sent over, but when had he actually set foot in a *theater*?

Could it have been with his mother, a decade back? What had they seen? With her, it probably would have been a character-driven film. Perhaps *Dances with Wolves*. Or *Pretty Woman*—yeah, that one would have appealed to her.

But no, he would have been too young. Maria Stark had been a forward thinker, but she was always mindful of her son.

He wistfully thought of his mother the rest of the ride home.

After an excellent meal, Stark figured the alcohol he had consumed would help push him over the edge, and he'd simply fall into bed.

Instead, all the relaxation seemed to give him a bit of a second wind. So rather than toss and turn, he found himself once more tinkering in the lab, playing with sonics, attempting to solve the jamming he feared would complicate the army network.

He spent maybe twenty minutes on it, then got distracted by some tweaks he had planned for the armor's internal diagnostics.

He was fidgety and distracted, awake but too tired to actually do anything; sleepy but too alert to actually try to sleep.

He needed someone to talk to.

The clock told him it was after an hour when polite people called one another. Instead, he decided to do what other Americans did when they couldn't sleep.

In what was still called the family room—despite his lack of a family—Stark sat with a tumbler of whiskey and the television remote. He drank with his left hand and clicked with his right, quickly noting how few shows he recognized.

Soon his second drink was gone without notice, and he settled on an old Walter Matthau movie that seemed engaging. He continued to sip at the liquor, slumped on the couch, more staring than watching the movie.

"Sorry, Happy," Tony Stark said as he got into the limo. He was still trying to tie his green-patterned tie while clutching his briefcase.

"It's fine, Mr. Stark, you're usually on time, so you can be late every now and then," Hogan said agreeably.

"How'd the Rangers do last night?" Stark asked brightly. Once he had drifted off, he had actually gotten some decent sleep.

"Night off," Hogan replied as they left the grounds and headed for Flushing. The two chatted amiably, though despite his rest, Stark still felt a little bit unsettled. But it wasn't anything he could put his finger on.

As he stepped off the elevator, Pepper not only had his coffee mug ready, but she had also made certain it contained a particularly potent blend from South America. She quickly reviewed the day's anticipated highlights.

He thanked her, slipped into his office, and kicked the door closed behind him.

His emails had been piling up for a couple of days now, so he tackled them first, firing off terse and not necessarily the most courteous responses. He cajoled his department heads to think more for themselves, he begged off charity requests, and he scolded a journalist who somehow had gotten his note past the normally vigilant Ms. Potts.

Once he was done with the several hundred notes, he returned the top-ten phone calls. He again found himself being curt, and even peevish, and paused to gather himself. *It's not going to do me any good to alienate people whose only offense is to catch me on a bad day.*

He realized that the problem was that he had gotten

some sleep. His somewhat rested mind was sifting through the mounting list of items that had been stolen, and that was just irritating him all the more, tainting everything else he needed to accomplish.

Around mid-morning, an encrypted email arrived from Gabe Jones at S.H.I.E.L.D.

At last!

It was a list of suspicious robberies that had taken place along the eastern seaboard, and sure enough, several of his competitors seemed to have been hit in one way or another.

So it's not *just me,* he realized with some relief, and a different picture began to emerge.

HYDRA was assembling an arsenal. He still couldn't figure out what the nonmilitary equipment was supposed to accomplish, but something was beginning to take shape in the back of his mind.

Regardless, a war was coming. That much was clear. And it meant that the clock was ticking.

Would Fury be ready?

Ever since the colonel had found an explosive aboard the helicarrier, everyone in S.H.I.E.L.D. had been on the alert. But he hadn't yet taken them into the field. During his service in the U.S. Army, he had been sergeant of some repute, highly decorated, but this was going to be a very different war.

Still, Stark had a business to run, and he forced himself to focus on that until late morning. Once it was tended to, however, he used the intercom for the first time of the day.

"Pepper, get me Fury."

"In person or on the phone?" she asked.

"Damn it, the phone," he said. *Tone it down, Tony.* He continued in a calmer voice. "I can't wait for him to fly over—let's just see if we can get him on the horn."

Minutes later, a secured line lit up. He grabbed the headset.

"Fury, this is Stark."

"What'cha need, Stark?" Fury sounded as if he'd rather not be wasting time on a call.

"It's HYDRA," Stark replied.

"Well, you can't have 'em," Fury said. *"I've already been promised the first dance."*

"Not funny, Fury," Stark replied. "Do we have any intelligence telling us where they're based?"

"Hoekstra tells me there's a New York cell, but we haven't been able to pin down a location," Fury admitted.

"Swell," Stark said.

"You have something?" Fury said. *"I can send some backup if you need it."*

"Just guesses and a hunch," Stark admitted, giving nothing away, secure line or not. "If I want to act, though, it'd be nice to know where to focus the heat. Have your guys come up with anything on the gas attack?"

"Yeah, Gabe was gonna brief you later today," Fury replied. *"The delivery device wasn't anything special, and we couldn't figure out where it came from. The gas, though, was something designed to disable, but not be lethal."*

"So much for that," Stark replied, a bitter edge to his voice.

"Amen to that. But its bark was worse than its bite, and it was something new for HYDRA's arsenal. They tend to prefer more lethal results when they go the gas route."

"Interesting," Stark replied. Something was off about that. Here was an assault on his home turf, yet they ratcheted back their approach. Why?

And would they be so reserved the *next* time?

"Don't go all rogue on me, Stark," Fury said, breaking into his reverie. *"If you come up with something concrete, let us know. You know how we hate it when you throw a party and don't ask us."*

"I'll make sure you get the first invitation," Stark replied. "Stark out."

"Fury out."

Pepper poked her head in the door to see if he wanted more coffee or maybe something more useful, like lunch.

"Too much on my mind," he said.

"I know lunch is for wimps," she said, "but you do know that was just a movie, don't you?"

"What? What movie? Oh, that one." He hazarded a smile. "Look, I'm not being macho—I'm just really busy. But I promise to eat something. What's the rest of the day look like?"

As she ticked off each item on his agenda, he had her reschedule two internal meetings and canceled a visit to Manhattan for a conference. Then he agreed to have her order a sandwich from the commissary.

"Well, all that leaves is your date with the mysterious green-haired woman," she finished.

That gave Stark pause, and he smirked a bit.

"It just irritates you, doesn't it? That I'm taking someone to dinner, and you don't know a thing about her." He softened his voice a little. "I can't always rely on you to protect me. And don't worry, Pep, it's not like she can pierce the armor with her fingernails."

Pepper looked hurt by his attempt at humor, and he didn't get it.

She excused herself and left the room.

Happy Hogan was loitering by her desk, chauffeur's hat in hand.

Pepper saw him, swallowed back whatever emotions she was feeling, and spoke.

"The New York conference is off. I don't think he'll be needing you until tonight."

"The boss has a big date, huh?" he suggested. "Is it that green-haired chick who was in all of the papers?"

"Do you know anything about her?" Pepper asked hopefully. "Even her name?" She knew from experience that Happy was more observant than most people gave him credit for. His spot in the front seat of the limo offered him a bird's-eye view, so to speak.

But Hogan just shook his head, looking glum.

"I think I heard him say the name Katalin, but that's all I got—they're meeting at the restaurant, so I won't know a thing until we take her home." Both were aware that, despite his reputation, Stark rarely had a woman spend the night.

"How does he seem to you?" she asked, concern edging her voice, earning her a frown. She knew he was conflicted about her relationship with Mr. Stark, especially since he made it no secret that he harbored a crush on her.

What she and Happy were to each other was something that was still evolving.

"Whatever's on his mind really seems to be eating at him," Hogan said.

"He's taking these attacks personally," she agreed.

"That and this HYDRA outfit. From what I've read, they're international terrorists, and that seems to bug him more than the garden-variety crooks we've got here at home."

"You seem to have read up on them, Happy."

"Don't sound so surprised, Pep," he said with pride. "I've gotta read the papers, just to keep up with you and Mr. Stark."

She chuckled at that, but then the two fell into an uncomfortable silence, both worried about the man each had grown close to.

Tony Stark stared at his reflection in the mirror.

Yes, he did look tired and worn. As a result, he gave himself extra time to dress for his dinner date. He shaved carefully, for the first time since the morning before. Then, he carefully selected a brand-new navy-blue suit, just arrived from a Hong Kong tailor. He selected a freshly laundered white shirt and a gold tie, plus cufflinks with the SI logo on them.

He checked the shine on his shoes, not up to Joachim's standards but passable, and finally felt ready to be sociable. That his date was such an utter mystery added a tinge of excitement, and fueled his enthusiasm.

Hogan was waiting with the car when he emerged from the mansion. They chatted amiably as they headed into Manhattan, and Stark used his driver as practice for the evening.

After all, he hadn't gotten far with Marquez, and was hoping to do better tonight.

The Quilted Giraffe was at Madison and Fifty-fifth Street, not far from the ancestral mansion, but he ignored any tug he felt to go visit. As he exited the car, Stark entrusted his briefcase to Hogan.

Once inside, he was warmly welcomed by Susan Wine, one of the owners of the establishment. Stark had been a regular since they had opened in this location a few years prior.

He liked the experimental menu they maintained, and they were particularly well-known for their excellent seafood. The sleek décor and granite tables never failed to impress the women he brought here.

Wine gave him a kiss on both cheeks and he inhaled her perfume, which mixed with the various cooking smells and indicated that she spent plenty of time in the kitchen alongside her husband, Barry, who was the head chef.

He suddenly felt ravenous, realizing that, despite his promise, the sandwich Pepper had brought him still sat on his credenza, carefully wrapped and uneaten.

He was early, so the billionaire industrialist decided against sitting at the table and instead chatted with Susan. Minutes later, however, there was a murmur at the front of the restaurant, and his date arrived.

This mystery, unlike what lurked back at the office, was one that intrigued him.

She stood like a vision, gorgeous in a plum Amanda Wakeley gown with a halter top and exquisite beading that accented her form. Her black hair remained green-tinted, long and covering one eye, but her makeup was understated and enhanced her attractiveness.

She extended a hand, which Stark bent to kiss with a showy flourish, earning him a smile. He then introduced her to Susan, hoping his date would finally offer up a surname, but he was thwarted.

Susan showed them to a table, and Stark immediately ordered a bottle of red wine without having to consult the list, earning him an approving look from the sommelier.

He asked her how her day had gone, hoping for a hint as to what she did, but beyond a hint that it had something to do with running a company with a fairly decent-size staff, he remained clueless.

When pressed, she said the firm specialized in "logistics," and while that meant she wasn't working for a competitor, they seemed to know a lot of the same businessmen.

The wine arrived, and after tasting it, he accepted the bottle and they toasted the event where they had met. They read through the menu, and Stark opted for his usual—lamb baked in corn husks—while he insisted she try the signature beggar's purses: tender crêpes filled with the finest caviar and crème fraiche and tied in a bundle with a strip of chive.

She agreed, and the waiter hurried off.

Stark felt relaxed and comfortable. She was certainly attractive, and heads turned to stare at them now and then. While all recognized him, none knew her, and he knew that would have tongues wagging.

He decided to watch his wine intake, preferring to focus on her and remain at his best.

"I saw the broadcast of your appearance in Washington,"

she said, and he loved the light accent in her voice. "You've had a busy week."

"It's the price I pay for doing what I do," he said, trying to sound offhanded. "Congress always wants their pound of flesh, preferably on camera."

"And Iron Man has been earning some frequent-flyer miles, as well," she added.

"Another price to pay," he said, trying not to allow his mind to return to the HYDRA issue. "With what the suit can accomplish, I have to lend a hand as time permits."

"And time permits for me?" she responded. "I suppose I should feel honored."

"Well," he said, drawing the word out. "It took a little doing. But here we are, Katalin, and yet, I don't even know your last name."

She smiled, sipped her wine, and put the glass down before replying.

"I like to keep the mystery alive."

"Well, from the look of things, you're an expert at it," Stark said.

She was enchanting, attractive, and clearly interested. It had been a while since he had felt any sort of connection like this. The other women he dated were athletes, models, and actresses, and were usually selected for their photogenic qualities, as opposed to any urge he might have to open up.

Katalin was different. There was a maturity—a gravitas— to her poise, and her conversation had something that he hadn't experienced in a long while.

Joanna Nivena had come closest. She was his first fiancée, and had they married before he left for Asia, his life might have been very different.

As it was, when he returned and made it through the healing process, he kept the secret of the armor. As they began drifting apart, however—due in part to his depression and drinking—he had revealed everything.

Something in her must have understood. She encouraged him to embrace the armor, but in doing so she ended the engagement, freeing him to focus on his new mission in life.

Then she vanished. He respected her enough not to seek her out.

He blinked away images of that first, burning love, and focused on Katalin.

Stark didn't love her, didn't even feel anything more than an intense attraction, but that alone was stronger than anything he had experienced in a long while.

"You work very hard, looking after the world," she said frankly. "I wonder, however, who looks after you?"

"Pepper and Happy, I suppose," he said.

"Are they your dogs?" she asked. "What breed?"

Stark chuckled and shook his head.

"No, Pepper Potts is my right hand, and Happy Hogan is my driver and bodyguard. He'll be taking you home tonight."

"Oh, will he?" There was something in her eye . . .

He laughed again and the meal arrived. It was everything he expected, and Katalin seemed equally satisfied. Shortly the plates had been cleared away, and he signaled for the waiter, ordering the gossamer chocolate soufflé tempered with a scoop of ice cream and the buttery pecan squares on the side.

Over coffee they continued to chat. She was knowledgeable to the nth degree about current events, and in general could cover any topic. He was thrilled to note that the topic of his armored life had not come up much—she seemed interested just in Anthony Stark.

Instead, they debated the new administration's goals toward scientific research and space exploration. She seemed to know as much about that as she did about what was popular on Broadway. As for him, he barely paid attention to the arts—despite the fact that he lived in New York City. After all, *something* had to give.

As he signed the check, Stark continued to study her. She had an intelligence in her eyes, and something else—something he couldn't quite label.

He held her chair, she rose, they gathered their coats, and Barry Wine came out to bid them farewell. He was still in his chef's whites. They left the restaurant, and once they were outside, Stark slipped on gloves and escorted her to the curb, where Happy waited. Despite the dropping temperature, he wore only his chauffer's uniform, and helped them into the limo.

"Where to, sir?"

Stark glanced at Katalin. She stared back with naked interest, and maybe hunger for something unattainable at the restaurant.

"Home, Happy," Stark said, and he settled back in the leather seat, enjoying the warmed air. He slid off the kid leather gloves, stuffed them in his pocket, shifted his briefcase toward the door, and positioned himself in the middle of the seat.

This crowded his companion somewhat, and she snuggled up against him. Their hands interlaced, and he felt a tingle—as if he was a teen again, on a first date.

He'd known many women, and had explored their likes and dislikes with great passion through the years. It never ceased to tantalize him, the beginning of a new relationship, and his breathing quickened a bit.

As they drove through Manhattan, Happy stayed silent, but he did turn on the radio, tuning it to an FM jazz station, which enhanced the mood as Junior Mance, McCoy Tyner, and the Brecker Brothers serenaded them.

His driver certainly knew how to lend a hand, Stark mused.

Hogan also knew better than to take the direct route home, and by the time the car had entered Central Park, they had embraced, and he tasted her soft lips for the first time. The lipstick gave them a waxy feel and they remained together as she returned his kiss, her nails tightening their grip around his neck.

Her nails were long and sharp.

When they exited the park again, finally headed for the tunnel leading back to Long Island, it was like a signal, and she parted her lips. Their tongues finally met and he responded to her hunger with one of his own.

The trip away from Manhattan to the mansion passed in blissful silence as they alternately kissed, embraced, and caressed each other through their coats. As the car slowed, they parted and arranged themselves for the exit. Hogan, without expression, helped them out of the car and handed Stark his briefcase.

"Thanks, Hap," Stark said with a genuine smile, the first he had displayed in some time. "You can pick me up the usual time tomorrow. Thanks for working tonight."

"Sure thing, boss. You have a good night. 'Night ma'am."

She nodded in acknowledgment, and began walking toward the door. Stark caught up and held her hand.

Once inside, a maid greeted them in the foyer and took their coats. She vanished without a word, leaving them alone.

"Nightcap?"

"Do we need one?" she asked, without taking her eyes off him. She reached out and took his hand, leading him toward the master bedroom. Considering the fact that she had never been here before, she moved with tremendous confidence.

Once the door closed, she turned and fell into his arms. Their lips met anew and his hand worked to unfasten her gown. Her hands returned the favor and undid his tie and began unbuttoning his shirt. They did this with quiet efficiency tinged with desperation, but they were adults—no need to rush and be sloppy about it.

Once his shirt was off, he was exposed to her. The metal chestplate that kept his heart beating was visible, and she ran both hands over the crimson metal, smooth to the touch. Her fingers lingered over it, tracing patterns as if searching for flaws.

He waited for the sight of the cold metal to cut into the moment, for he had seen that expression before, combining pity with quiet revulsion.

To his surprise, she seemed entranced by what she saw, staring at it as another woman might at a diamond necklace or a rare artifact. In fact, her breathing seemed to deepen with excitement.

She then ran her fingertips down his waist.

His hands equally explored her bare skin.

They broke the clinch for a moment and he raised his right hand to her face. His fingers touched her hair, felt its smoothness, and then moved it away from her face.

Another surprise as he saw puckered, scarred skin left by an injury of some sort, and then he moved in to kiss her once again. His kisses worked their way up, from lip to cheek to the scarred skin, and he was gentle. Her hands clutched him, and her breathing quickened again.

After countless dates, endless kisses and flirtations, he was as naked as he dared allow himself to be. Exposed to this woman he barely knew, but could not get enough of.

xiii.

Two men arrived at a pocket park near Harlem. They carried with them a satchel filled with cash, and they wore overcoats.

The exchange went easily enough, since they were working through an intermediary who had little to gain from crossing either side. Thus, just as quickly as they arrived, they left, returning to a town car, stuffing their purchase into the trunk with more than a little disgust.

Once within the waiting vehicle, they turned up the heater and drove off.

"Well, we make terrific errand boys, don't we?" the passenger upfront grumbled.

"That's all we've done for a week now, and it's beginning to piss me off," the man who was driving said. His accent indicated that he had been raised in the deep South. Yet none of his associates knew his name. To them he was just number 267.

"How much longer is this crap going to go on?" the man beside him—number 145—grumbled.

"As long as Madame Hydra says it's gonna," the man in the back—number 389—replied. "She has her list and her schedule, and it looks like we have another week of this."

"Wouldn't it go faster if we just divvy up the list, and blitz these places in, like, two nights? Then we'd be ready."

"Maybe," 145 said, but then he added, "Ready for what?"

"Yeah, like she's gonna tell any of us," 389 said scornfully.

"Does the equipment make sense to you?" 267 asked.

"Well, I get all the guns and stuff, and god knows we've got enough of those to kill every cop in the whole friggin' city," 389 said, and there seemed to be relish in his voice. "The rest—geological maps, land surveys, deeds . . . nah, I can't figure it out."

"She tell anyone?" 267 pressed.

"Not that I know of," 389 said.

"Damn."

145 spoke up. "She's been talking to some of the tech geeks. There's definitely something on her mind. Trust me, we're not spinning our wheels and just stockpiling this stuff. There's a plan."

"Just nothing the bitch will share," 267 grumbled.

"Would you?" 145 asked.

They sat in silence as they drove back to their warehouse. Lookouts spotted them coming and the door was unlocked and easily rolled open to admit them. The car was swarmed by a half-dozen agents who took out the purchased equipment and quickly checked it off on a clipboard, then stowed it on one of the empty metal racks.

The conversation repeated itself as they did.

The man known as 389 listened, and then looked at 145.

"It sounds to me like there's not a lot of love lost for our fearless leader."

"She makes speeches, and doesn't tell us a damned thing," his comrade agreed. "I can understand the whole 'need to know' thing, but this is just plain stupid."

"It's not like she's the Grand High Poobah, though," 389 noted. "Isn't there someone we can complain to, higher up the food chain?"

"Nah, the Supreme Hydra doesn't seem to give a damn," 145 said. "He seems to think she's the hottest thing in town, and just leaves her alone."

"Well, we might need to make a few changes around

here," 389 said, loud enough that those who stood nearby could hear him. Suddenly conversation dropped off, and more than one man glanced around nervously.

More than few heads nodded in agreement.

Gabriella Marquez was returning to her apartment after a very late night at Stark Industries.

Her oversize shoulder bag fairly bulged with the odds and ends she had managed to gather—all from her father's shopping list, plus a few things that caught her trained eye. Despite their heft and her sore shoulder, she knew it was too little, and there'd be hell to pay once more.

It was something she was growing tired of. After all, she hadn't invented the Marquez persona just to be a simple industrial thief. Instead, unlike her money-hungry father, she was thinking long-term.

Crime in New York was changing. On the one hand, there were the immigrant gangs from South America, Russia, and Asia. They imported their own rules, and as often as not life was cheap to them. As a result, they callously shed blood to take one street corner after another. Or they imported their relatives and sold them into prostitution or slave labor.

The police commissioner, funded by additional money from Washington, had a real reputation for cutting down on crime, but he had just managed to drive it out into the suburbs. So while it was becoming harder to do business in the traditional places—like Times Square and Hell's Kitchen—crime was up in places like Coney Island and Long Island. Well outside of the Maggia's traditional sphere of influence.

Where outfits like the Maggia customarily did business, the old-time gangs were being subsumed—one after the other—by Wilson Fisk, the Kingpin of Crime. Thus, if anyone conducted illegal business in New York, Kingpin demanded—and got—his tribute.

Though her father was unaware of it, she made her own regular "contributions," and so was left to her own devices. The people under her command continued their day-to-day activities, but it fell entirely on her shoulders to find new revenue streams. Since her current activities were outside of the norm, they had managed to remain beneath the Kingpin's radar.

But sooner or later that might end. And if it did, there would be blood shed.

Hers.

Eventually, she imagined, there'd be a terrible war between the criminal organizations, and she wished to see the Maggia emerge unscathed. As a result, she was slowly redirecting their efforts to "cleaner" criminal activities, such as corporate espionage, and Stark was the ultimate example of that. It was much simpler to steal information than objects.

She had always had an affinity for technology, and as soon as she had turned her attention in that direction, she discovered how easy it would be to infiltrate such companies, and use fences to move stolen ideas. With miniaturization, moving vast amounts of data was becoming easier by the month. She had targeted Stark Industries, figuring they were cutting-edge, and knowing the CEO was as often as not distracted by other concerns, such as saving the world.

Stark was a test, and, if successful, she'd train others to engage in similar operations and seed them across the industry. New York was filled with opportunity.

Besides, she considered as she placed the objects in a locked cabinet in the living room, if everything went to hell, she'd need her own exit strategy. Her father wasn't going to help—he had made it clear that he considered her an accident of birth.

It was ironic, really. She had grown up thinking of herself as Whitney Frost, daughter of a Wall Street tycoon.

Byron and Loretta Frost had been loving, attentive parents. She was part of Manhattan's social world, and she adored the role of debutante.

Everything changed when the Frosts died suddenly. Shortly after the funeral, Count Luchino Nefaria approached her and told her the truth.

Frost had been his employee, and had agreed to adopt her and raise her, not in Rome, but New York. Whitney was really Giuletta, and Nefaria wanted her to be his heir.

From there her world had shattered, and before long the only person she had left was her father—her *true* father.

He trained her both physically and mentally, encouraging her natural talents for math and science. In time, he returned her to America, where Whitney Frost became a cover for the Maggia's regional director, Madame Masque.

Giuletta—or Gabriella or Whitney—undressed for bed, yawning along the way, and carefully peeled away the layers of appliances that turned her scarred features into the soft, smooth, and attractive face that had Tony Stark so intrigued.

The sun was starting to set in Austin. The horizon was streaked in yellows, pinks, and oranges as the orb lowered itself toward the horizon, painting the flatlands outside the city in vivid colors.

In the air, however, there were red and yellow beams of light cutting through the sky, flickering in and out like a visual Morse code. Accompanying the light show was the sound of explosions ranging from brief pops to extended deep-throated rumbles that could be heard a mile away.

On the outskirts of the city stood a factory owned by Stane International. Atop its flat, gray roof, a swarm of green-suited HYDRA agents had staked out positions and were firing with abandon at people scaling the building or on the ground, scrambling to take aim. In total, there were maybe just under two dozen people using the location as a battleground. Already, fallen agents of HYDRA and S.H.I.E.L.D. were dotting the ground, their blood mixing with the gravel and oil on the paved pathways.

Nick Fury, vigorously chewing the end of an unlit cigar, gripped his pistol as he hurled himself over a totaled car, seeking cover. As he tumbled and heard his business suit jacket rip on impact, two magenta beams of light flashed over his head. A second after the lights vanished, Gabe Jones jumped over the car and landed with a dull thump beside his old comrade.

"This sucks," Fury said. "I gotta get out of these suits. You know how much this cost me?"

"About eighty-five bucks at Syms?"

"Hardy-har-*har*," Fury said, surveying the area. Signaling to his men, he positioned them away from the concentrated enemy fire. *The weaponry got fancier*, he thought to himself, *but tactics remain pretty much the same, all the way back to biblical times.*

HYDRA had the high ground, giving them a tactical advantage. Unlike the armies found in the good book, however, the S.H.I.E.L.D. agents had access to the high ground's *interior.*

"Any civilians left inside?" he asked Jones, whose dark features were covered in grime.

Jones just shrugged. He peered over the top of the crumpled car, then fell flat to the ground as a new round of energy beams shot out. One of the fenders shattered into scrap.

Kenn Hoekstra came scrambling from behind them, a rifle at the ready.

"Sir," he said, acknowledging Fury.

"Sit rep."

"HYDRA has the doors and windows covered or booby-trapped, Colonel. From what we can tell, the civilians were herded out before we arrived."

"And how did you figger that out?"

"We . . . er . . . peeked through the windows."

"That'll do," Fury said.

"Orders?" Hoekstra was young, but he was a pro—the kind Fury hoped would be in the majority of his new organization.

"Get me four other men, heavily armed," the colonel said. "We're going to blow out a window and take the building."

"Sir?"

"What's the problem, Agent . . . ?"

"Hoekstra."

"Hoekstra—got it. So what's the problem?"

"Well, we're outgunned. Their weaponry is superior to ours," the agent said, sweating despite the cooling air around them.

"So I see," Fury replied. He took Hoekstra's firearm. "Can your rifle break glass?"

"Yes, sir," Hoekstra snapped.

"Get me the men, and you'll see how we did it in Berlin," Fury said and winked at Jones.

Hoekstra shot his commander a confused look.

"Buy me a beer and I'll tell ya the story," he continued. "Now *git*."

Hoekstra got.

In less than a minute, he returned with four men, all crouched low, arriving by zigzagging across debris and bodies. The scene was all too familiar to the colonel. He hated writing to the next of kin, but it was no less than the soldiers deserved.

Of course, in the beginning of his career he tended to know all his men personally. Now they were just cooling bodies in blue uniforms. He doubted he'd ever get used to that.

Fury assessed the men, made certain they were all armed. He nodded at Hoekstra, then Jones, and rose to a crouch, taking point. They huddled around him and he gestured at the building.

"We'll split in two. I'll take Hoekstra and you two," he said, pointing. "Gabe, you got the other two. Find a better position and fire at everything moving up top. Keep moving so they have to concentrate on you guys, and not on us.

"We'll get around and blow through a window and scramble inside, then take them out."

"Just the four of us?" one of the agents asked, looking concerned.

"Yeah, I know, used to do it with two, but I ain't that young anymore," Fury snapped, spitting out the chewed up, severely misshapen cigar butt. "Okay, on my mark.

"Go!"

He and Jones had done this sort of thing countless times in the past, often with men they didn't know well, or facing superior numbers and firepower. Usually both. This was old news to them, and neither seemed concerned.

That seemed to reassure the men they were leading, and everyone moved forward with purpose.

Duckwalking like Chuck Berry, they moved away, Jones moving off to the right, firing first, and taking out a surprised HYDRA agent who wasn't paying attention. That brought a slew of weapons to bear on him and his two companions, so they moved quickly.

Fury ditched the jacket altogether. He, Hoekstra, and the other two agents—a man and a woman—waited a beat, then broke to the left. Thanks to Jones and his group, they weren't fired upon.

As they moved, Fury did a headcount of dead S.H.I.E.L.D. agents, and was up to six by the time he scurried around the corner.

That was too many. Clearly, they needed better weapons, maybe even better uniforms and other protective gear. He had to get Stark on line for these tools of war, once he was done with the mission. The colonel would not send his men out this poorly equipped—not again.

Once around the corner, they hugged the building in the

shadow cast by the setting sun. He found a window that looked likely and signaled for Hoekstra to take it out while the other two covered him.

Signal given, the men fanned out. Seconds later the *rat-a-tat-tat* of the rifle sounded and the window shattered, setting off what appeared to be a grenade.

Glass, metal, and brick flew with dizzying speed at the agents. They dove to the ground.

The man panicked and ran from the pack.

"Penn!" Hoekstra yelled.

"Shut it," Fury hissed. At that moment a high-intensity beam flashed from the roof, striking the man squarely between the shoulders. He went down like a sack of flour, then lay there, his uniform smoldering.

Stoner's reports had insisted that the agency was months away from operational combat, and this was proof that his predecessor had been right.

Too bad Stoner wasn't around to hear it.

The remaining woman bent low, cupping her hands. Hoekstra stepped on them and hoisted himself through the ruined wall where the window had once been. Fury followed.

His hand in the air to stall the others, Fury scanned the room. It appeared to have been a break room for the workers—shattered coffee mugs and a ruined pot had fallen into a sink, while plastic chairs and the cheap wood table were scattered.

"It's clear—let's go," he told the others, eliciting nods of agreement. On the way out he grabbed an emergency-procedures card that showed the layout of the floor.

They moved through the door, which was remarkably intact, and emerged into the factory itself. The aisles and corridors were devoid of life, and he listened intently, hearing the muffled firing that continued from the ground and the roof above them.

He pulled out his radio.

"Gabe, we're in."

Nothing.

"Gabe?"

Still nothing. There could have been any of a number of reasons for the silence, and he couldn't dwell on it. He'd already lost one man to this shindig.

We've been through worse, he mused. *I'll see him again.*

The emergency card showed where the fire stairs were located. He led the two men toward the stairwell, and checked the door frame. No traps were visible.

The door opened soundlessly and they crept up a flight of stairs, then another, then another, pausing at each landing to make certain the sounds of fighting had not changed.

At the top of the stairs was a doorway announcing that the roof lay beyond. Fury tested the handle, noted nothing out of the ordinary, then eased it open a crack. Warm, moist air mixed with the air-conditioned cool of the factory. The firing sounded louder and he checked the men.

Hoekstra was set and determined. The other agent was breathing rapidly, but had a ready look.

Probably the kid's first combat, Fury thought.

Gripping his pistol tightly, he kicked the door open and shouted a banshee wail that sounded like that of a howling commando. He fired to one side, then the other, each shot precisely aimed, keeping the HYDRA contingent off balance until the other two could get into the open.

The HYDRA agents were leaning over the rooftop's edge, firing down at their targets below, so they were taken entirely by surprise. Bullets and the occasional yellow beam of energy fired back, and Fury wondered how many were left.

Once all three had clear lines of fire, they began firing at will, shooting to wound but willing to kill if necessary. Those had been his orders when this intervention had begun, and he expected his men to follow them implicitly.

A pair of the enemy charged at Fury, and he shot one in

the kneecap, then moved in close and planted a left upper-cut on the next, sending him flat on his ass. Ending up in the middle of the HYDRA group, he easily flipped another one over his shoulder, then kicked an agent flat on his back.

His every move was designed to disable an opponent with the minimum effort and the maximum effect. Hoek-stra and the other S.H.I.E.L.D. agent fought less elegantly, but with more intensity.

In mere minutes, the rooftop was cleared. The HYDRA agents were either wounded, unconscious, or dead.

Fury peered over the edge, and was relieved to see his old friend, skin intact. Nearby on the ground lay a scatter-ing of debris that looked suspiciously like the remains of a radio.

I knew it. He's too damned stubborn to let hisself get shot by pikers like these.

As the field agents cleaned up the area and emergency medical personnel were allowed through the cordon that had been set up a mile away, Fury and Jones slumped atop a car and reviewed the situation.

"We won," Jones said.

"In spite of ourselves," Fury grumbled. "We were out-gunned. I had a man panic. We were sloppy. If it weren't you and me in the lead, the outcome might've been differ-ent."

"I agree," Jones said somberly.

"These HYDRA bastards are tough," Fury said with grudging admiration. "They fought like a unit, and knew their weapons. Sloppy on the inside, but that was over-confidence. These goons are here for good, and this was one way of rubbing our noses in it."

"What did they want?"

"Don't know. Our intelligence says that this factory man-ufactures gear for miners—go figger," Fury said. "Right now, I don't care. What I care about is leveling the playing field."

"And how do you propose to do that?"

"First, we head back to the helicarrier. Once you eat and get some sleep, you're off to see the wizard."

"Stark?"

"Stark."

#

"Stark?"

He had been staring intently at his computer screen. He blinked his eyes several times, and then focused on the figure looming over him.

Gabe Jones.

An unhappy-looking Gabe Jones.

He hadn't heard the man enter. What was more disturbing was that somehow, he had made it past Pepper.

"What is it?" he asked. "What's wrong?"

"We had our asses kicked last night," the S.H.I.E.L.D. agent said flatly. "In Austin. They hit Stane."

Stark rose from his desk, allowing this to sink in. Just then, Pepper walked in carrying a tray set up to serve coffee. She quietly poured two mugs, handing one to Stark's unexpected visitor. Stark caught her shooting him a particularly nasty look, one reserved for those who got past Tony Stark's gatekeeper. It was a look he never wanted directed his way.

"Milk . . . sugar?" she asked, her tone bland, hiding her annoyance. Jones shook his head. As they moved to the guest chairs, Pepper set down the tray within easy access and closed the door behind her. Stark settled into one, while Jones sat stiffly in the other.

He's not in a good mood this morning, Stark observed.

"One of Stane's buildings?" he asked once he sipped from the cup. "What was taken?"

"We're not sure—maybe nothing," Jones admitted. "It

was a mining equipment factory, and we may have stopped them before any got away."

"Okay then," Stark replied. "Why the personal visit?"

"We'd like you to look over their captured weaponry, and maybe the factory itself, and see if you can bring us up to parity with HYDRA."

Great. As if I don't have enough on my plate already. He was growing to really hate the terrorist operation.

"Stane's going to love having me poke around his stuff."

"I know you're competitors, and don't necessarily get along—" Jones began.

"He's a psychotic, pure and simple. That plant in Austin is the one he uses in corporate PR, to show the world that he's not all about munitions."

"Which he is."

"Which he is. So that begs the question, why did HYDRA attack Stane's one nonmunitions plant? Helmets with built-in flashlights aren't exactly going to strike terror into their enemies."

"Well then, how about a trip to Austin?"

"I need answers, Gabe," Stark said, rising. "I'll have Pepper clear my schedule, and I'll fly down immediately. Where are the captured weapons?"

"On the helicarrier, awaiting your arrival."

"I'll fly up when I'm finished in Austin," he said. The two men shook hands, and Jones left by the front door. Stark noted he wisely avoided contact with Pepper as he left. It's the only way he made it off the floor in one piece.

Flying high above the Atlantic, Stark waited until he had bypassed any major commercial air routes, then turned to the southwest, crossing almost immediately over the coast and continuing above dry land.

He barely acknowledged the fall chill that spoke of short days and hearty meals. In fact, he'd be lucky to get back by dusk, and would most likely have to make do with whatever he could find in the helicarrier's commissary.

Somehow, he doubted that their first recruits had included a four-star chef.

The long flight south to Texas allowed him time to order his thoughts. First, Katalin. When he awoke that morning, the other side of the bed had been empty, and the sheets had been cold, indicating that she had left sometime earlier, in the middle of the night.

She had no last name, no known address. *How on earth do you send flowers to someone like that?* And why had she left?

He wasn't sure how he was feeling about her. She intoxicated him with her accent and beauty and air of mystery. Even more, she hadn't been chased away by his ironclad alter ego, despite the fact that there was no escaping him. No, she had actually seemed *fascinated* by the chestplate. Not drawn to him like a superhero groupie—he'd seen more than his share of those, and could identify them twenty yards away.

No, this had been deeper, though he couldn't quite figure out where it came from.

There was far more to her than she let on, and he loved it. Together, they had performed flawlessly, and he smiled at the recent memory. His body hadn't felt this way in a long, long time, but his mind cautioned him to learn more before things got out of hand.

After about an hour of such musings, his mind turned to HYDRA. The Austin attack was distant from the other sites they had hit in the past week, all of which had been in the Northeast. That had led them to believe that it was a single branch of the group committing all the assaults. Was this a change in tactic, or a broadening of their scope?

And what was needed from the mining equipment Stane manufactured in Texas? He tried to come up with a link between mining, communications, gyroscopes, and the other items they could link to HYDRA. But without any luck.

They were a global threat, and that was the very reason S.H.I.E.L.D. had been formed. What if there *wasn't* a connection? What if he was making this trip, only to discover that it was a wild goose chase?

As he rocketed across the land, Stark began to think that he needed a faster way of traveling. The quinjet the Avengers had recently received from the African nation of Wakanda would do the job, but it was designed for multiple passengers. He needed something self-contained, just for himself. Something that would attach to the armor, with its own power supply, but that could be jettisoned, then retrieved.

For the next half hour, he sketched out some schematics in his head.

By the time he began his approach to the factory, Stark had already dictated several pages of notes about various devices he nicknamed "rocket sleds." He was actually looking forward to playing with the designs, once this HYDRA mess was resolved.

The factory grounds had been cleaned up, so there were none of the bodies he had seen in the photos, and the ground just had dark patches where the blood had dried or soaked into the dirt. Bright yellow police tape surrounded the entire building, and no one was present beyond a small contingent of the locals, and Stane's security people.

He landed in the late morning and noted that it was in the mid-fifties, far warmer than New York.

No sooner had he landed than two security guards, guns drawn, approached him.

Despite the fact that he had royally pissed her off, Pepper had worked with Jones to warn them that he was coming, and to arrange full clearance. Stane wasn't happy about it, but he had acquiesced to the federal request.

It certainly helped to have both federal approval as an Avenger, and international credentials from S.H.I.E.L.D.

"I'm here to help," Iron Man said, realizing immediately how lame that sounded.

"Do you have any ID?" the foremost guard demanded.

"You're kidding, right? Who else wears armor like this? I'm sure as hell not the Titanium Man."

The guards exchanged glances, shrugged, and holstered their guns.

"Sorry, sir. Mr. Stane insisted that we ask."

"He's just jerking my chain," Iron Man said, and even more than before he disliked his competitor.

"We were expecting you, and you have total access, although Mr. Stane asked that we accompany you at all times. He also, er, wanted to repeat that no pictures were to be taken. If there's anything you want to have recorded, we'll take care of that and supply you with the imagery."

"Always worried about corporate espionage," Iron Man replied with a cold chuckle. "Follow me, then. Let's get this show on the road."

The trio approached the building and eschewed the doors, which had remarkably remained intact. Instead, they entered through a blown-out hole in the front wall.

Within, the factory was a shambles, and at a glance Stark could tell it would take a few million and probably six months to fix everything up. *Hope Stane's been keeping up on his insurance premiums.*

"I'm not going to take pictures, but I'll need to take a series of spectroscopic readings," Iron Man said as they stood by what had once been a conveyor belt.

"What's it do?" asked one of the guards, a burly man with a handlebar mustache.

"It'll allow me to locate any energy signatures that would tell me what sort of weapons were used. Think of it as a variation on the Geiger counter."

They glanced at each other again, turned back, and nodded.

*If we have to make every decision by committee, this is
going to take all day,* he thought grimly. But he didn't say
anything. *No sense in making it worse.*

He opened a panel in the wristband of one of his
gauntlets, revealing a miniaturized control panel, tapped a
couple of touch-sensitive buttons, then threw a switch. Immediately the circular chest piece began to glow.

One of the guards took a step or two back, but the other
held his ground.

Stark's helmet readings indicated that the sensors were
recording all the data he would need, and that things were
nominal so far.

"This is going to take time," Iron Man warned the
guards. "We have three floors to cover, plus the roof."

"Anything yet?" the mustache asked.

"Actually, no," he replied.

The three men silently walked through the carnage, stepping over bits and pieces of company equipment and task-
specific machines that were designed to produce the mining
materials. Stark recalled seeing a press piece on it when the
factory had opened, and thought the bald man was grand-
standing. Looking closely at the equipment now, he admired
the elegance Stane brought to the hand-tooled devices, but
took no pictures.

First he established the readings he would get when
there *wasn't* anything out of the ordinary. That would allow him to recognize any anomalies that popped up.

Walking the three floors took them more than an hour.
Dust, debris, and fire-retardant foam was everywhere,
making a mess in varying degrees.

The third floor was particularly innocuous looking, and
also the least damaged. Thus far there was nothing unusual, and he assumed that when the HYDRA agents had

been inside of the building, they hadn't employed any unusual weapons.

On the rooftop were scorch marks and deep divots dug out of the brick and concrete by the bullets that had been fired by Fury's men. There were plenty of new readings, as well, indicating that HYDRA's weaponry had been discharged, striking some of the structures on the roof. He walked the perimeter, then focused on the center before turning off the scanning.

"Get any good information," the clean-shaven guard asked.

"Enough to give me something to work with, but I'll need to analyze it."

"What were they using?" the guard continued. "I was here yesterday and it scared the living crap out of me."

"Energy weapons—but you already knew that—and more sophisticated than lasers, it appears," replied Iron Man.

The guards nodded in unison.

"I'm done here," Iron Man said finally, and he extended his hand. "Thanks for your time." The men readily shook it and smiled, looking relieved that things had gone smoothly, and that there hadn't been any sort of confrontation.

"What happens now?" the mustache asked.

"Stane rebuilds. And I go figure this out," the armored Avenger replied. "Stand back now."

As they stepped away, he gave the command that ignited the boot jets and propelled himself into the sky, waving once at the men who watched in rapt fascination.

Away from the surface, the sound of his jets faded as he gained altitude, and he opened a signal to the helicarrier, getting a fix on its current position. It was over Ohio, so he adjusted his course.

While flying, he had his internal systems begin an analysis of the readings, but he recognized that it would take plenty of time, and doubted there'd be anything conclusive until he could download the data into S.H.I.E.L.D.'s mainframe.

Once that was running, he checked in with Pepper to make certain the campus was intact. Ever since the two attacks he'd been thinking about ways to improve security, and found that he disliked being so far away. Yet, he knew that when he wore this armor, his responsibilities extended well beyond the two square miles of his home base.

It was a bonus that the Stark subsidiary plants around the country hadn't been similarly assaulted, which provided some comfort. It also led him back to the theory that the incidents were being carried out by a Northeastern branch of HYDRA.

From a distance, he saw the bulky silhouette of the heli-carrier, nestled between two thick cumulus clouds just over the border where Ohio gave way to Pennsylvania. He pushed the jets a bit for additional thrust, and then received a warning that he'd need to recharge while visiting with Fury.

Once aboard, Iron Man was escorted to the data center, where he found a connection and downloaded the information he had recorded just two hours earlier. As he did, he realized that it had been many hours since the coffee, nor had he eaten. He paused to calculate, and realized he'd been on the go for about eight hours straight—not unusual in his life, but the week was taking its toll.

No wonder he was feeling lightheaded.

Fury found him just then, looking freshly pressed in a new suit, and his stubble appeared only a day old this time—which for him was clean-shaven. They shook hands, and then the colonel got straight to the point.

"What'd you find?"

"Don't know yet," Iron Man replied. "We need to run a full analysis, but those energy weapons of theirs are pretty potent."

"I coulda told you that," Fury replied. "Try being on the receiving end of 'em. What I want to know is, where'd they come from, and what can I do to protect my men?"

"Feed me, and we can talk," Iron Man said, admitting that he needed to recharge, not only the armor, but the body. "Make sure we sit near an electrical outlet."

The colonel nodded once, and the two men headed for the nearest commissary, walking in silence.

Sure enough, the fare wasn't ready to be reviewed in *Gourmet* magazine, or even *Zagat,* but he wasn't feeling picky. Iron Man picked out foods designed for sustaining energy, and then something sweet to treat himself. When he couldn't find the chocolate soufflé, he settled for cookies.

Once he had a tray full of food, he followed Fury back to his office, where they could talk in privacy. After setting the tray down, he opened up one of the circular pods at his hip and withdrew a cable. He attached one end to the smaller circular access port on his right side, and the other end went into a specially designed outlet Stark had cannily included throughout the helicarrier when the plans were being drawn up.

As the charge began, he took off his helmet and settled back to eat.

Fury fiddled with some papers on his desk, waiting for Stark to get comfortable, then asked again about the weaponry.

"I'm seeing wavelengths being used in the infrared spectrum the likes of which I've never encountered before," Stark said. "This is really sophisticated equipment, certainly nothing available on the commercial market."

"Well, if it's what I'm thinking of," Fury said, "then I know why. Imperial Industries International."

Stark put down his carrot stick and raised his eyebrows in surprise.

"Leslie Farrington's company? What's he got to do with this?" While he didn't know Farrington personally, he couldn't help but see Triple-I's name in numerous trade publications. And Farrington was well-known for taking very good care of his employees, which enabled him to recruit some of the best. In some ways, Stark admired their work, and might even have been subconsciously steering SI toward the Triple-I model.

"Our intelligence shows that he may have links with AIM. There's a very real possibility that he's been diverting a lot of their tech to building weapons and vehicles for them, skipping the free market," Fury said, tapping the papers on his desktop. "That would give them cutting-edge weaponry, advanced submarines, and top-of-the-line fighter aircraft.

"If that's the case—and I think it is—then I need you to help counter them."

Stark chewed and nodded.

"HYDRA was an abstract concept," Stark began slowly. "A costumed terrorist operation dating back to World War Two—that always struck me as something from an Ira Levin novel."

"Says the man who took on Ultimo," Fury said.

"Touché," Stark responded. "Hearing about Atlanta, and seeing Austin, I get it. They're prepared. And by contrast, the free world is not."

Fury nodded.

"We're getting there, but I gotta level the playing field with something more than this flying bathtub."

"You'll have it," Stark promised. "I admit to being, *ahem*, gun-shy about building fresh munitions, but I can see the need."

"And just because the Council rubs you the wrong way," Fury added, "it doesn't mean they're wrong."

Stark grinned and nodded in agreement.

"That they do, and you're right. Anyway, I have some things in development that should at least give you the firepower."

They were interrupted by a flashing red light on Fury's desk. He grabbed his handset and said, "Send her in."

A blond female agent walked in, saluted Fury, and dropped off some printouts. She nodded toward Stark.

"That'll be all, Agent 13. Thanks."

Stark's eyes followed the attractive woman out of the office.

"Eyes front, Shellhead," Fury said, and tapped the papers. "Here, this is what we got from your scans in Austin. Turn it into English."

Stark studied the documents, quickly flipping through the printouts, then went back to the beginning and reviewed them more carefully. His lips pursed and his mind went into overdrive.

"The weaponry discharges highly powerful energy from compact cartridges constructed with something I've never seen before."

"If you've never seen it, where'd it come from? Latveria? Wakanda?"

"No clue," Stark admitted unhappily.

"Well, you got the degrees, so it's all Greek to me," Fury admitted. "Still, if it has you puzzled, it has me worried."

He reviewed the papers one more time, then tossed them on Fury's desk.

"Triple-I is a key," Stark said.

"How do ya figger?"

"What HYDRA was trying to take in New Jersey was supplies from a Triple-I competitor. They wouldn't need to do that if they were getting their equipment from Triple-I. So it seems like two different factions of HYDRA have been involved. And I'm betting that the East Coast attacks are coming from one cell."

"And Austin?"

"Most likely a different faction entirely."

"What I can't figure out is just what they're trying to do?" Stark said.

Fury chewed it over silently for a few moments, then spoke.

"They're putting us on notice."

"How so?"

"Why attack Stane's plant without taking anything obvious? They did it to show us they can, and that we can't stop 'em."

"Yet."

"Yet," Fury replied, and he smiled.

Somehow, Stark felt as if he'd been neatly led to this moment.

"Nick, I have to admit, it's got me baffled," Stark admitted. "Gyroscopes, sonics, communications. I just can't piece it together."

"Well, you're gonna have to," Fury said without a trace of antagonism in his voice. He was simply stating fact. "If you don't, we're in for a world of hurt, and god knows where it'll stop."

"Exactly."

With that, Fury went to his sideboard, poured them two glasses of scotch, and returned to his desk, handing one to Stark before sitting behind his desk.

For the next hour, they sat uninterrupted, and reviewed everything that had happened over the past week.

All Stark omitted was Katalin and Marquez.

XV.

As Madame Hydra was returning to the Manhattan apartment she was using, there were a few other men and women on the cold, dark streets, scurrying furtively, doing what had been nicknamed the "walk of shame."

She felt no shame, though. Madame Hydra had gotten through to Stark in ways his other opponents had never been able to. She had him utterly mesmerized by the persona she had carefully crafted to keep the attention on the mystery, and not the details.

Both Iron Man and Tony Stark had to be distracted while HYDRA readied itself.

And the experience had been intense. Stark's chestplate had fascinated her, at once a cold, unyielding barrier and a thing of power. She had been repulsed by it, drawn to it, and challenged by it, all at the same time.

Coupling with him had meant revealing herself to him in ways she had not done in a very long time. Allowing him to touch the scars had at first caused her skin to crawl—she was used to covering them up, employing the look to lend her the air of an enigma. In permitting him to get so close, she had, in essence, removed the mask and left herself vulnerable.

And his reaction to them had come as a surprise. Rather than being repulsed, he had shown a tenderness she had not understood, and still could not grasp.

But no matter—they were still scars, and they served her well, reminded her of a past she would obliterate along with any who stood in her way, Stark included.

And while her body had betrayed her mind, responding in ways she had not intended, in the end it proved the perfect tool for keeping Stark entranced. The release their liaison provided her had been pleasant, in its way, but she could not allow herself to be swept up in the emotions the same way she wanted Stark to be.

No, such things lay in her dim past, and were better left there. The only emotion of any value was anger—a fire that would bring down the world, one piece at a time.

At the same time as she was seducing Stark, her Midwest counterpart had succumbed to her manipulations, hitting Stane's plant and obtaining the device she required. Each HYDRA cell needed to be properly funded, and the fact that she was willing to pay had provided incentive enough—as had the possibility that the plant might also yield some munitions.

No doubt the device was already en route to New York. Suddenly, something was wrong.

Breaking out of her thoughts, Madame Hydra realized that there was a car approaching from the front. A quick glance over her shoulder registered another approaching at exactly the same speed.

They seemed inconspicuous, but something about them . . .

Her hands were deep in her overcoat pockets, but she quickly withdrew them, each clutching a pistol, small and of unusual design.

As her hands cleared the pockets, she extended her arms and fired once from each gun. Magenta light burst forth— narrow at first, but widening as it crossed the distance—and struck the cars, blowing out the windshields. Whoever was driving lost control, and the two vehicles crashed into parked cars on either side of the street.

Return fire was almost immediate, two shots from the nearest car, three from across the street. The walk of shame became a sprint of fear as people scattered to get clear.

With practiced ease, she tucked her shoulder and dove for cover, firing without letup and with unerring aim. This effectively prevented her opponents from targeting her. The cars were pierced repeatedly, damage to the engine block preventing them from driving off. The occupants returned fire or died trying, and in less than a minute both cars were devoid of threat.

Sirens began wailing in the distance, magnified by the crisp, clear air. She knew that she had only moments, so she investigated only the closest vehicle. Acrid smoke rose from seared flesh and smoldering metal and made her cough once, but she checked their imbedded IDs and discovered that the assassins came from within her own ranks.

She was impressed by their initiative, but disgusted by their failure.

They had deserved to die.

"Imperial Industries International," Stark muttered out loud.

Pepper was wearing a floral blouse and black skirt, and she cocked an inquisitive eyebrow in his direction.

"Beg pardon?"

"Just thinking out loud," he said quietly. "Just ignore me." She nodded and let him brood.

He had returned to SI's headquarters just as the business day was winding down. Most of the staff were already leaving—those who had lives—but not Pepper. She announced firmly that she wasn't going to leave her desk until Stark said it was fine.

So they had reviewed the day's activities and the revised schedule for the next morning. There had been back-to-back-to-back meetings on the calendar, and when he groaned, she had shown little sympathy, but had begun adjusting the schedule.

That task complete, she had showed no sign of departing, and Stark appreciated that it was out of concern. How many days and nights had she remained on call, lending him a hand far beyond the limits of her duties?

No man could ask for a greater friend or ally.

"So, what caused you to think about Triple-I?" she finally prompted. He jumped, suddenly realizing that he had left her sitting there while he mused in silence.

"Turns out they're mixed in with HYDRA, and I never saw it," he confessed. "Here I thought they ran such a tight ship, while someone at Imperial was funneling their best designs to an outfit that wants to take over the world."

"Sounds pretty shortsighted to me," she said. "What happens when you take over the world? First you have to feed and clothe and house and rebuild. Then you've got to run it. Is it really worth the effort?"

Stark blinked at her comments.

"And if you ran the world?"

"Equal the playing field, I think," she said. "The people who really run things should be given the benefits, and the people who *think* they run things should be forced to work for a living."

"From secretary to mogul, you mean?" She was hitting kind of close to home, he thought with a mixture of amusement and chagrin.

"I'm no one's mogul," she replied with a grin. "I'd settle for benevolent despot."

"Well, Ms. Despot, would you do me a favor, and ring Ms. Marquez's office to see if she's free for dinner?"

"Two women in two nights? That's busy, even for you," she said with a disapproving tone. "Especially when one of them is your own employee."

Ouch.

"It's just dinner," he said, but he didn't succeed in keeping the defensive tone from his voice. "I'm hungry, and I don't want to eat alone."

"I could always order out for Chinese," she offered.

*   *   *

Twelve hours after the abortive attempt on her life, Madame Hydra returned to the New York headquarters deep beneath the Manhattan skyscrapers.

She noted more than a few surprised looks, tough to see from beneath their cowls, but evident when jaws were dropping like the temperature.

Her lieutenants—145 and 389—were standing at attention by the main communications panel. Neither seemed surprised to see her.

"We managed to obtain the electronics you wanted," 145 said by way of acknowledgment.

"The package from Texas is in your office," 389 added.

"Very good, that's one less thing we need," she replied.

Stepping close to the two men so no one else could hear them, she added, "I can't tell you how much I disapprove of the initiative you two are showing. We're getting close to our goal, so I will keep you alive, but do not think that you will receive a second opportunity to show such an opportunistic streak."

The men nodded subtly.

"There are many ambitious people in this base, some more loyal to our ideals than you seem to be," she continued, practically hissing in their ears. "*No one* is irreplaceable."

She stepped back and studied their body language.

They were not done.

However, the backbone they had exhibited, combined with the fire of competition she had fanned, would lend new intensity to their efforts. She would watch them carefully; take full advantage of their anger.

And then be done with them. *Cut off a limb and two more shall take its place!*

"Status," she said to the man behind the console.

He swiveled around and in clipped tones recounted reports from other HYDRA cells. News that Iron Man had been in Austin was of concern only because she hadn't foreseen it. She had presumed it would be S.H.I.E.L.D., and had hoped to cripple their forces in that section of the country. They were still building, and any losses would be devastating.

And Fury would now have a greater understanding of their actions. He was smart in an entirely different way from Stark, and both men were adept at connecting the dots. Worse, she had no way of distracting Fury.

It was time to make a statement of their own, let the agents of law and order understand just how powerful HYDRA was. Along the way, some of her *personal* goals could be served.

"Get me all information on the Lincoln and Holland tunnels—I want it in my office before day's end," she commanded.

"Yes, Madame Hydra," the agent said, and he grabbed a headset.

"Agent 145," she called out. The lieutenant was at her side in moments.

"We meet in an hour. A new mission has begun."

"Hail Hydra," he said, sounding like every other agent. Nothing in his voice indicated a personal agenda.

She would need to watch him with particular care. . . .

All Stark really wanted that night was someone to have dinner with, someone not actively working for S.H.I.E.L.D. or Congress, someone who wouldn't be making demands on him, or pinning him under their value judgments.

He was delighted when Marquez appeared by Pepper's desk—which was finally deserted, since he had convinced her to go home.

Gabriella even smiled when he emerged.

"Hope you don't mind, but I want to keep it local and simple," he said, closing his office door.

"Not at all, sir," she said.

"Tony."

"Sorry. Tony."

"Well, I know we had hoped for something more formal tonight. . . ." he began sheepishly.

"To start the weekend off right, you said," she offered. "That doesn't have to be formal."

"True. Events have a habit of derailing my best-laid plans," he agreed. "I'm just getting used to it, but others aren't always so understanding. I appreciate it."

"I've read about your . . . exploits, and understand the extraordinary demands on your time," she said, the first affectionate hint he had heard in her voice.

Maybe all was not for naught.

"So then, you up for Mexican?"

She nodded, and soon they were being driven to a mom-and-pop restaurant Happy had recommended to him some weeks earlier. The owners were unaccustomed to seeing limousines pull up, so there was more than the usual amount of gawking. At least no paparazzi were on hand, since celebrities and superheroes tended not to dine in the neighborhood.

Once inside, they sat, ordered margaritas, and chatted. She outlined her day and the department's efforts until he waved a hand in the air between them.

"Too much work," he interrupted. "Please, tell me about yourself instead."

"There's nothing to tell," she said. "I'm pretty much a run-of-the-mill SI employee."

"Tonight, I'll take run-of-the-mill. Truth is, I don't see much of that anymore," he replied.

"I can imagine," she agreed, and she seemed far more interested in talking about him. "Your world is certainly a very different one than mine. What's it like wearing the armor?"

She stopped herself, and then continued.

"If you don't mind talking about it, that is."

He drank slowly from the glass, licking a little of the salt from the rim.

"When I'm in the suit, I feel powerful," he began. "It gives me control over situations others couldn't handle, and it feels good to help out."

"With the rate at which technology is advancing—much of it due to your efforts—how do you keep up?"

"Well, I'm always upgrading the armor, trying to see how much I can pack into the circuitry without becoming too bulky. In that way the advancements offer a tremendous benefit.

"The weight concerns are more than just convenience, too. You know, this all happened because of my heart."

She nodded.

"I can never take off the main chestplate," he continued. "I feel its presence every waking minute, and sometimes that makes me feel, well, trapped."

"Do you . . . how does that affect how you relate to other people?" she asked. "Do you ever feel cut off from the rest of us?"

He studied her eyes, noting the intensity behind the questions, which was surprising. She was looking for something, but he had no clue what.

"Sometimes, but I don't let myself go there," he admitted. "I still have my brain, my emotions . . . the armor lets me still run the company. While not perfect, it doesn't keep me from being human, if that's what you're asking."

She thought about that for a moment.

"And yet, rather than limit yourself to the chestplate, which can be hidden under a shirt, you put on a full suit of armor, which entirely blocks you off from the rest of the world. How is that not hiding?"

"I'm not hiding, but using it to help," he said, suddenly feeling adrift in the conversation. "There's a big difference."

"So do you wear the armor to erase that feeling of isolation?" she pressed. "Turn being trapped into being something *more*?"

"I've never sat on the couch and had it analyzed—and perhaps I should—but I'm sure there's some validity to that." He couldn't quite put his finger on what she was talking around, but at least she was talking.

Their conversation continued, and by the time they were driving home they had talked about him, his life, his world, then politics, monetary policy, and travel, but very little about Gabriella and her life away from SI.

She was still an enigma, and he was still fascinated by her.

As the limo pulled up to her apartment building, he turned and took her hand.

"This was very nice. Thank you," he said. "Now, when can we schedule that formal date I promised you?"

"Is that appropriate, sir . . . er, Tony?" she asked, yet he didn't think she sounded disapproving.

"Don't worry—one date won't raise HR's legal hackles," he said. "If there's a second one, we can discuss it then."

"One date then," she agreed, gave him a peck on cheek, and left the car.

As they pulled away from the curb, he realized that while she had agreed, they hadn't said *when*. Somehow, he had a feeling she had wanted it that way.

XVI.

It was Saturday, and he decided he didn't have to go into the office. He woke up, hoping for a genuine day off so he could tackle the growing mental list of things he wanted to build.

Rather than indulge his creative side, however, he got a call from Fury with word that a HYDRA ship—probably one of the ones built for them by Triple-I—was attacking an incoming freighter. The helicarrier was over the Canadian Rockies, the Coast Guard was too far away, and the vessel and its crew were in danger of sinking into the Atlantic Ocean unless help arrived.

Within minutes of hanging up, Iron Man was rocketing across Long Island Sound connecting with S.H.I.E.L.D. to acquire the correct coordinates. It took perhaps seventeen minutes before he spotted the bright bursts of fire from the HYDRA craft. The small, sleek vessel was circling the far larger and dowdier tanker, sizzling sounds filling the air as the Golden Avenger neared.

"Repulsors, energize. Standby mode."

Iron Man angled low, gaining speed.

Just as the HYDRA attack ship came around the prow, Iron Man interposed himself between the ships. In doing so, he received enemy fire. The magenta energy blasts packed far more oomph coming from hull-mounted guns, larger and deadlier than the handheld pistols he had swatted away in Boston. He shuddered, biting his lip and drawing blood, but managed to remain aloft and spared the tanker further damage.

Both gloves aimed at the center of the HYDRA craft.

"Activate repulsors, eighty percent."

Twin impacts dented the hull, sending sparks from the gun mounts.

A second barrage and the guns were crippled, and there was a noticeable breach on the port side, well above the water line.

It was just then that something was thrown at him. The object arced through the air at a leisurely pace, and so his sensors didn't immediately identify it as a threat. The gray device, about the size of a softball but shaped more like a cigar, lit up brightly and shed sparks, emitting some form of energy discharge.

The discharge laced into his armor, which absorbed some of it, but his sensors quickly showed that the circuitry would overload if the assault continued.

The device reached the apex of its arc, and began to fall back toward the sea. Iron Man kicked out, managing to catch an end and sent the weapon away from him even faster. As soon as it struck the surface, there was a small explosion, a burst of steam, then nothing.

Anger getting the better of him, Iron Man fired his repulsors again and again. The HYDRA engines began to emit thick smoke, then flames began shooting out from the rear. His heads-up display indicated the ship was rapidly losing power but not taking on water.

Sirens sounded in the distance, audible now that the shooting was over. Iron Man moved in close and a quick scan enabled him to identify a major structural support beam. He grabbed onto the HYDRA ship, dragged it away from the tanker, and accelerated across the water, tugging the vessel toward the oncoming Coast Guard vessel.

Quickly the HYDRA craft was surrounded, and Iron Man hovered above, waiting until its crew could be off-loaded, hoping to have the opportunity to ask some questions.

There was an explosion beneath the surface, sending a

plume of water and steam out from either side as a self-destruct mechanism imploded the vessel, breaking it in half and rapidly sinking it. Screams came from the nearest Coast Guard vessels as scalding steam swept across the sides closest to the doomed boat.

Almost immediately, the only signs of the HYDRA attack were scraps of debris and floating bodies, dressed in their green uniforms. There was nothing to salvage, nothing for S.H.I.E.L.D. to study, and no one to interrogate.

While the tanker was safe, nothing had been learned.

He radioed the status to Fury, asked for a copy of the tanker's manifest, and then flew back to SI. He needed a stiff drink, and to forget that the day had ever happened.

Stark landed just outside the rear of the mansion and was through the doorway when he heard the phone ringing. With the majority of the staff enjoying the day off, he instructed his helmet to make the connection, and answered the phone himself.

"Stark."

"Tony, it's Leticia Dandridge." That she was calling on a weekend wasn't a good sign, nor was this a conversation he felt up to having.

"How can I help, Leticia?"

"What's going on with you and Congress? I just watched the C-SPAN rerun, and you looked terrible."

"Thanks for the vote of confidence," he said archly. He was out of breath and sweaty, despite the armor's environmental controls.

"You sound strange," she said. "Are you all right?"

"I'm fine, Leticia."

"Well, are you going to lose us the army contract?" *Straight for the jugular.*

"Not at all," Stark said, wishing he could tell her to go to hell and let him get out of the damned armor. But he knew better. While he was in charge, the fact that his was a publicly traded company meant having a board, and people like Dandridge sitting on it. As much as he hated the corporate bullcrap, he had grown to enjoy running Stark Industries, although his preference remained to tinker in the lab.

He also treasured the link to his parents, and would never allow SI to slip from his grasp.

"Look, Leticia," he continued, tamping down his frustration. "We got robbed, and Congress had every right to ask. I've taken steps to improve security, and we still have the network plans. In fact, this gave us the time to improve upon them.

"The bottom line is the Army will have their network, and they'll be thrilled."

"I wish I had the votes, because I'd love someone in that chair who would run the company 24/7 and not go fight the Misfits of Evil."

"Masters," he corrected.

"I wish I could believe you," she countered, "but time and again you've let me down."

When did it become all about you, Leticia?

"You want to stop making munitions and save the world," she continued without a pause. "And as long as there's a dividend, most of the shareholders won't care. But some of us on the board aren't happy that we're moving out of a profitable field just as this country needs to hold on to its dominant position in the global community. Have you seen the headlines, or are you too busy flying around in that ridiculous suit and sleeping with everything in a skirt?"

"That's unkind to women, Leticia," he responded. "After all, you're no doubt wearing a skirt right now." He swore he could hear her mouth drop, and he forged ahead.

"Yes, of course I see the headlines. I receive reports not that dissimilar to what the NSA presents the president every morning. And yes, it's a scary world out there. That doesn't mean I want to build countless missiles that can be used by any group of fanatics crazy enough to attack an army base.

"Making this world a safer and more secure place remains a new and very worthy goal for me, and for Stark Industries."

His words—the force and passion behind them—seemed to mollify her.

"Tony, I'm just doing my duty."

"As am I, Leticia," he said calmly. A beep interrupted their conversation, and rather than put her on hold, he took advantage. "Someone else is calling, so I'll talk to you during the week."

He pressed the flash button.

"Hello?"

"Tony Stark? Please hold for Senator Byrd."

Dropping his voice, he said, "I'm so sorry, but Mr. Stark is out for the day, and can't be reached. Excuse me— incoming call . . ."

With that he quickly hung up.

Moving to his master bedroom, he shucked off the rest of his armor. He'd return it to the lab after he got dressed and made his way downstairs.

As he slipped into pants and sweater, the phone rang again and he debated letting the machine get it this time. But the readout identified it as Pepper's extension.

What the hell is she doing in the office?

He sighed and answered.

"Hi, Mr. Stark," she said. "Sorry to interrupt your relaxing weekend, but Garrison Quint needs to see you."

"Now? Can it wait?"

"He's standing at my desk," she said, as if that answered his question.

"It *is* Saturday, you know," he said.

"Says the man who just saved a ship at sea," she said.

Damn, she's good.

"Is Happy around?"

"Already halfway there," she said brightly. For someone working on a weekend, she sounded awfully chipper. *I need to check her salary—there's no way I'm paying her enough.*

Stark decided not to change, but grabbed a snack from the kitchen and munched as he repacked his armor in the briefcase. His afternoon was likely shot—as would the evening be, no doubt.

He found Hogan outside. Both he and the car were idling. *He's not being paid enough either for the hours I make him keep.*

They headed to SI, and for once Stark used the chitchat time to force himself to calm down and focus on what he needed to do.

The building had subdued lighting, and just a single guard was visible at the station as Stark and Hogan entered the pristine headquarters. They rode the elevator in silence, and an immaculate yet casually dressed Pepper greeted him with a mug of coffee, then handed one to Happy, as well. Quint stood off to one side, and Stark nodded in his direction as he took a long sip.

Ahhh, Celebes Kalossi. Perfect. Happy looked as if he was in heaven, but he suspected that it had nothing to do with the coffee itself.

He thanked her and walked right to his desk, Quint on his heels, booted his computers, and sat back thinking to himself, *no rest for the wicked.*

As his systems came to life, he sipped the coffee and felt he was ready for whatever news his head of security had to offer.

"So, what's so important that you had to drag me in here on a Saturday?" Stark asked, though he was careful not to make it sound as if he disapproved that the man was doing his job.

Physically they were a rough match, although Quint had a fuller head of brown hair, and a thicker mustache. His navy pinstripe suit came off the rack, and his shoes needed a shine.

Despite Stark's attempt to keep things relaxed, he looked deadly serious, which worried the industrialist.

"We've discovered something," Quint said, and more than his expression, Stark didn't like the tone of voice. There was a pause, then he spoke up again. "Sir, we've discovered several breaches, and a number of items that have gone uncatalogued and are now missing. We have photo reference off of the security system, but the items themselves are there one day, and gone the next.

"These appear to be small prototypes from Electronics Design, the Biochemical building, and the Computer Sciences building."

Stark's mouth ran dry, and suddenly he wanted something stronger than the coffee.

"How much?"

Quint handed over a sheet of paper and Stark was relieved that it was a single sheet.

"Seven items in all. What's common is that they're all small, easily carried or concealed."

Stark came to the same conclusion as he studied the sheet. Nothing tied these items together, and frankly, their randomness bothered him. No rhyme, no reason, and therefore no obvious culprit. It didn't sound like HYDRA this time, but . . .

"The security cameras show us anything else we can use?"

"We're checking those now, but nothing has turned up. The swipe-card records are also being checked, to determine if and when personnel were away from their departments."

"Smart. Now what?" Stark was getting grumpy, and fast.

"We keep following the protocols, and hope something

turns up," Quint said. "We're still running all the background checks, and my people all checked out. Found a couple of minor concerns in the clerical staff, but nothing that would explain what's been happening." With that, he went silent, and looked as if he was steeling himself for a verbal onslaught.

Normally Stark would have cut his man a break, but today it was all getting to him.

"You have twenty-four hours, Quint," he finally said. "Get me something concrete to work with or I'll have S.H.I.E.L.D. down here to take over."

Quint blinked once, which was the most emotion he'd displayed since walking into the office.

"S.H.I.E.L.D.?"

"Remember those guys who were here for the computer break-in?" Stark said. "Guy with an eye patch? Like we said, they're government, but not a branch you know. This is a new outfit."

"Sorry, sir, I've not been made aware of them. Where are they based?"

"They get around," Stark said, allowing himself a slight smile. "I'll give you the full picture as soon as I can. And you'll know when they arrive, if it comes to that."

"Then I best get back to it," the security man said.

Stark nodded. He had been hard on the man, and needed to contact Fury about bringing him into the fold. If they were going to work closely with S.H.I.E.L.D., it only made sense.

"Garrison, please know that I appreciate your efforts, even on a Saturday," Stark said firmly. "*Especially* on a Saturday."

"Of course, sir. Thank you for that."

Once the man was gone, Pepper entered and announced that Gabe Jones had called during the conversation.

Doesn't anyone know what a weekend is?

He asked her to return Jones' call. Minutes later, a fresh

mug of coffee—laced with a shot—rested in his hand as Stark picked up the receiver.

"Before you start, if this isn't something we need to address immediately, why don't we take a different track?" Stark offered, and he suggested that the agent join him for dinner.

Jones agreed.

Well, so much for a hot Saturday night date. Instead, he had Pepper order the kitchen to prep something, since it was likely to be a working night. At least the food would be top-notch—unlike helicarrier fare.

She offered to stay, but he was mockingly dismissive. He also ordered Hogan to go home.

While waiting for his dinner date, he tried to focus on the torrent of emails he had been neglecting, but kept pausing, sidetracked by an uneasy sense he couldn't set aside.

He felt violated. This was his family's company, and someone had been helping themselves to *his* things.

That had to stop.

He gulped down the coffee and fumed.

Stark was still preoccupied, and had barely made a dent in the emails, when Jones strolled into the office.

"So what's this all about, Gabe?" he asked as he sent a quick note to the kitchen.

"We're getting hit pretty hard," Jones said, adjusting himself in the chair. "We've got to get up to speed, and we need to do it sooner, rather than later."

"HYDRA?"

"Yeah, and we think they're targeting us specifically," Jones said. "The thing in Austin could have been written off as simple theft, but Fury thinks we were their real mark, and I have to agree."

"This may force you to go public soon, and it may be just as well," Stark replied. "My own security chief never heard of you, which is both good and bad."

"Yeah, well, *you* try and get all the countries to agree to how to make the announcement," Jones said with a cold chuckle.

Stark nodded, and he could only imagine. There were days when total control felt good.

"And someone's going to notice the helicarrier one of these days," Stark said. "Sooner or later there's going to be an amateur astronomer, trying to explain what just blotted out the moon."

"Yeah, well, hopefully it'll be later," came the answer. "It's getting serious, though. Austin was a love tap compared with the assault they mounted in Cheyenne."

"What the hell's in Cheyenne?"

"Air Force testing base," Jones said. "Rhodey's out there now, looking over the damage."

"You could have called me," Stark said in a tense voice.

"You were already at sea," Jones explained, and he continued. "Tony, you're just one man. And S.H.I.E.L.D. has to be able to stand on its own. But right now, we're not done with building the infrastructure and training the troops."

Here it comes. . . .

"We need your tech, as well."

He had hoped to have this conversation when he was ready, but there it was. And he couldn't argue the point.

"Given how long it will take for you to gear up," Stark said, "I don't think you can wait. Yes, those pistols of yours pack a wallop, but HYDRA's pack a bigger punch."

"Very true, and the colonel doesn't like sending his men out at a disadvantage."

"Admirable. Where is he now, by the way? I'd have expected him to be here backing you up."

"He's training division leaders," Jones said.

"Doesn't he have people to do that?"

"He does indeed. Led by a great guy named Dum Dum Dugan," Jones said, flashing a smile. "But they'll be doubling up to speed things along."

"What kind of name is Dum Dum?"

"An old nickname, to be honest," Jones admitted. "He prefers it to Timothy Aloysius Cadwallader Dugan, and god help anyone who calls him anything other than Dum Dum."

"Yeah, well god help anyone who's being trained by a guy named Fury, for that matter," Stark said, and Jones agreed emphatically.

Then he spoke up again.

"Stark, I'm getting nervous. We're not ready for prime time, and HYDRA is. We'll need help, and sooner rather than later."

Stark eyed the man and considered his words carefully, not wanting to wound an already damaged pride. Fury certainly knew how to pick people.

"You want me to call in the Avengers?"

Jones shook his head. "And send them where? We're still gathering data on where the HYDRA bases are located and how they're organized, and frankly, we're not making the progress we need.

"Besides, think about the big picture. We were organized on an international level to combat this terrorist threat. Then, before we're even public, we have to be rescued by a team of superheroes—a team based in the United States, and seen as American.

"After that, who would support us? How could our international sponsorship withstand the criticism?"

Stark thought about this as he poured two drinks. Dinner was due to be brought up within the next half hour, so he thought a cocktail was perfectly in order.

He handed one glass to Jones, who tipped it with thanks in his direction. They drank in silence as Stark considered what had just been said. Savoring the burning sensation in the back of his throat, he realized that this was geopolitics on an unimagined scale. There was also the issue of the collateral damage that would be created by an all-out war between the two sides.

They continued to talk logistics through a second drink, and then during the dinner that was probably the most complete meal Jones had eaten in days. Then the discussion turned to specifics.

By the time he left it was late, and Stark quickly fired off an email to his department heads, with a priority list of the raw materials they would have to acquire in order to manufacture the items S.H.I.E.L.D. would need soonest.

He sent a second note to a select few, asking them to start teams for developing new weapons, gear, and uniforms.

Finally he sent a note to Pepper, asking her to coordinate with the department heads in order to hire the staff that would be needed to mount the effort.

This was going to be a multimillion-dollar spike. *How's that, Leticia—maybe now you'll be able to get those jowls tucked, or your fangs sharpened.*

But then his thoughts turned to the real enemy.

If HYDRA wanted a war, Stark would see to it that the good guys would win.

xvii.

The next morning, Stark was in the armor and flying across New York State before the sun was even up. It was cold out and he pushed the internal temperature in the armor up as he headed north by northwest.

Fury himself had called to wake him with news that a S.H.I.E.L.D. training exercise had been attacked. Three were dead and HYDRA had destroyed the facility. Brazenly, HYDRA hadn't even bothered to cover their tracks, so the Armored Avenger was following the path.

Although the incident had occurred hours earlier, the energy signature from their atomically powered vehicle was glowing like a sunbeam in his sensors. The path took him through the Southern Tier, near the Pennsylvania border, and it was in the mountainous region just by Route 80 that he spotted it.

Abandoned.

Approaching cautiously, he scanned for life signs, then, finding none, for any nasty surprises they might have left behind.

They were taunting him, and he rose to the occasion, beating the craft with his fists, crumpling the front end, yet ensuring that the nuclear power cell wasn't ruptured.

He shredded the metal, and the rage was pure and fueled him for minutes. Finally, breathing hard, he cursed one more time, kicked out the last tire, and reported to Fury.

Flying back toward Long Island, he started to contact Pepper, but reminded himself that it was Sunday.

At least she'd better *not be there.*

En route, he picked up a local police call over Middletown. It was a routine bank robbery, but it served to remind him that he wore the armor to help—not just pound on inanimate objects.

He adjusted his course, slowed his speed, and dove down through the clouds, zipping past a startled police cruiser that was already doing eighty. Seconds later he caught up with the cherry-red Camaro. Magnetizing his gauntlets, he gripped the vehicle's trunk, crushing the metal, and accelerated, taking control of the car.

The air began to stink of burning rubber as the driver attempted to brake. Metal groaned, something snapped, and he continued to push the vehicle forward.

The man in the passenger seat turned around to gape at the red-and-gold figure. He raised a pistol—a simple .38 special—took aim through the rear window, then dropped it, recognizing it would do little good.

Finally, spotting a nearby park, he shoved the vehicle onto a grassy expanse, which turned out to be the outfield for the local Little League. He slowed down, and then came to an abrupt stop, which he figured would be the end of it.

But the driver continued to gun the engine, perhaps in a panic, perhaps as a last-ditch attempt to escape. Iron Man held tight, and a quick systems check showed a slight strain, but he wanted to prove a point.

To them, or to himself—he wasn't sure.

The car's engine finally seized up from the strain and cut out, smoke rising from beneath the hood.

There was the sound of an approaching siren, and he waited until the police car arrived. The men within the Camaro sat silently, shaking visibly—and not from the temperature.

Once the patrol car arrived, he saluted and took to the air.

At least *something* productive had come of the day.

He resumed his course and continued to jet through the bright blue skies. As he neared the tip of Long Island, his radio activated, and he heard Fury's voice.

"We've got something going on at Groton," the colonel said. *"We're on our way, but you can be there faster."*

"Damn it, Fury, I'm not your errand boy," Iron Man growled.

"I know, Stark," Fury replied, the frustration clear in his voice. This was hard on him, too. *"But you're knee-deep in this and we need your help."*

"On my way," he grumbled, and he cut the signal.

As he adjusted his course, the internal navigational computer synched with a weather satellite and he triangulated his best course to Connecticut's submarine base. He considered ways of storing navigational data in the armor, so he could ascertain his whereabouts more quickly.

He had 150 miles to cross, and as he did, his anger began to subside. Even though it was past prime leaf season, the countryside was beautiful, and his mind turned to more pleasant considerations.

What the hell . . . might as well give it a shot.

He spoke Katalin's number, and heard the connection go through. But all he got was a recording, as her European-accented voice announced that she'd return his call.

"It's Tony. I was hoping that we might get together again." He hoped that didn't sound too eager. "Call me when you get this message."

He cut the connection, and then refocused his thinking on the sub base.

HYDRA already had subs built from Triple-I's designs, so what would they need at Groton's facilities? It wasn't a S.H.I.E.L.D. facility, so this wasn't a direct assault, as had been the morning's incident.

If not the subs, then perhaps their supplies? Repair materials?

Flying up the Thames River past Fort Trumbull, he opened up his electromagnetic sensors. All the readings seemed nominal for a base with nuclear subs.

As a result, he almost missed the burst of energy that occurred along the coast. It was followed, seconds later, by another charge going off farther away.

A chain reaction of explosions rocked the Connecticut coast, leading away from Groton and extending to the tourist destination of Mystic Seaport. The explosions all registered as simple dynamite—not typical of HYDRA.

He'd fought enough supervillains and other crazies to recognize that he was meant to follow the line. Certainly they knew he would smell a trap, but they also likely counted on him recognizing that civilians were being endangered by the blasts, and that he'd have to help. That would keep him away from his primary goal in Groton.

Fury and his team were still an hour away, he estimated, so HYDRA would have free rein to accomplish whatever they intended to from the outset.

He had come to really despise them.

Kicking the boot jets into a higher gear, he propelled himself to reach the area of the first explosion. Sure enough, cars had careened off the road, one building looked ready to crumble, and people were screaming in panic.

Pretending he was a robot and not a man in a robotic shell, Iron Man methodically worked his way around the area, listening intently to the police bands and determining where he was most seriously needed. In all, there were a dozen blasts, and he had to perform triage.

A loud buzzing sound made Stark wince as he was hoisting a car away from a telephone pole.

"Audio off."

A quick analysis showed that the painful sound was no accident—it was a second wave of distraction courtesy of whatever terrorist group was responsible. He'd be effectively blind as he tried to pinpoint where he was most needed, and that would cost him precious time.

Worse, the interference seemed to be screwing with his computer systems, including radar and sonar systems. He hovered for a moment, then dove into the water as his helmet sealed itself and his oxygen supply was activated.

Beneath the surface the interference diminished. He regained radar first, then sonar, and he was able to access situation maps maintained by local law enforcement. Thus, he could identify the locations where he was most needed, and he managed to maneuver up the coast to the seaport.

As he emerged from the water, his sudden appearance at first elicited shrieks from the witnesses nearby. He was quickly recognized, though, and they cleared space for him to work.

By the seaport's entrance, three cars had piled up and firefighters were trying to get to an elderly woman trapped beneath the wreckage. Using a pinpoint laser from his chest mount, he cut away bits and pieces of the three cars, which had twisted together into a grotesque parody of pop art. Paint peeled away, metal softened and began to warp. His sensors constantly monitored wreckage to ensure that the cars wouldn't crush the woman. It took precious minutes, but he had to be precise.

As bits fell to the ground, firemen pulled them away, keeping the area clear. Behind them waited emergency medical rescue personnel. He heard the whirring blades of helicopters overhead.

The Armored Avenger shut off the beam. Bracing his feet against the pavement, he clutched the metal with both hands. Maintaining precise control, he hefted the metal and slowly the cars rose up an inch, then three, then a foot.

Firefighters scrambled beneath to where the woman had been pinned. She was unconscious, her pink overcoat soaked blood-red, but she was breathing. Carefully, they eased her out from under the cars, which were beginning to tremble in Iron Man's hands.

The strain on his systems was starting to show and his power reserves were dipping to the 50 percent level.

Fury was half an hour away by now.

He dropped the red-hot wreckage safely to the ground. The metal groaned as it settled on the roadway, hissing on contact with the cooler ground, and the throng of witnesses burst into applause. Iron Man looked around and saw people taking pictures or simply gawking. He waved in their general direction, then walked over to the EMT team, which was checking the woman's vitals.

"Should I fly her to the hospital?" he asked.

"She'll be fine in the ambulance," an Asian woman said, listening with a stethoscope. "Good work, Shellhead."

He really needed a new nickname.

He took to the air and hovered at an altitude that would allow him to assess the situation. He tried the audio again, and found that the interference had cleared. The explosions had stopped, as well.

HYDRA may well be gone by now, Iron Man realized, and he felt a bitter pang in his chest.

He checked the law-enforcement frequencies as he gained altitude. It seemed the worst was over and adequate police, fire, and EMT staff were on hand.

He pushed the jets and flew north, and in five minutes was over the submarine base at Groton.

There were military personnel everywhere, but it looked as if all nonessential staff had been evacuated. Curiously enough, though, there was no sign of violence—nothing on fire, no wreckage, no bodies. He flew lower in an aerial reconnaissance loop around the 500 acres.

The base personnel were converging on a warehouse that was missing a door—clearly it had been forcibly removed, and lay on its side, the edges charred.

A quick check showed that the warehouse belonged to

General Dynamics, one of the base's contractors. Without landing, he entered the warehouse, only to find it stripped clean.

Whatever HYDRA had wanted was gone.

He landed inside the cavernous space and approached the commander of the security team. He requested a full accounting of what had been taken, hoping that *this* might give him a clue as to what HYDRA was up to.

S.H.I.E.L.D. arrived too late to do anything but clean up work, but Iron Man lingered long enough to speak with Fury.

Wearing just a suit, the colonel looked cold, but he was steaming from anger. He chomped on a cigar, and studied the now-empty building.

"Another day late, and a dollar short," he muttered.

"I need to get back, but tell me what *should* have been here. We'll figure this out, then make them eat it," Iron Man said, not bothering to hide the anger from his voice.

"Only if I can watch," Fury added. Then he added, "Thanks for expediting the equipment."

"If I have it, it's S.H.I.E.L.D.'s," Iron Man replied. "Anything to shut these bastards down." With that he propelled himself upward, and turned back toward Long Island Sound and home.

As he rushed over the water, he noticed his reserves were getting low, faster than he had anticipated. He opened a channel and called Hogan.

"Happy, meet me at the mansion," Stark said.

"You don't sound so good, boss," Hogan said, the concern obvious in his voice.

"I may sound bad," he replied, "but I feel worse."

And it was true. As his armor routed power to the jets and environmental systems, it came at a cost to the magnets that kept his heart from being shredded. He wasn't in any immediate danger—not *yet*—but he felt the grip tightening in his chest, and he began to sweat uncontrollably.

He was fatigued and erratic as he flew over the mansion. He smiled, though, as he saw the limo in the driveway. Cutting the jets, he began to descend, but not properly, and he landed with more than a thud.

The landing actually cracked the blacktop driveway, a spiderweb of cracks radiating outward.

Hogan, in a heavy black coat, came hurtling out of the car and grunted as he tried to help his employer to his feet.

"You putting on weight, Mr. Stark?" Hogan asked, earning him a grunt and what might have been a chuckle.

"Need to recharge, and fast," Iron Man said, sounding out of breath.

"Let's get you inside, then," the chauffeur said, and muscles bulged beneath his coat as he helped the armored figure move slowly toward the front door.

One of the butlers had the front door open and came out to assist them entering. Stark directed Hogan to take him to the underground lab. It was slow going as Hogan had to shift position and pause to regroup his strength.

Despite the exertion, Stark found himself thinking about lighter alloys for the next-generation suit, but then his mind clouded and he struggled to remain conscious.

The pain in his chest increased.

"Hurry," he said, and Hogan grunted and shoved the armor down the hallway.

Finally, they reached the lab, and Iron Man slumped against a wall.

When he finally constructed the Model 4 armor, he had been conscious of the increased demands the new computer systems, turbos for the boots, and increased weaponry would place on the power cells. As a result, he had devised an induction matrix, woven into the metallic mesh of the armor, that allowed him to absorb energy in large amounts.

He had to talk Hogan through locating the right connections and cables to set up the charge. Then he slowly raised his hands and removed the helmet, which was covered in grime from the day's efforts.

The connections were made, and Hogan threw the switch.

Within moments, the surging energy eased the pressure in his heart and chest.

He smiled at Hogan, who flashed him a thumb's-up, then rubbed his shoulders as if he were a prize fighter.

"I owe you big-time, Hap."

"Only when I save your life," Happy Hogan shot back. It was how they had met, and here he was doing it again.

"Trust me, my appreciation knows no bounds," Stark said.

"I'll think of something," Happy said, "and get back to you."

"Without a doubt, but can I have a drink first?"

Hogan went toward the sink on the far wall, but Stark called him off and pointed him to the scotch he kept in a cabinet nearby.

Hogan shrugged, filled a tumbler with the amber liquid, and handed it to Stark, who gestured for the bottle, too.

They sat silently as Stark sipped the single malt and his armor supped on electricity.

xviii.

His power levels were at 68 percent, and he'd been sitting there for almost an hour.

Not good enough, he thought. *There has to be a better way. . . .*

"Iron Man, this is Quint."

"Go," Stark said, putting the glass down and reaching for his helmet, from which the voice had come.

Hogan, who by then had been dozing, stirred to semi-alertness.

"We've got a situation out here at the airfield," his security chief said. "They're wearing green uniforms, and from what you've told us, that means HYDRA."

Damn.

Stark ripped out the power connection, and began affixing his helmet.

"You fully charged?" Hogan asked somewhat sleepily, but he was rousing quickly. He was on his feet and straightening his tie.

"Nearly seventy percent. It'll be good enough," Stark said, sounding more confident than he actually felt.

Hogan eyed him, silently challenging his boss, but Stark refused to slow down and explain himself.

"You know, I've had a little experience in the suit, and it ain't a good idea to take on the enemy without full power," Hogan said, his tone light but his eyes serious.

"Happy, HYDRA's on our doorstep right now. I don't have another twenty minutes to wait for a full charge, do I?"

Hogan opened his mouth to say something, thought better of it for a moment, then opened it anyway.

"You got a spare suit?"

For a brief moment, Stark was tempted. He kept intact versions of the previous models, a testament to his ingenuity, ability to learn from experience, and a certain sense of nostalgia.

Other men collected coins or comic books. He collected armor.

Any of the suits could be put on and used, but there was no way he would risk Hogan's life. An "Iron Army" would come in handy right about now, but no, this was his baby, and he intended to keep it that way.

HYDRA has enough of my tech, and is using it to kill people, he thought darkly. *The one thing they'll never get their hands on is Iron Man.*

"Sorry, Hap, but you're grounded," Stark said.

Hogan nodded and Stark thought he detected a hint of relief in his friend's eyes. Hogan had heart all right, but was also a practical man.

He paused and considered summoning the Avengers for support. But he wasn't certain whom he would get, and he wasn't certain they would arrive in time.

No, HYDRA had been dogging him for a week now. It was time for payback.

"Get Pepper," Stark said, sealing the helmet and booting up his systems. "Keep her away from there, and have her call the department heads. The plant is closed until I say otherwise.

"Once that's done, get out of here."

The armored figure walked over and placed a reassuring hand on the chauffeur's left shoulder.

"And thanks for offering, Hap," he said before turning away and accessing one of the escape passageways that would get him to the surface quickly.

On his way out, he checked the radio frequencies and heard Quint directing his men toward the main buildings, to protect them from invaders, but the green-suited clods seemed more interested in ripping up the airfield. The only reason he could come up with was that this assault was designed to lure him out—which also meant they were armed to the teeth and were gunning for him. It was bold and audacious, and it just might work if he didn't quell this in short order.

Hurtling through the tunnel, he contacted S.H.I.E.L.D.

"This is Iron Man for Nick Fury."

Moments passed as the tunnel led him to the grounds.

"Fury."

"They're in my backyard!"

"The plant?"

"Yes, damn it," Iron Man said, irritation evident in his voice. It quickly gave way to a fresh wave of anger.

"We're coming."

"Bring everyone you got," Iron Man said and cut the signal.

If Fury were smart, he'd be keeping the helicarrier in the northeast, since that was where most of the fun had been taking place.

The chronometer read four minutes past two in the morning, and Stark was worn. Rather than drinking, he should have been sleeping, but he could never have predicted that HYDRA would come knocking.

He flew in a shallow arc, more concerned about speed and distance. SI wasn't far away, and in the still of the night he could see the red, yellow, and orange flashes showing that HYDRA was taking target practice with his people. Stifling a curse, he kicked in the jet boots' turbo chargers, and noted that the energy reserves had already dipped 2 percent.

No time to be fancy, but brute strength will do. It was

something he had learned from dancing with the Hulk on more than one occasion.

Before he could even enter SI airspace, his armor detected something small speeding his way. He expected to be assaulted, but not in the sky over a residential area. Presuming it was a heat-seeker of some sort, he arced upward and went for altitude, veering away from the neighborhood below.

The object stayed on his tail, and closed. Whatever it was, it would hit him in twenty seconds, even with his increased speed.

He charged his gloves, slowed, and acrobatically adjusted his position in midair. He extended his right arm and let loose a torrent of energy, which met the missile perhaps one hundred yards away.

The bright light caused his eye shields to darken, and a moment later he heard the concussive explosion. Whatever fell to the ground would be small enough to do little damage, and with luck the light breeze would scatter the pieces.

His sensors indicated that two more such missiles were headed his way, from two slightly different vectors. Seeing little choice, he flew in their general direction at his top speed and used his internal computers to lock onto their heat signatures as he readied both gloves to fire. He wanted to time this just right, so at the 150 yard mark, he let loose a five-second burst of power and kept on flying forward.

Twin beams of energy lanced through the air at skewed angles. Sure enough, the repulsor rays made contact and both missiles detonated upon contact. He gritted his teeth, closed his eyes, and applied more thrust, flying straight through the coruscating energy, hoping to limit his exposure through speed. He was buffeted first on the right, then on the left, and it felt as if he was flying through a whirlwind.

The rocking jarred him, but within moments the flight smoothed out, and he was that much closer to SI.

The missiles had either been a welcome gift or a wake-up call. Either way, Iron Man was angry, and ready to fight back.

His onboard computers detected energy signatures on the far end of the main runway. Those were likely the vehicles HYDRA had used to access the campus. To his surprise he saw that HYDRA had actually erected temporary enclosures, dark green and trimmed in yellow, built on the airfield to protect them from opposing fire. His armor couldn't pick up the body-heat signatures well enough to provide an accurate number, but he ascertained that some three dozen HYDRA agents were present.

On *his* property.

Three dozen? And to think he had considered summoning the Avengers. He would handle this on his own, and enjoy doing it. Grinning coldly behind his helmet, he waded into battle.

Swooping low and fast, he was an iron bullet, barreling right through the first enclosure, which seemed to be made of a flexible metal alloy. His speed and metallic form tore it apart like so much cotton candy, and he held on to a large piece to use as a battering ram. He was moving so quickly that he didn't stop to count the bodies, but they offered no resistance and he kept moving.

As he cleared the first structure, Iron Man took aim at the second, but by then the HYDRA agents had gotten themselves organized. They were moving with practiced ease, and he raised the gain on his external microphones, hoping to catch their shouted orders.

They were too far away, and all he heard were muffled voices and the rushing sound of the cold night air in his speakers.

What he *felt*, though, revealed the orders that were being given.

Still in midair, he rocked as he was struck by multiple

impacts, and even through his protective shielding he began to feel traces of heat.

They were firing particle-beam weapons at him, filling the sky with streamers of yellow and magenta. It appeared as if they were being careful not to intertwine the energy beams, which probably meant they were on different cycles, and might cancel one another out.

He shrugged off the first three or four hits, and landed as his armor began to glow with the absorbed energy. Unfortunately that energy didn't flow into his depleted power cells, and he didn't want to risk overloading his defensive systems.

With the sixth or seventh beam that struck him, Iron Man noticed that he was staggering. He leapt into the air and fired his boot jets, dodging the onslaught as well as he could, and the farther he flew, the less impact each beam yielded. As he reached fifty feet up, he twisted around and took aim with his gauntlets, then kicked the boot jets into turbo mode.

Hurtling down, he fired off rapid pulses of repulsor energy, knocking men and enclosures to the ground.

Several of his opponents were down for the count, others were scattering, and a few were reaching for other weapons, now that he was a clear target in the air once again.

More small missiles came his way, as did something big and bulky that seemed to have been launched from a ground-based device. Twisting and turning in a way that Captain America had taught him, he avoided one missile and actually managed to swat the other away with a boot jet, which caused him to somersault in the air.

The larger object, however, reached him—and to his surprise, it affixed itself to his left leg. The thing was gray and dark in the night, and he saw several small lights winking green toward the center. He jetted far from HYDRA's cluster and reached to pull it from his leg. Its magnetic lock was powerful, and he failed to yank it free.

Worse, the device had barbs along its bottom edge, scraping and clutching on to the armor.

If this was an explosive, at this proximity it might breach his armor and take his leg with it.

His sensors registered other missiles closing on him quickly. He spun and fired a fresh repulsor burst, causing the nearest one to explode, too close for comfort, as shrapnel went skittering and sparking off his armor. *So much for the paint job,* he mused, frantically trying to figure out what to do about his leg.

He needed leverage in order to apply brute force.

Spotting the nearest building, a hangar, Iron Man deftly landed on its roof, then kneeled, hearing the crunch of gravel and concrete under his weight. Gloved hands gripped the device, which continued to happily blink green at a steady rate. He applied pressure, and heard the barbs digging into the armored skin, a loud piercing sound that made him wince and feel sorry for the suit.

The thing didn't budge.

The green lights began blinking faster.

He applied greater pressure, not caring about being gentle. He felt movement; the thing was beginning to give.

Shrieking metal continued to echo through the night and made him wince. He was winning, but would it be in time?

Just like that, the bulk was free from his leg, and he hurled it like a discus. It sailed away from the hangar, toward the field, and skittered across the asphalt.

There was a sudden, concussive detonation, and even with his shields he shut his eyes.

Shock waves followed the explosion, rippled through the air, and buffeted the armored form. The bomb left a crater in the tarmac, at least three feet deep and four feet wide.

His sensors alerted him to the next assault—grenades, which must have come from shoulder-mounted launchers. Rather than risk the hangar, which might have personnel in it, he leapt into the air and engaged the jet boots, instantly becoming a fast-moving target.

The grenades exploded harmlessly beneath him.

As he flew, Stark looked down for a brief moment to assess the damage to his leg and saw that several layers of the armor had been nicked and the enamel paint ruined, but no circuits had been exposed. The entire section would need replacing, though. In a calculating way, he admired the device and wondered which of his rivals had manufactured it. It was a practical device for wartime use against planes or boats, or maybe even submarines.

He neared a trio of HYDRA agents and slowed enough to reach out and grab one of the launchers, ripping it from the man's hands. As he did so he heard the sharp pop of a bone cracking.

Hefting the device, he saw the Stane logo on the barrel and frowned. Using the launcher as a club, he swatted the other two men to the ground, and then hurled the weapon at another agent who was trying to take aim.

Someone else was swifter, and a grenade landed between him and the downed agents. Scooping it up, Iron Man went into a baseball windup and threw it back their way, intending to land it close enough to disable them without being fatal. He took too long, however, and the grenade detonated while in the air, fairly harmless in terms of destruction, but damned loud.

He landed again and waded into a cluster of men, some of whom were trying to grip their pistols, but without success. With one hand, he picked up the nearest man and hurled him into others, then grabbed a pistol out of a woman's hand and crumpled it in his fist, enjoying the bending metal despite the loud *screech* it made in protest.

The HYDRA agents began to scatter, and Iron Man noticed that two men toward the rear of the airstrip were shouting. They had to be the field leaders, and he was determined to grab them and hold them for Fury.

The agents nearest the leaders snapped into action, and unpacked different shoulder-mounted weapons that looked to pack more of a wallop than conventional grenades. The black metallic weapons were uniform in appearance, and once again he could see the telltale logo from one of Drexel Cord's outfits.

Too much death could be delivered from too far away, he thought quickly, taking the human factor out of the equation. A man should be able to look his opponent in the eye on the field of battle.

There'd be fewer wars if the rulers had to fight one another, hand to hand, winner take all.

Suddenly he staggered under the impact. The weapons were charged particle beams of a higher order than the pistols, and worse, one struck his damaged leg, and he felt circuits overloading. A thin trail of smoke escaped from a puncture, and he ordered systems to be rerouted.

He had exerted a lot of energy flying, fighting, and withstanding attacks. His power levels had dipped below 40 percent, and would drop even faster if this kept up.

Okay, maybe summoning the Avengers might have been a wise idea.

Two blasts hit him squarely in the chest, right on the tri-beam emitter, and he saw the sparks before detecting the acrid smell of burning circuits. No doubt this suit of armor was done for, but he couldn't return to the lab for repairs until HYDRA was off his property, even if it took every last erg in his reserves.

A new sound caught his attention, mostly because it was human and came from behind. As he began to turn, he didn't know whether he would find a new assault, or Happy on some crazy suicide mission.

Instead, he discovered that the landing strip behind him was crawling with agents from S.H.I.E.L.D. Fist fights were becoming as common as exchanges of weapon fire. It quickly grew very loud on the airfield, and he found that concentrating wasn't as easy as it had been minutes ago.

At a glance, he recognized Kenn Hoekstra leading four men who were taking out the enclosures to his right. Farther behind was Gabe Jones, and there was that attractive blonde he spotted on the helicarrier, but most of the others were unknown to him.

Where was Fury, though?

The time he took to gawk allowed HYDRA to throw more weapons at him, and he was beginning to stagger under the barrage, which was relentless. He was going to be sore for days when this was done.

It built until it was like the crescendo to a fireworks display, as every last firecracker went off at once. He was blinded, deafened from the constant concussive blasts around him. His armor was holding on, but the power levels dipped faster and faster, falling below 30 percent. The leg damage was worse than he feared.

He crouched, and realized that there was nothing he could do. The killing blow was certain to land any moment.

Then there was silence.

Iron Man paused, then stood straight and looked all around him.

Fury was standing behind the HYDRA leaders, a rather impressive-looking pistol in his left hand and a victory cigar in his right. The leaders were on their knees, guns trained on them by flanking agents.

All the HYDRA agents were dead, unconscious, or surrounded by S.H.I.E.L.D. agents.

"Glad you dropped by for a nightcap," Iron Man called out.

"You look like hell," Fury said.

"I can't look as bad as I feel," Iron Man admitted. At least he was close to his lab—which remained unscathed—and could get out of the armor.

The colonel walked over to the avenger and they nodded toward each other.

"It's getting worse," Fury said.

"This was more than a calling card," Iron Man agreed. "This was a declaration of war."

"They manage to take anything?"

Iron Man shook his head; the movement made him feel a little woozy.

"I'm not sure the objective was to steal anything," he replied. "I think this was meant to take me out of the game."

Fury nodded.

"Your driver is still waiting for you," he said. "Good thing he didn't keep the meter running.

"Gabe'll oversee the mop-up, and coordinate with your man, Quint," the colonel added. "We'll compare notes tomorrow. You go home and rest—we've got it."

Iron Man checked his systems, and saw that he had enough power left for a short trip without risking his systems. He gave Fury a thumb's-up, then stepped back, igniting the boots and lifting into the sky.

The short hop took him right to the main administration building, where he spotted the black limousine sitting under a street light. He landed gently beside it and saw that Happy was inside, reading a book.

Some people had all the luck.

He opened the rear door and carefully entered, knowing his armor's weight would cause the car to sag, despite the fact that he'd had it reinforced. Once the door was closed, he noted the heater had been on, and his cold armor misted a bit as the temperature equalized.

"You okay, boss?"

"Not in the slightest, Happy," he admitted.

He had wanted to hand HYDRA their heads, but he'd let himself be overconfident, and had nearly lost everything. He was angry that they brought the war onto his property, and that he hadn't been able to defend it.

One of his chief rivals had manufactured the equipment that might actually breach his armor.

No, it had been a horrible night, and one he'd like to obliterate from memory.

"Home," Stark said, and Happy pulled away even as Quint's men began fanning out, keeping a vigil across the campus while S.H.I.E.L.D. herded the captured and loaded the dead into vehicles they'd brought with them.

The drive was quiet as Hogan kept his thoughts to himself and Stark dozed, utterly spent.

Once back in the mansion, Stark again needed help to get out and then down to the lab. This time, he took off the entire suit of armor, disgustedly tossing each component into a heap by his fabricators. Once the shell was entirely off, he told Happy to go home and sleep.

While he stood in his underwear and chestplate, Stark poured a fresh glass of whiskey and plugged in, ensuring that his heart would remain beating when he went to sleep.

Not that sleep would come easily, despite his exhaustion.

The adrenaline was still in his system, waging war with the alcohol, and his mind wouldn't stop thinking about all that had occurred. To date, he had seen captured weaponry used against him, but there was still nothing to indicate what the gyroscopes were needed for. It might well be HYDRA was already using the pilfered communications network, but that was a pure guess.

No, things refused to add up, and the engineer in him abhorred that.

Stark Industries had lost non-military devices and items that could be used offensively—*his* weapons, which placed any fatalities on his head. The items from Rand-Meachum, Richmond, and elsewhere were all offensive.

They had tons of matériel, which meant they needed plenty of space. S.H.I.E.L.D. had the sky, but did they have the ground, or the sea?

Who was the HYDRA mastermind, and why these blatant attacks on him and S.H.I.E.L.D.? Did they really think they could take out the opposition so easily?

If so, they have another think coming.

Nothing was making sense, and he was lapsing into cliché. He couldn't hold a coherent thought long enough to pursue it to its logical conclusion.

As he sipped his second glass, Stark noticed a winking red light in the distance. Phone calls. He staggered over to the answering machine.

"Play."

Worried calls from Pepper, Quint, and even Burstein. He smiled that Marquez had also left a message, but had a broader smile when he heard the accented voice that belonged to Katalin.

He didn't have the energy, however, nor was he in the mood, to return any of the calls.

xix.

Two men found their way off the Stark campus, and despite the late hour, actually flagged a passing livery.

It was quick work to kill the driver, dump the body, and drive off.

As they drove across the 59th Street Bridge, the two used their communicators to report in. Madame Hydra's voice did not sound at all pleased.

"Satisfied?" she hissed at them.

The men—234 and 543—remained silent, knowing better than to speak to their leader when she was like this. Instead, they heard her cut the signal, and knew she'd prefer to yell at them in person.

They could take it if that was all she intended to do.

Abandoning the car on the West Side, the two men, still in their green-and-yellow uniforms, hijacked a cab, tossed the driver to the curb, and sped off. They then drove to Lower Manhattan and left the cab, walking the distance to the warehouse. In this neighborhood, at this time of the night, no one was on the street to see them.

They were fairly chilled by the time they entered, but Madame Hydra, in her sleek uniform, stared at them with cold anger that made them shiver.

"You didn't have the courage to hold your ground?" she said, her voice rising with each word. "Were you trained to *run* when things got difficult?"

She spat at their feet, the spittle making a wet sound in the dust.

"I need intelligence, so there's a benefit to your cowardice. Attend me."

Madame Hydra turned and walked away, heading for her office. The two followed, looking confused and keeping several feet between them and their leader.

Within the office sat her lieutenants, designated 145 and 389, who were slow to rise when she entered. Clearly, they were up to something.

"Report," she ordered.

With as much detail as possible, the two recounted the battle, making certain to note how damaged Iron Man had been. Her eyes gleamed with glee when she heard which weapons had managed to affect their enemy most.

The lieutenants probed and did all the questioning as she listened, breathing quickly.

When they were done, she nodded at them in appreciation, then nodded to the seated men.

The lieutenants withdrew guns and fired.

Magenta energy pierced the uniforms, instantly killing the men.

"You see," she said, ignoring the bodies at her feet even though the air was rapidly filling with the stench of blood and other fluids leaking from the bodies. She then fixed her cold glare at 145. "You wanted to test the weapons on Iron Man and be brazen. I let you, and what did that gain us? S.H.I.E.L.D.'s intervention."

"They got their asses kicked in Austin," agent 145 countered.

"Do not underestimate Nick Fury," she said. "He is very good at what he does. That he lives today tells you how good he can be. S.H.I.E.L.D. will continue despite our best efforts. We have to adjust our tactics, and we must prepare for what is to come."

Everything in her life had prepared her for this. As a

young child in Eastern Europe, she had been deprived of her parents and watched as her older sisters were raped and left for dead. Escaping across the landscape, seeking the border to a friendlier country, she had experienced the accident that scarred her face, so that people would forever avoid meeting her eyes, or showing her pity.

Her instinct for survival led her to hone her wits, using any means necessary to find food and shelter. She taught herself to read and write, and to fight, starting with a kitchen knife and working her way up to firearms. She came to revel in wanton destruction as a form of revenge against a callous world.

Calling herself Viper, she traveled to Southeast Asia and the tiny nation of Madripoor, where she gained a reputation as one of the world's most dangerous criminals, sought by Interpol and other agencies. When she discovered HYDRA, it became clear that this was her means to an end.

And now she was poised to begin the endgame.

"I thought they did fairly well tonight," agent 145 challenged.

She blinked away the reverie and eyed the man.

"What exactly did they accomplish?"

"They enabled you to plunder the Richmond warehouse in Jersey," the man replied, glancing at his compatriot for confirmation. But 389 sat and watched impassively.

"It cost us three dozen men for that raid," she said coolly. "Do you really expect six dozen to materialize in the morning?"

"Of course not."

"Did they destroy the Stark plant?" she hissed. "Did they eliminate Iron Man?"

"Well, no . . ."

"Buffoon." She spat again. "I tire of your 'initiative,' which borders on insubordination."

The two stared at each other and for a moment she considered killing him outright; she was feeling tense and needed some form of release. Stark wasn't likely to return her call anytime soon considering what her men had just done to him. So 145 would have to suffice.

"Come here," she ordered him.

The men exchanged glances and then looked at their leader. She returned their gaze, and her left hand curled once, gesturing for 145 to move.

Finally, he flexed his fingers, ready for a fight he knew he would lose. It was all in his body language.

She hoped he would last at least two or three minutes.

She stood impassively, body loose, eyes alert. She'd wait him out, get him nervous.

Sure enough, he lowered his head, rushing her.

"Fine, I'll take you down and *really* control this operation!" he bellowed.

Madame Hydra gripped his shoulders and took control of the momentum, ramming him into the nearest wall. Quickly, she lashed out and kicked his feet out from under him.

To her surprise and pleasure, he kicked out his feet, arched his back, regained his balance, and rose. Fists lashed out in a forward attack, then he spun and managed to land a kick at her hip, actually staggering her.

Excellent.

She kicked back, sending 145 back into the wall. He bounced off and landed a right jab before she gripped his arm, hyperextended it, and dislocated his shoulder. The groan of pain came through clenched teeth.

He reached behind her head and forced it down into his upraised knee. She actually saw bright spots in front of her eyes for a moment. He was better than she thought.

He may last longer than I could have hoped.

He pressed his advantage and landed an elbow to her

back, between the shoulder blades, forcing her to the ground. When he raised his right leg to bring his boot on her prone form, she rolled to her left and scissor-kicked in the air, catching him between her legs and sweeping him from his feet.

Side by side on the concrete ground, they lay opposite each other, close enough to be lovers. But he was trapped between her legs and she began to exert pressure, feeling her knees squeeze against his organs, just below the rib cage.

One arm useless, he flailed at her with the other, and the blows hurt but were diminishing in impact with every passing second.

His breathing became ragged, and he was having trouble getting a good breath. The counterattacks slowed, then stopped. She gathered her strength and exerted one final bit of pressure, and he stopped moving altogether.

She held the position for a count of ten, then removed her legs from the limp form. Rising to her feet, she studied the body. Though still, he was breathing. Then she looked at 389, who was still seated and observing the proceedings.

"Kill him."

Agent 389 pulled his gun again, and fired point-blank into his fellow's skull. It shattered, and sent up a beautiful red spray.

Then he turned to her again, awaiting instructions.

"Have you any thoughts along the lines of your former ally?" she asked.

"None whatsoever," he answered.

"Excellent—that's just how I like my first lieutenants," she replied.

"Hail Hydra," he said with quiet conviction.

"With S.H.I.E.L.D. making itself more of an imposition, we need to move up the timetable," she instructed. "Are the plans in place?"

"Yes."

"Then begin executing them," she said, and she walked out of the office.

The fight had lasted perhaps three and a half minutes and had taken the edge off, but it hadn't been enough.

XX.

Gabriella Marquez didn't often drive from Manhattan to her job at Stark Industries. However, she intended to load her trunk this evening, and needed the space.

She had driven to the campus once a week for the last three weeks to establish a pattern with security. Always on Mondays, so there'd be nothing unusual about her arrival.

Today she had the heater on, the radio playing NPR, and a cardboard cup of coffee that was half empty. It was a typical fall day, cool and crisp, the sun shining, and—to everyone around her—all seemed right with the world.

A dark red sedan appeared in the rearview mirror, a mere three car lengths behind, and switching lanes swiftly.

When she changed lanes, seeking to give it a clear path to move on past, the car eased closer, and suddenly it was right behind her.

Across the median, the Long Island Expressway, at this hour of the morning, was jammed with commuters heading into New York City, but in reverse—the way she was driving—there was a lot more flexibility, even though there still was a good amount of volume.

The car then crept up on her and tapped her rear bumper once to make sure they had her attention.

What the f—

Marquez began to sweat, not a good thing to do with the facial appliances she was wearing. Her gun was in the glove compartment, and a can of acidic pepper spray was more easily in reach, inside the pocketbook on the seat next to her.

The car eased back for the next quarter mile, but then moved up again to crowd her, forcing her onto the Exit 20 ramp. She had little choice but to leave the expressway and take the service road.

Her eyes darted left and right, seeking a clear street that would allow her to make a run for it. Futile, she realized, since they likely knew where she worked, and where she lived.

The hell with it, she decided.

With a jerk of the wheel, she came to a rest at the curb and let the engine idle. The maroon car came up behind her and stopped, a trail of exhaust curling straight up in the still air. Three men emerged, leaving the driver within. From the mirror, she tried to identify them, but none were familiar to her, meaning they were imported talent.

As they flanked the car, one man came to the driver's window. As he leaned over and gestured for the window to be lowered, she complied, but also used her free hand to reach for the spray.

"Good morning," she said, feigning cheerfulness.

Without preamble, the man spoke in a voice that was as rough as the pothole-strewn streets.

"The last set of schematics sold for a nice bit of change. But they proved worthless, outdated. The Big M had to issue a refund, with interest. As you can imagine, this did not go over very well."

"That's always the risk with these deals," she said. That Francois had not informed her directly was of major concern. Had he been co-opted by her father?

"Not good enough for the Big M," he said. How she hated that code name. "He dislikes disappointment."

"Don't we all?"

"Don't make this harder than it needs to be," he continued, leaning closer. He was definitely not going away, but she doubted he was going to do her physical harm in broad daylight. "You know the family's needs, and he's counting on you not to . . . disappoint him . . . again."

"I'm doing everything I can," she said with steel in her voice. "You can assure him of that."

"That's what he's worried about," he said. Then he straightened up. "We'll be watching."

"You could be helping instead," she suggested, but his impassive response told her she was on her own. If she wanted to lead New York, she had to deliver on the promise, and renew her father's trust in her.

The man cracked his knuckles and stood there, as if considering saying something more, then turned and returned to his car. It spun away from the curb and drove off the moment the door closed.

Masque sat there, collecting her thoughts, willing her heart to slow down. She closed her window and sat in silence for several minutes, then pulled away from the curb and found the next access ramp that would take her back to the expressway and her office.

Suddenly, she had a long day ahead of her.

Tony Stark hadn't felt this spent since the injury that had changed his life.

He'd had difficulty sleeping, and ached as he rolled out of bed. Covered in black-and-blue marks, he felt like a sleepwalker as he showered and dressed, selecting favorite clothes that brought him comfort: a dark merino wool turtleneck, a windowpane blazer, and light gray pants and loafers. Good enough to look professional, but comfortable enough that he could get through the day.

He would have preferred taking the day off, but there was no chance of that while HYDRA was active and S.H.I.E.L.D. was still getting its act together.

He walked downstairs to the kitchen for coffee, and was surprised to find both Pepper Potts and Happy Hogan in the foyer awaiting him. She was in a teal dress that showed her knees, while Happy was in his usual chauffeur's uniform.

They shared the same worried look in their eyes.

"Problem?" he asked as he walked the final steps.

"No, sir," Pepper said with a shake of her head, her red hair barely moving. "We're just very concerned about you. This has been a difficult week or two."

"I didn't know you had the gift of understatement," Stark said without a hint of humor. He headed for the kitchen, his employees in tow. "And it's not getting any better."

"We know, and we're concerned," Happy added.

Stark grunted and accepted a cup of coffee from Constance, the day cook. She offered cups to the others. Pepper accepted, and Happy did not.

Stark drank in silence, brooding and feeling irritable.

"What's going on at the airfield?"

"S.H.I.E.L.D. has the whole field cordoned off, and has cleaned the area, but say they still want to study the scene," Pepper told him. "We've given the airfield staff a paid furlough, and told them to return Wednesday."

Stark nodded.

"Mr. Quint says he expects a report from them this morning," she added, then finished her cup and handed it back to Constance, a plump older woman with steel-gray hair.

"May I fix anyone breakfast?" Constance inquired.

"We won't be staying to eat," Stark said, and Happy looked disappointed. "Let's go to work." Without waiting a response, he hurried from the kitchen out to the foyer and helped himself to a black overcoat and a patterned scarf that he hastily threw around his neck.

Hogan had to rush ahead to get past him so he could have the car door ready and waiting. Stark eased in gingerly, gripping his briefcase. Priority one had to be replacing the damaged armor, he decided. He had the component parts, and was tempted to devote the day to upgrades he had in mind.

On the other hand, he wanted a suit that would be ready for action at a moment's notice. The internal debate continued, and he was oblivious as Pepper joined him in the backseat, and the limo pulled away from the mansion grounds.

"Mr. Stark, you need to rest," Pepper said softly. "The place can run itself for a few hours. A day even."

He stared at her for a moment.

"Actually, it runs fine without me as long as you're there. Don't sell yourself short. But I'm the one the board and Congress want to yell at. I'm the one who made the campus a target."

"Guilt doesn't become you," she said softly.

"It's not guilt, Pepper, but a fact," he said, and then he turned away from her, staring out the window and letting his mind once more review the list of things that had been stolen. The locations, the timing . . . and he tried to find the elusive pattern.

The limo pulled through the gates twenty minutes later, and nothing new had suggested itself, which only darkened his mood. As they neared the headquarters building, he finally spoke.

"Have there been any calls this morning?" He knew she would have checked from the mansion.

"The usual two dozen. Department heads, that woman from *Esquire,* and two calls from Katalin," she said, studying him for a reaction.

His eyes must have given him away, and she had an expression on her face he found tough to read.

"Once we're inside, I need to tend to the armor, then business," he said. "Rearrange the schedule as you see fit, and let me know if something comes up that I can't afford to put off. We'll return calls at four, and we'll all try and have a normal day."

"Aye, aye, sir," she said with a mock salute. He didn't react but stared ahead.

That Katalin had called—twice—only piqued his interest

for a moment before new designs for the armor's heat exchange suggested themselves.

Stark decided to drop his briefcase in his office before proceeding to the sub-basement. He walked quickly, not wishing to waste time, but as he crossed the threshold, he stopped in his tracks.

Gabe Jones sat there, and beside him was Rhodey in full uniform. They studied him, much as they did prey, and then stood and extended their hands. Stark eyed them himself, and shook their hands in greeting.

Rhodey finally smiled, but still looked worried.

"How do you feel, Tony?" he asked.

"Like hell, Rhodey, but you can see that," Stark said. He placed the briefcase beside his desk and sat down. To his surprise, Pepper walked right in with a tray and three mugs of coffee. He noticed that it was the dark French roast Rhodey favored.

"Change of plans, Pep. Business first, armor later."

"I'll try and keep up," she said with a straight face, and exited.

"Last night was a mess," Jones said. "But we didn't lose anyone and they lost seven, plus three in the hospital. Your own people seem to have stayed out of the line of fire, so there were only minor injuries, and the maintenance crew says the damage will take at least a week to repair."

"Thanks—can I bill S.H.I.E.L.D. for the repairs?" Stark asked archly.

"Your tax dollars at work," Rhodey quipped.

Stark turned his attention to his friend.

"What was it like at Cheyenne?"

Rhodes shook his head slowly, eyes looking at the carpet.

"A bigger mess. They were savage with the people and the equipment. I really hate these guys, Tony."

"Join the club," Stark said.

"Stark," Jones said, directing the attention back his way. "We were at a disadvantage, and there's no use repeating our needs. I know you told the colonel that matériel will be en route, but we need schedules."

"Pepper should have that information later today, but what you *really* need, Mr. Jones, is to find HYDRA's New York base." Stark stared at him with an uncompromising expression. "I want the coordinates, and then I want an army to follow me through the front door," he added.

"A frontal assault isn't likely to be the wisest course—" Jones began, but Rhodey cut him off.

"I know you're angry, Tony," Rhodey said. "But look at you. The rings under your eyes say that you're not sleeping. You have a leg injury, and the pounding can't have been good for your heart. HYDRA is S.H.I.E.L.D.'s problem."

"My heart has been fine," Stark shot back, not even trying to disguise the anger in his voice. "Want me to take an EKG? I can waste the time if you can. If not, I have injured people to check on, and a suit that needs to be repaired sooner rather than later."

"One more thing," Jones said smoothly. Stark arched an eyebrow his way, daring him to say something useful. "Colonel Fury wanted me to remind you that while we appreciate all Stark Industries is doing for S.H.I.E.L.D., he'd also like to extend an invitation for Iron Man to become a deputized agent."

Stark was surprised by the statement. It wasn't at all what he had expected, though as he considered it, it wasn't so surprising. If Stark *and* Iron Man were both attached to the operation, Fury and the Executive Council could count on him day and night.

"I'll give Fury my answer in person, but thanks, Gabe," Stark said, softening his tone.

Stark appreciated seeing Rhodey, despite the circumstances. It comforted him to know that he had an independent ally within the helicarrier. He instinctively liked Fury, but was still learning about him, and certainly didn't trust the Executive Council.

Once they left, he debated between the needs of Stark Industries and the needs of Iron Man. Suspecting that HYDRA, having been badly trounced, wouldn't attack so quickly again, he decided to handle the company business first.

Pepper brought him a fresh cup of coffee and then guarded the door, allowing him to try running SI for a while. She did such a good job handling the minutia that he found himself doing the "touchy feely" management that his father had done so well, pounding out cajoling or encouraging emails to staffers, department heads, suppliers, and others.

He then allowed himself an hour to troll through the company's intranet to see for himself the progress being made on a variety of projects.

One project particularly interested him—the space program, building the next-generation spacecraft. He'd love to tinker with that himself, and even thought the heat-shielding technology might be adapted to a high-altitude version of the armor.

As his mind shifted from blueprints and schematics to transistors and microchips, he knew the time had come to tend to the hero. So he informed Pepper that he was gone for the day, and went below to sub-basement five.

The lights sensed his arrival and switched on, and he felt like he was finally getting to be himself. With a refreshed eye he looked over the components for another Mark 1, and determined what he had time to modify. He loosened his tie and picked up a soldering iron.

Stark worked without break, barely noticing the time as he made minor modifications to the gauntlets, the energy pods, and the tri-beam emitter. He even downloaded a new rev of the operating software that had been finished just before all this hullabaloo had begun.

He examined each component part, blew compressed air to clean out crevices, and then ran a chamois over the polished metal, buffing out any flaws.

By the time he looked up, it was nearing seven o'clock, and he realized he hadn't eaten. On the other hand, he now had a fully functional suit of armor at the ready, so it wasn't exactly wasted time. But he was hungry, and craved the companionship of someone who didn't want a paycheck or a favor.

He grabbed the nearest phone and dialed Katalin's number, which had been imprinted on his mind.

"Katalin, Tony Stark," he said, then silently cursed himself for sounding so formal.

"So nice to hear from you," she said on the other end. He heard clanking sounds, metal on metal, but couldn't identify the source.

"I know it's late and probably a breach of someone's etiquette, but might you be free for dinner?"

"There may be rules of some sort, but honestly, I tend to make my own," she said. "I did have somewhere to be tonight, but I can certainly change the plans."

"Great. Can I pick you up this time?"

"Let's make it a late dinner, just in case," she said breathlessly and he liked the husky accented sound.

"Nine, then," Stark suggested.

"Perfect," Katalin said, the clanking sounds fading away, robbing Stark of a clue as to her whereabouts. "Yes, pick me up." She gave him an address, and rung off.

Stark carefully secured the new armor in his briefcase, and caught himself whistling happily.

She definitely had an effect on him.

xxi.

Burstein finally went home to his wife and unfinished novel, leaving Gabriella Marquez alone.

She had spent all day creating a reason she needed to be at satellite factory number two clear on the opposite side of campus. It was one of the few places on campus where munitions still were manufactured and stored. When Stark decided to wind down the programs, he farmed some of the remaining contracts out to the plants in Detroit and Portland, and many of the storage facilities were elsewhere, as well.

What remained at corporate were the experimental models designed specifically for the armed forces and S.H.I.E.L.D., and that was exactly what she needed. Weapons—not plans for weapons—always sold for top dollar, and that was what she desired so she could take the pressure off, once and for all.

And to prove to her father she could be trusted.

Since laser-sighted rifles used new microchip technology, they had to be programmed, so Marquez crafted a series of emails between herself and the factory's foreman, Adam Colan, which led him to invite her to come see the chips in action.

This way, when Marquez's swipe card showed up on the security logs, it wouldn't raise any red flags should someone scour them later. The development building ran two shifts, and had just shut down for the day, so at most there would be a skeleton crew, which could easily be avoided.

Not wishing to risk things, she wore her dark spandex

outfit under her clothes and carried a cloth mask in her oversize bag, nestled next to an empty carryall.

Despite the cooling temperatures, she decided to take the long walk from her building to building 2. This gave her a chance to check on current security and refresh herself on potential escape routes, should something go wrong. After all, every other theft had gone smoothly, so the law of averages said that something was due to go ass-over-tea-kettle.

Some twenty minutes later, she swiped her way into the darkened building. Safety lights hung overhead, and red exit lights glowed at regular intervals. The place was large, silent, and filled with parts for weapons, as well as racks of finished models waiting to be shipped and tested.

Any criminal organization would have sold their mothers to obtain the goods contained within this one building. Not wishing to waste time, she quickly doffed her outer clothes and slipped her mask into place.

She hefted one of the rifles to get a sense of its weight. *Not too bad,* she decided, and she withdrew her carryall. Smoothly, she slid three of the rifles into the bag, and then started grabbing components—including the programming chips that were the key to the weapon.

As she lifted a handful she heard a rushing sound outside and suspected the worst. Sure enough, the outer wall began to shudder and crack, spilling concrete chips and metal fastenings to the ground.

It took Iron Man a matter of seconds to burst through the wall and then land. While he adjusted the tri-beam emitter to act as a spotlight, she had already run to the far wall, from which the security systems were operated. Flat hands slapped at controls, activating various devices, and within moments hidden panels revealed themselves, allowing articulated cables to snake out.

The end of each cable had a heat-seeker attachment, and they sought out the one form emitting the most heat, which happened to be the Armored Avenger. Instantly they wrapped around his arms and legs, beginning to constrict and immobilize the suspected intruder.

Madame Masque watched in fascination as Tony Stark was stopped dead by his own inventions. There was some justice after all.

Turning, she sprinted for the nearest exit and kicked at the handle, breaking a seal, which set off the piercing wail of a siren and activated emergency lighting. She shuddered but kept moving, hoping Iron Man had seen only a dark silhouette.

Moments later she was out the building and sprinting toward the employee lot where Marquez's car waited. As she moved, Masque saw several SI security vehicles approach building 2, their lights flashing.

She shoved the carryall beneath blankets in the trunk and withdrew a spare winter coat, which she put on over her outfit. The mask came off and she knew some of her facial appliances were marred, but hoped that in the dark, the security guards at the entrance gate wouldn't look too closely at a member of the staff.

Moments later she was at the gate, where she was stopped by a barrel-chested ex-football player turned night guard.

"You'll have to wait a minute, ma'am," he said. "There's been some sort of incident." He stepped back into his booth, and she sat while a few other cars began to line up behind her.

So much the better, she thought. *This way I won't stand out.*

The guard stepped back out, and to her relief he smiled.

"What's happening, Phil," she asked sweetly, keeping away from the window so not too much light made its way to her face. She casually handed him her laminated badge.

"Nothing to concern you," he said, and he handed back her ID. "Have a good evening."

*   *   *

Iron Man cursed himself as he struggled against the titanium steel coils. Every time he pulled against them, they responded to their programming and tightened to hold him in position, theoretically until security came and took him away. The angle gave him no leverage whatsoever.

If I get my hands on the guy who invented these . . .

Everyone had called him crazy for such an elaborate system, which simultaneously identified the intruder and what they had stolen, and then immobilized the person instantly. Now he felt vindicated and pissed off at the same time.

He'd focused on the sites that dealt with munitions, and if only he'd had systems like this in all his buildings, none of the break-ins would have succeeded. As it was, en route to building 2 he had checked the status, and the restraints hadn't deployed for some reason.

Hence the dramatic entrance.

The metal was almost as unbreakable as adamantium, the hardest alloy on earth. *Almost* being the operative term, as the fully charged hero began exerting more and more pressure against the coils. The thin smell of burning fumes reached him, and he knew he was burning out the control mechanism, which would then render the coils useless.

More and more, he flexed and pulled, feeling muscles begin to complain. Finally, he heard crackling from behind a wall and knew the system had been fried. The coils lost their tension, and he shrugged them off.

His internal systems told Stark that the figure was gone from the building. Thanks to his state-of-the-art security, he hadn't been able to capture a clear image before he had slipped away, and a quick scan showed that three of the laser-sighted rifles were missing.

Each one would fetch thousands on the open market, more on the black market.

No sooner had he stepped away from the useless restraints than a quick-hardening riot foam began spewing from the sprinkler system, adding insult to injury. The foam would harden on contact with the air and be as stiff as concrete within seconds. The floor puddled with the foam, preventing his boot jets from engaging.

Since he had already ruined the wall, a little more damage was nothing to be concerned about. He activated his repulsor rays, took aim, and let rip, destroying the nozzles one by one.

He then pulled himself free from the hardening foam. While it was far less restricting than titanium steel, it rendered his jets useless. With mounting anger, he knew that his prey had long since escaped—and thanks to his own ingenuity.

Though it had all seemed to take place in slow motion, mere minutes had passed, and his security team charged the building, their weapons drawn. They blinked in the glare of the security lights.

"It's Iron Man," he bellowed as the men approached.

"Sorry, sir," the lead agent, a dark-skinned man named Vance. He signaled for the others to stand down.

He gestured for Vance to follow him to the rack and pointed to the empty spaces. The security man nodded in understanding, and began his analysis of the crime scene, which the hero knew would yield nothing useful.

But there was nothing more he could do, so he stalked off in search of the solvent he would need to clean the armor before he changed for a dinner date that had suddenly lost its appeal.

Miles away from SI, Marquez pulled over and used her portable phone to place a call.

"It's me," she said in a rush. "I have something you can move quickly, but I need cash. Tonight."

The man hesitated before answering, then confirmed he could meet her and asked for a number. When he heard it, there was a low whistle and another pause.

"Tonight?"

"Tonight," she said emphatically.

Another pause.

"Eleven, the usual place," he said and clicked off.

That left her time to clean herself up, double-check the equipment, and stash one of the microchips. After all, if the Maggia was to evolve, they needed to stay atop the latest technology.

As Marquez, she'd heard enough from Stark about HY-DRA, AIM, and other outfits—all with top tech, and it made her feel as if the Maggia's time had come and gone. She was determined to keep at least the New York operation relevant.

Her father could worry about the rest.

Microchips might well be the key to the Maggia's survival.

Happy Hogan pulled up at Katalin's address just before nine, but she was already waiting in front of the building. She was wrapped in dark fur, the green highlights in her hair providing a marked contrast. She wore no earrings or obvious jewelry, something Stark found odd for a glamorous woman.

He was having trouble focusing. Twice he barked at Hogan, becoming the worst of backseat drivers, and each time he apologized. He needed to get a grip on his emotions, and hoped a calm dinner with a beautiful woman would do the trick.

The limo wound through the canyons of Manhattan until it arrived at a small, dimly lit restaurant down near Greenwich Village. Stark told Hogan he could return for them in two hours, which earned him a curious look from Katalin.

"Just an estimate, based on previous experience," he said with a shrug. "Hap, I know it's a late night, but I'll make it up to you."

"No prob, boss," Hogan replied, closing the door behind them.

Stark approached the door, briefcase in one hand, Katalin in the other, and it seemed to open automatically. In fact, it had been opened by a towering man who he always thought resembled Punjab from *Little Orphan Annie*.

The décor within was exaggerated Indian with Pakistani touches. Spices filled the warm, thick air, which automatically made Stark ravenous.

Katalin inhaled deeply and nodded with approval, earning her a grin.

"I thought this would be good for us both," Stark said.

Punjab greeted Stark by name, and then escorted them to a table against the wall. It had a large candle in the center that flickered, casting moving shadows. They ordered drinks, then settled in. The sounds of a live sitar player drifted over them. He gazed into her eyes.

"And how was your day?" she asked.

"Don't ask," he said with a wave of his hand, as if the day was a bad smell that could be blown away.

"Oh, but I did," she insisted. "What happened?"

"Just problems in one of the factories, and I could have handled it better. I'm just mad at myself," he admitted without elaborating. She placed both her hands around his, and held them in comfort.

He smiled, and enjoyed the feeling of being taken care of.

The cocktails arrived and Stark drank deeply, signaling for a second round while the waiter was still within earshot. Katalin sipped at her martini, quickly falling behind.

Menus magically arrived and the waiter, speaking in a thick accent, worked his way through the lengthy specials.

Stark nodded along with each item while Katalin sat impassively, just listening. Her calm seemed appealing, and he wished he could feel that sort of inner peace. There was so much he wished to learn about her.

Once the waiter had finished, he ambled off and they were finally alone.

"Do you like music?" he asked.

"Of course. Doesn't everyone?"

"I would think so," he replied, "but I have no way of knowing what your likes and dislikes might be . . . apart from the obvious, of course."

"It's the beginning of a relationship," she said softly, her voice soothing. "I don't even know your favorite color."

"Cherry red," he responded, instantly earning him a smile. He liked when she smiled. "Let me guess, you like green."

Her fingers touched the hair that covered the left side of her face, and she nodded.

The two talked, ordered food, drank, talked some more, and the night passed quietly. He could feel the anger ebb from his bones, and allowed himself to forget HYDRA, to forget industrial espionage, and most important, forget the foul-smelling solvent he had used to remove the even fouler-smelling foam.

He doubted he would ever get the stench out of his briefcase, and was grateful that it was airtight.

As they talked, Stark found out that she liked ballet, but not baseball; *Masterpiece Theatre,* but not the network news. She ate spicy seafood and never broke a sweat.

He found himself telling her about his childhood, times with his mother, and what it was like when his parents died. He was opening up in ways he hadn't to anyone in a very long time.

Was he falling in love with Katalin?

As the meal drew to an end, and he wasn't feeling any pain, he felt like taking her back home, dismissing Happy, and losing himself in her softness.

*　　*　　*

The HYDRA agents fanned out across the river, once more in New Jersey, surrounding one of Drexel Cord's facilities. It was inland, away from the river, and sprawled for hundreds of acres.

The Cord logo shone brightly in the night light and the security building at the front gate was a large, formidable structure, intended to keep prying journalists away. It was a squat concrete building, and anyone driving up couldn't see who was behind the smoked-glass partition.

All communications were done by speakers and electronics.

Within were half a dozen guards armed with tasers, pistols, and extra cartridges, known to fire first, apologize later. They trained every day to be ready for all manners of intruder.

The high-speed hovercraft blew right through the wood and metal gates.

It was green, yellow, and black, with opaque screens, and was moving at forty miles an hour without pausing. Alarms sounded, echoing throughout the entire complex, sounding eerie in the evening air.

A second hovercraft flew behind it, with enough lag time that the six men had time to react, charging out with guns waving in the air. But the craft's momentum quickly took it out of range. The crack of the guard's pistol was lost amid the sirens.

More security men poured out of a building toward the edge of the complex, a barracks for the staff. They carried rifles, and one hefted an axe as they rushed out onto the roads and pathways. They focused on the hovercrafts and missed the dozens of uniformed agents now scaling the walls, easily breaching the electrified fences thanks to energy dampeners they had brought with them.

Suddenly the roads connecting the modern-looking buildings were filled with green-and-yellow figures firing magenta beams that burned into the bodies of all who stood in their way. As blood began to flow freely, men and women turned to flee. Several managed to get away, while others were cut down.

The invaders had five minutes to breach the defenses and make their way to the warehouses. Additional empty hovercrafts awaited a signal that would cause them to move in and be loaded with the goodies that were essentially unprotected.

"Stark," the rough voice said out loud, easily heard over the sitar music.

Tony Stark looked to his right, and saw a frowning Nick Fury standing by the table, wearing a camel's hair overcoat, a yellow scarf around his neck.

The man seriously needed a shave.

"Fury," he replied by way of greeting, but his voice sounded thick.

At the sound of the name, Katalin jumped noticeably, a reaction he couldn't quite read. She remained silent and fixed in her seat, eyeing the intruder warily.

"I'm sorry, ma'am, but I need to speak with Mr. Stark rather urgently. His driver will take you anywhere you want to go," he said to her, and he seemed to be studying her with his good eye.

This is all very strange, Stark mused.

"Hap's a good driver—you'll be safe," Stark said confidently. He was buzzed; no, he was drunk, and he was going to hear about that from Fury.

But the colonel's presence also spoke to the urgency of whatever was happening.

Katalin rose and Fury held her chair. She leaned over the table and kissed Stark on the cheek, then left the two men, moving quickly but with a sway to her hips Stark could still appreciate through the haze.

"Pretty woman," Fury said, taking her seat.

"Yeah, that she is," Stark happily agreed.

"Once I get the coffee into you, we're going to Jersey," the colonel said.

"Without dessert?"

"One of life's little disappointments," Fury said.

xxii.

It was cold, and the last place Madame Masque wanted to be was standing in Washington Square Park.

Drug dealers darted here and there, arms wrapped tight around their bodies to try to keep warm.

Francois was running late, and while her outfit kept her warm, the air was still chill enough to seep through the layers. Having stowed the carryall with the rifles and chips—all but one—in a bush behind a park bench, well out of sight in the poorly lit park, she walked to keep the blood pumping and distract herself.

As a result, she almost missed the telltale sound of knuckles cracking. She turned around and her father's burly representative was standing on the path, flanked by his three associates.

"We heard there was an incident at Stark Industries," he said in that rough voice that irritated her. "Fast work."

"I want the debt paid, and Big M off my back," she said from behind her golden mask.

He nodded in agreement.

"That's why we're here. To ensure that our mutual leader gets every nickel. Your fence will be along shortly."

She was done with this. She had served her father well, done as he had bid, and was *still* under watch. What would it take to gain her independence?

It was time, she considered, to take a stand.

"What right do you have to interfere with Maggia business?" she demanded. "What right do you have to interfere with *my* business?"

He stepped closer, no longer massaging his gloved fists, letting his arms hang loosely at his sides.

"I have done everything asked of me," she continued, taking a step toward him, keeping her eyes on him. "I have served the Maggia well, as I suspect you have. But this is a breach of trust."

As she neared, she noted that he hesitated, and the others had crowded behind him, all bunched together.

"As leader of New York, this is my turf," she said louder. "My turf, my city, and my operation. Interference will not be tolerated. In fact, it will be punished."

On the last word, she rushed forward, head low, and butted him in the chest, the momentum carrying them both into the men clustered behind. Two fell, while the third struggled to maintain his balance.

Her target staggered a few steps, but straightened up quickly.

He growled. He actually *growled,* and rushed her.

She used his speed against him, pirouetted out of the way, and kicked out, landing him on his ass so that he sprawled on the leaf-covered grass by a bench. The landing was a solid thud, so she quickly spun and took three steps toward the still-standing thug and struck with a right jab.

The strike was followed by a right cross. By then the other two men were on their feet and trying to join the melee.

One wore a ski parka, which she grabbed by the puffy fabric and used to swing him three-quarters about and right into a lamp post. She then kicked out at the other man, but only glanced off his arm.

Trying to press her advantage, she rushed him, only to have her legs kicked out from under her. It had to be Mr. Rough Voice, and as she landed she braced for an attack. Sure enough, he straddled her, using a knee to pin one arm to the ground and grabbing the other with his right hand.

The left was holding a switchblade, which reflected the weak light from the lamp.

"You're a disobedient bitch, truth to tell," he said. "And the Maggia wouldn't be in trouble if you had paid your fair share."

It was an old argument, and he was just parroting what Count Nefaria had been saying all along. She was tired of it, and tired of her father.

Vibrating with righteous anger, she managed to wriggle her legs free before he could carve her with the blade. She pulled them in, tucked them against her stomach, and then kicked out, dislodging the disagreeable weight from her chest. He flew backward and away, letting her regain her feet.

Suddenly she found herself in a weak bear hug from one of the others. Fueled by adrenaline, she pummeled his ears, causing him to break the grip. Moving away from him, she lashed out with her left fist, breaking his nose. The breaking cartilage sent a satisfying sound to her ears.

He was down for the count. Three to go, including the ringleader, who bellowed his indignation.

Once more he charged her. They went over a set of bushes and sprawled on the grass. He landed several punches that were blunted by the coat she wore, but she noted the power behind the blows. She needed to deal with him once and for all.

As he reared back for a stronger punch, she rolled to her left at the last moment and his fist hit the ground. There was a crack and she guessed he had busted a knuckle or perhaps even broken a finger or two.

Her elbow flared up and caught him on the jaw, making him arch his back. Another punch to his gut stunned him, and she regained her footing. Quickly she reached into her coat pocket, withdrew her pepper spray, took aim, and squirted a fine mist right into his eyes.

His screams were bloodcurdling, but immensely satisfying.

Whirling about, she pocketed the spray and looked at the other two men, who were still standing.

They stared at her, glanced beyond her to their writhing leader, and shrugged.

"No more," one said with an Italian accent. Interesting, but their surrender spoke of how the Maggia had fallen. The two men turned and walked away from her, practically daring her to strike them down.

She had made her point, and would add a punctuation mark to the entire matter when she wired the money to her father. Then she would quit SI and move on before her disguise was pierced. While Stark's interest was flattering, now was not the time.

As the men departed, Masque stood rigid, trying to control her breathing, control the steam that was coming in rapid puffs. She was winded and realized that she had been behind a desk for too long.

A clapping sound surprised her and she turned, reaching for the spray. Instead, when she recognized Francois, she withdrew her hand and bowed gracefully.

"Smoothly done," he said softly. "But now we must hurry, because surely someone has dialed 911."

"In this park, at this time of the day, I doubt it," she replied. "But why take the risk?"

She walked over to the bench and then behind it, where she retrieved the carryall. Masque handed it to him and he, in turn, passed her a blue satchel that had the right kind of heft for the cash she had demanded. There was no need for her to count it any more than Francois needed to check the merchandise; they had done enough work together to earn a measure of trust.

However, there was one issue she needed to clear up before she would trust him entirely.

"You had a problem and went to the Big M and not me. Why?"

He studied her carefully before responding.

"Because, my dear, when I deal with the Maggia, I know that I deal with the entire operation. When there's a problem that affects *my* reputation, I go straight to the top. The Big M is the top."

She nodded, but didn't like the answer she had received.

"We're going to be finished for a while," she told him, wishing to snap his neck, but restraining herself.

"Pity," he said with a bow. "I was earning some nice commissions, and the holidays are coming. My wife's tastes are . . . expensive."

"Yeah," she said with a little regret. "I hear money's tight all over."

 xxiii.

"How are we getting to Jersey?" Stark asked as he downed a large cup of coffee. He was still feeling bleary, but the pleasant glow was being washed away.

"I brought the car."

"Cool."

"So grab your briefcase and let's get out of here. We don't have a lot of time," the S.H.I.E.L.D. director growled.

"I'm coming," Stark said, and he grimaced as he noted that his voice sounded petulant.

He shrugged into his coat and followed Fury out of the restaurant, giving the waiter a sloppy salute. Once they were outside, the cold air was like a slap, and he took several deep breaths, a sip from a cup, then more deep breaths. His mental faculties were coming back on line, and he was finally absorbing the urgency of the situation.

"What's going on, Nick?"

Fury eyed him and grinned, walking over to a bright red muscle car that was parked in a no-parking zone.

"Welcome back. She's some dish. Where'd you find her?"

"I just turned around, and there she was."

"Some millionaires have all the luck," Fury said and eased Stark into the car, which hung low to the ground. Stark placed the briefcase in the rear, followed it there, and buckled up, admiring the leather and new-car smell.

"HYDRA's hit Drexel Cord's place over the river, and I need Iron Man," Fury said as he pressed his thumb against a sensor and engaged the engine. The sound was soft, like a purr, and barely caused the vehicle to vibrate.

"Better take the tunnel at this hour," Stark began, sounding a little less slurred. "It's faster."

"I have a better idea," Fury said. He pulled away from the curb and braked, then opened up a panel next to the radio. His fingers worked several buttons, and the entire vehicle shuddered. A deep throbbing sound began as a different sort of engine was engaged.

"My way's *really* fast," the colonel said.

The car seemed to rock in place for a moment. Then it began to rise into the air.

"Drink up," Fury began.

"You bet," he said absently, but he was staring out the side window. Each wheel was parallel to the ground, and was acting as a vertical-takeoff-and-landing jet. "Damn, I wish I could have designed this."

"You've been missing out, riding in that tin can of yours," Fury said as he turned sharply to avoid a flagpole.

"Each wheel doubles as a mach-turbine with enough lift and thrust to get us anywhere pretty quickly. The alloy for the shell is lightweight and aerodynamic, but on the down side, I hear it has pretty lousy gas mileage."

Stark laughed.

"Yeah, but with gas at one seventy-five a gallon, we're doin' okay," he said. "Of course, the nice thing about the helicarrier is that we can always find the stations with the lowest prices."

Stark sipped the cooling liquid caffeine and began imagining going into battle at less than peak form.

Well, he'd done it before, and no doubt it'd happen again.

"Where're your troops?"

"Coming," Fury said bitterly. "HYDRA distracted them, just like at Groton. It's why I need Shellhead."

"One Shellhead coming up," Stark replied. He retrieved the briefcase, snapped it open, and made a face as he caught a whiff of the smell.

"What the hell is that?" Fury demanded.

"Don't ask," Stark replied, trying desperately not to vomit.

Fury wrinkled his nose, but concentrated on gaining altitude as they headed for the Hudson River.

Stripping off his suit coat, tie, and shirt, Stark focused on the change from inventor to Avenger. It was cramped, but he urged his fingers to work without error. As they were nearing the Jersey docks, Iron Man was powering up behind Fury, who nodded with silent approval.

"ETA, four minutes," Fury warned him.

"I'll bail out here," Iron Man said. "Give me a chance to get there faster. Air will clear my head, too."

"Ya know, Shellhead," Fury began, "relaxing is fine and all, but you seemed pretty far gone, which isn't a good way to treat your date."

"I know, I know," Iron Man replied. "I've been letting everything get to me. And she's a real find, too—the sort who deserves to be treated right."

"So I saw." With that, Fury hit a switch that unlocked the passenger door.

Iron Man tumbled out and began to free-fall, the shrill sound barely audible as he cut through winds off of the river. Within seconds, though, he engaged the boot jets, and with a wave toward Fury flew a loop around the vehicle, then shot straight ahead, gaining speed with every foot.

He opened a couple of exterior vents, strategically placed so that they wouldn't affect the aerodynamics of the suit. Glancing at the various readouts in his helmet, he quickly checked his onboard status and saw green lights in each and every instance. He was brimming with power, and he liked the rush of cool air that filled the helmet and made him alert.

No, he felt *alive*.

He reveled in flying, and once he was in the armor, he actually became someone else. Tony Stark's crises could be put aside as Iron Man focused entirely on dealing with the global terrorists.

He wouldn't bother holding back this time. This was an opportunity to smash them and deal them a serious blow. If his rival's factory got bashed up a bit—oh well, there was *always* collateral damage.

He smiled, imagining the repair bill that would land on the old man's desk.

Bright pulsing lights attracted his attention as he neared the facility, and he scanned the situation. Iron Man's sensors seemed to send him conflicting information, however, perhaps due to the distance, so he ignored them and went for a purely visual study.

There were sleek aircraft parked outside the plant, and just beyond, a sea of green and yellow. Beams of red and yellow light flashed from several locations at once. The entire place was overrun, and he estimated that at least four dozen enemies were helping themselves to Cord's goods.

"Repulsors, energize. Standby mode."

Iron Man activated his offensive systems and received green lights, telling him that he was weapons-hot and ready to rock-and-roll.

"Boot propulsion, seventy-five percent."

As he neared the perimeter, he lowered his altitude, took aim, and let loose. Repulsor blasts from both gauntlets tore through the parked vehicles, and as their engines and fuel systems were compromised, they exploded in flames.

His armored form was moving so quickly that he was already within the facility by the time HYDRA agents could focus on the cause of the explosions. Instantly he came under fire, but he twisted and rocketed left, then up, evading most of the blasts.

Several hit the armor, however, and he rocked in the air,

but he steadied quickly as he absorbed the impacts and his gyros kept him from being thrown off course. For all his confidence, Stark knew he was outgunned, and even Fury's imminent arrival wasn't going to change the odds too much.

He needed to take out large numbers, and quickly.

This was Stark's element. His head felt clear, his mind sharp. He spotted a huge water tower toward the rear of the building, adjusted his course, and rocketed toward it. He grabbed a major support and tore it loose in a single motion, steel buckling like cardboard. A single shot from his left glove punched a hole through the tilting tank and a rush of frigid water poured out, the torrent of painfully chilled water engulfing the HYDRA agents below.

Iron Man adjusted his chest-beam emitter and sent out pulses of energy that would scatter agents who stood farther away from the water.

The tank finally succumbed to its own weight and tore from its foundation with a shriek, and Iron Man gripped it, adding thrust to keep it under his control.

With a great effort, he hefted it over his head and hurled it forward. Agents scattered as they saw the large form sail through the night sky, and it came down on one of the invading craft with a rending sound as metal ripped into metal and split apart. Whatever water remained within splashed out and formed rushing streams in all directions.

Debris knocked HYDRA agents to their knees or flattened them, pieces of metal ripping into their uniforms.

Now you know how it feels.

He had hoped to take out all the aircraft, and some of the debris seemed to accomplish that, but he had misjudged the throw.

"Boot propulsion, fifty percent."

He jetted up and headed in a different direction, toward the burning remains of some of the vehicles. He hovered just beyond their weapons' fire range, and as he did he

spotted Fury's vehicle. He contacted the colonel on a secure frequency and told him where best to land.

Finished playing traffic cop, he zipped back over the factory and then dove low, fists extended. He withstood pun-
ishing energy beams licking against his armor as he bowled
over agent after agent. They fell like tenpins and he completed one pass, and then swung about for a second.

As he swung about, the second pass was interrupted
when a withering onslaught slammed into him. The bright
yellow energy was stronger, and was likely delivered by
something other than the pistols. HYDRA was rolling out
the heavy artillery.

So would he.

Iron Man landed, turned, and sought the source of the
beams. He spotted a platform with a long turret and a
transparent shield protecting the seated agent who was
controlling the weapon. In turn, he extended his right arm
and unleashed his own onslaught. A sustained repulsor
blast tore into the weapon, bending the shield's frame and
super-heating the turret.

The energy feedback seemed to take the machine off-line.

He swung about and found five agents charging him,
and smiled behind his mask. He stood his ground, letting
them slam into his body—and bounce off him, as well.

When five more leapt at him, the sheer weight and momentum finally staggered him, but also provided him with
several new weapons he could use. Iron Man grabbed two
of the agents by their uniforms and swung one into the
other, trapping two others in between. Various groans and
grunts greeted him, and he grabbed one woman and tossed
her atop several other men, knocking them all to the
ground.

A different sound—more of a popping one—could then
be heard nearby, and Iron Man braced for a new attack. Instead, he saw Fury round the corner of the main factory, firing a S.H.I.E.L.D. weapon he didn't recognize. Whatever it

fired wasn't bullets, nor was it a laser like the HYDRA weapons.

He'd study it later, but noted that it was effective, as enemy agents fell with each strike.

Fury spotted Iron Man and gave him a thumb's-up, then decked a charging foe with a right cross.

Stark turned to focus on a quartet of agents trying to build some sort of modular weapon. He strode over and scattered them with the equivalent of metallic love taps, and then began crushing the metal and ceramic parts that were still awaiting assembly. Enough to disable, but leaving plenty to examine.

Several more laser blasts ricocheted off the armor, and he shuddered a bit with the pounding.

As he fought, Iron Man failed to notice a female silhouette that rose on the nearest rooftop.

She, in turn, silently watched him at work.

A roar of human voices washed over him, attracting his attention as a phalanx of newly arrived HYDRA agents stormed the area. They were all equally uniformed and equipped. Immediately they began firing, but were aiming wildly, with most of the energy beams missing him entirely. The sheer number of HYDRA soldiers gave Stark a new appreciation for their motto, "Cut off an arm and two more shall take its place!"

He checked his power and saw that the pounding was beginning to take its toll. That meant the sheer numbers would begin to work in their favor, and he again began seeking a way to put them out of commission until S.H.I.E.L.D. could arrive en masse to even the odds.

The discordant sounds of HYDRA pistols, Fury's single weapon, and the roaring voices of the newly arrived enemies filled the night air with a cacophony that made him engage the noise-dampening function in the helmet. He was careful to allow some sound to enter, though, so that he wouldn't become functionally deaf.

There must be a way to add a filtering function....

He waded into the nearest cluster of opponents and began manhandling them, scattering the men and women, bending pistols in his gloved hands, or crushing them beneath his boot heel. There was little time for elegance. He heard bones crack along with the sound of twisting metal, and voices crying out in pain.

Fury issued the occasional expletive-filled quip, clearly audible over the chaos, and he seemed to be relishing getting his hands dirty. Always keeping his back to the wall, he fought with practiced ease, a combination of pugilism, street fighting, and a dose of martial arts. This was someone who had seen combat, who knew how to fight in close quarters, and in some ways was better equipped for it than he was.

The hand-to-hand combat kept him surrounded, and therefore he wasn't an easy target for long-range weapons. For a while the green shapes obscured his field of vision, but then a cluster of enemy agents suddenly broke off and headed away from the fight.

A part of him just wanted to unleash his onboard weaponry and damn the consequences, but he refused to allow himself to take human life so callously. Yet if help didn't arrive soon, he would run out of power—both physically and mechanically—and then HYDRA would win through sheer force of numbers.

Suddenly the noise level skyrocketed, and at first he could not tell where it was coming from. Then he saw Fury scramble atop several unconscious HYDRA agents and wave his arm.

S.H.I.E.L.D. had arrived.

The blue-uniformed agents came charging from a darkened corner, their arrival entirely without warning. They still appeared to be outnumbered, but Iron Man surmised that their presence would more than tip the balance in favor of the angels.

These were men and women culled from the best intelligence and military operations from around the world, and sure enough, he spotted several displaying their fighting prowess as the battle was joined.

The element of surprise fading, several green-clad agents closed on him and targeted his helmet's mouthpiece, so he crouched, engaged his boot jets, and went aloft, leaving his enemies tumbling to the cold ground. Once he was twenty feet up, he hovered to survey the scene.

Several flying vehicles of a different make were approaching, others were landing, and the entire Cord complex filled with S.H.I.E.L.D. agents. The difference in their uniform colors allowed him to tell the good guys from the bad. There was something to be said for colorful outfits, but they had to be uniform, he mused, otherwise it got confusing.

On more than one occasion, he had nearly punched out a fellow Avenger, rather than a Master of Evil.

The sounds changed timbre as S.H.I.E.L.D. and HYDRA pistols exchanged fire along with fists, feet, and the occasional head butt. He couldn't spot Fury for a moment, but then saw a figure go flying and the colonel rising from the ground, actually bothering to dust himself off before decking an attacker.

Iron Man decided to change tactics and charged his repulsor rays. He fired off quick pulses, knocking people down and scattering clusters. Try as he might, though, it was tough to target HYDRA personnel without also hitting S.H.I.E.L.D. agents.

At that instant something hit him on the back with a wallop, and all the green lights switched to red. His systems went off-line, his boot jets ground to a halt, and he fell like a stone. There was no way to guide his descent—no spoilers, no wings or parachute.

He twisted in the air so he could see where he was going,

and pushed his arms forward in an attempt to steer himself into a parked security vehicle—as opposed to living beings. He misjudged and fell on a rooftop above the fray, unseen by S.H.I.E.L.D. or HYDRA.

Furiously, he tried to calculate how long a reboot would take, and judged it to be three minutes at minimum. The battery pack was tasked to energize the chestplate and keep the shrapnel away from his heart, but otherwise he was powerless and way too vulnerable.

He lay there and listened for his attacker—a second jolt might permanently deactivate the armor. And he dearly wished he could get his hands on the device, to reverse engineer it before turning it into scrap metal.

Remaining still, controlling his breathing, Stark tried to get a sense of his surroundings. With the armor off-line, he began to notice how cold the night air was, and watched steam rise from his helmet. He was on a factory building, maybe three stories up, and peering to the side he noted that the roof had tears in it, and needed a fresh coat of tar or some other sealant.

Then he spotted a green boot reflecting light from the nearby firefight.

With some effort he turned his head and looked up.

Tony Stark's jaw dropped, and he was confronted by the image of Katalin leaning over him, hair dangling before her face, her puckered skin exposed. He was thankful that she couldn't see his expression.

Her green hair, her mysterious background . . .

She was with HYDRA. It all added up now, and he felt like an idiot.

"Hello, Tony," she said in that lovely, accented voice.

xxiv.

"Who *are* you?"

Iron Man heard the painful rasp in his voice.

She stood over him, a metallic apparatus cocooned around her. Her expression was blank—no sentimentality, no rage. It seemed devoid of feeling.

"I am a woman who did what so many others could not," she said. "I got to your heart, even more than those insignificant bits of metal."

Indeed she had, and he cursed himself for letting himself fall for it.

Katalin—or whoever she was—began to release the straps around her waist and arms, sliding out of the sonic device, lowering it to the ground in silence. It was smoldering, and he guessed that it had been able to sustain only one charge.

That will buy me some time.

Stark mentally counted down to the reboot, hoping to keep her distracted.

Below, the sounds of the battle continued, and sooner or later, Fury would realize that he was AWOL.

"I needed Iron Man preoccupied so my people could complete their tasks," she said, towering over him. His teeth began to chatter in the chill, and he clamped them shut.

"You were perhaps my most pleasant diversion in many a year," she continued. "I so rarely allow myself dalliances, so each must be savored. And I savored you, Stark, savored knowing I was making love to a man I would destroy."

"What are you doing?" he asked. "And *why?*"

She walked around his prone form, admiring the armor up close, running her hands over the chestplate in a familiar fashion. Then she replied, "HYDRA's goals are to destroy the world governments. Once we take out the largest— starting with your America—the others will fall in line."

"And you had to seduce me, while robbing my company?" He felt the emotional paralysis lift as a fresh wave of anger slowly built in the pit of his stomach. It was a warm ember he hoped to fan into a bright flame.

When she didn't reply to his question, he asked another. "Is your name really Katalin?"

"You may think of me as Katalin, if you like, in the few minutes you have left," she said. "The world shall know me, though, as Madame Hydra."

Fury told him the terrorists were led by a "Supreme Hydra." Was this his wife? Mistress?

Was she even known to the S.H.I.E.L.D. director?

Madame Hydra kneeled down and reached for his helmet. Her gloved fingers sought a release mechanism. Finding nothing, she affectionately stroked the faceplate, but her eyes were devoid of feeling.

She was toying with him. As her fingers traced the outline of the mouth, a thrum of energy rippled through his armor. She sensed it, her fingers flying away, and she scrambled to her feet, reaching for her pistols.

Iron Man's reboot was quick, prioritized to provide power first to life support, then mobility, then weaponry. While she was withdrawing her guns, he was already rising to his feet, an imposing figure compared with her form— nice as it was.

She backed away while taking aim, and fired off a shot from each gun. The bullets struck the armor, ricocheting off the helmet near the eyes. He admired the skill that went into targeting his apertures. Had they hit the lenses, it might have seriously screwed up his vision.

He stepped menacingly toward her, hoping to subdue her easily and then present her as an early Christmas gift to S.H.I.E.L.D. But she avoided his first attempt at a grab and gracefully moved away, putting more distance between them.

The anger that fueled him swept aside his exhaustion. He killed his external speakers so she couldn't hear him.

"Repulsors energize, forty percent."

He decided to blow the roof out from under her feet and let the fall put her out of action.

"Rapid pulse."

He moved quickly, sweeping one arm in a feint, and fired with the other, targeted where he thought she would step.

Madame Hydra reacted faster than he thought possible, and cartwheeled away from the white beams of energy.

Then she laughed at him.

Everything contained in that laugh mocked his emotions, his vulnerability, the fact that he had felt anything for her. Anger flared with bright intensity, and Iron Man charged her, deciding to deal with her personally.

She tried to dodge, but ran out of space on the roof. Her pistols futilely fired at him, but he ignored each shot and kept coming closer and closer.

Careful not to use lethal force, he let loose with a right jab that went into her solar plexus. On impact she crumpled, the wind whooshing out of her lungs, and a gagging sound replacing the icy laugh. He prepared for a second blow, but stopped himself, feeling some of the anger begin to ebb.

Madame Hydra collapsed at Iron Man's feet, and Tony Stark took absolutely no joy in his victory.

Let S.H.I.E.L.D. have HYDRA, he thought. After this, he was done.

"I think we should see other people," he said to her still form.

* * *

Madame Masque had a decision to make.

Maggia had its money, so her father could launch his assault on Washington, but she needed her own personal operating capital. She brooded in her apartment, still in full gear, and considered her options.

She had the radio turned to CBS, the all-news station, and the name Iron Man caught her attention. According to the report, he was fighting someone or something in New Jersey. That left SI unprotected by anything other than the paid guards.

There were still things to plunder, baubles that would bring her the cash she desired. Since Gabriella Marquez was about to leave Stark's employ, she would need some severance pay. . . .

Less than an hour later, she drove onto the company campus. This was the last time she would do so—after this she would simply vanish.

While she had carefully avoided pilfering her own department's work as much as possible, now she could help herself without fear of anything coming back to haunt her. In fact, she knew exactly what she wanted, and what it would fetch on the open market.

Kenn Hoekstra was happily pummeling a HYDRA thug as Iron Man lowered himself to land right beside him. He was carrying Kata—Madame Hydra, and turned her over to another S.H.I.E.L.D. agent.

"Watch her," he said. "We'll need to talk to her later."

The tide had turned in their favor. Not that their work was done by any measure, but fresh reinforcements had arrived, and the remaining terrorists were outnumbered. With luck, the New York cell had been emptied for this assault.

Stark's energy reserves were dipping below 30 percent, but he took careful aim and let loose with several low-yield repulsor bursts to take down HYDRA craft that were attempting to flee the vicinity. S.H.I.E.L.D. aircraft were also patrolling the skies surrounding Cord's factory complex, which had been pretty much trashed.

Before the night's events, he would have taken guilty pleasure in that. Now it didn't seem to mean as much.

Gabe Jones was directing several men and women to corral the captured HYDRA forces into a specific area, which was ringed with heavily armed agents. While the mop-up was proceeding, there remained pockets of resistance as HYDRA agents attempted to slip away. It fell to Hoekstra and other agents to track them down.

The young man sprinted toward the remains of the water tank, waving for three others to follow, which they did without question, working silently and taking up positions around the twisted, torn metal. With hand signs, Hoekstra placed them at the ready while he crawled underneath. Dropping to his hands and knees, a knife held in his teeth, he worked his way between gaps in the metal.

Iron Man heard human and metallic sounds but couldn't tell exactly what was happening within the wreckage. In a matter of moments Hoekstra was shimmying out again, a cut on one cheek and his navy-blue jacket shredded across the eagle logo. Once he cleared the gap, he reached in with both hands and tugged.

"Allow me," Iron Man said. The S.H.I.E.L.D. agent looked up and grinned, then scrambled away.

The Armored Avenger pulled the metal apart and reached down to withdraw a female HYDRA agent, her own green-and-yellow uniform torn in several embarrassing places. She had several cuts looking worse than what the S.H.I.E.L.D. agent sported. He hefted her and then handed her over to the awaiting law-enforcement personnel.

"Thanks, Shellhead," Fury said, a fresh unlit cigar in his right hand.

"You know I hate that name," Iron Man said.

"Yep," Fury said, then he turned and directed several of his men for a moment.

"Are we secure?" Iron Man asked. "I need time for a recharge."

"No Duracells tucked in a pocket?" Fury asked, lighting up what appeared to be his victory smoke. "Yeah, go see if you can find an outlet in this mess."

"I'll do that, and then I have a surprise for you," he replied wearily. Somehow, he couldn't bring himself to think about her just yet.

Iron Man walked slowly toward the least-damaged building, thankful that a simple outlet would do the trick, presuming there remained any power in the entire complex. All he could see at this point was weak emergency lighting, no doubt coming from battery power—which was what he would be using if he didn't power up.

He kicked in the door, just to spite Cord, and found the nearest outlet and a metal chair that could support him. He disliked doing this in public, especially when enemies were within the area. Still, beggars couldn't be choosers.

He settled in place, withdrew the cord, and began sucking in raw voltage. Fortunately, there was some.

As he was forced to remain in one spot for a time, the exhaustion caught up with him. The next thing he knew, a voice roused him.

He blinked to clear his vision and saw Hoekstra standing in the doorway.

"Sir, I wanted to thank you again for the assist," he said. "Just to be safe, me and the others are standing right outside the door . . . just in case."

Iron Man wearily nodded in appreciation. Hoekstra began to turn away when he spoke.

"Where have they taken Madame Hydra?" he asked. "She has a lot of 'splaining to do."

Hoekstra seemed confused.

"Sir?"

Uh oh . . .

"Knock off the 'sir,' but go find Fury or Jones," Iron Man instructed. While not exactly a member of S.H.I.E.L.D.'s hierarchy, he suspected in the grand scheme of things, superhero outranked field agent.

A few more minutes passed, and while his gauges showed a substantially more reassuring charge, he also suspected that he'd be unable to top off the tank anytime soon.

Hoekstra and Fury came charging through the smashed doorway. Although the cigar was lodged firmly between the colonel's teeth, Iron Man saw the expression.

"Where is she?" he demanded.

"Gone," Fury said in disgust. "The guys who were guarding her didn't know who she was, and put her with a bunch of her underlings. They launched a suicide run that gave her the opportunity to slip away, and we didn't realize she was gone until it was too late—"

Iron Man interrupted him, anger also in his voice.

"That's sloppy."

"No kidding," Fury said. "We're learning how to work with these numbers. It wasn't like this in the European theater."

"Not you—me," he countered. "I shouldn't have left her until I was certain she was secure."

"Well, it don't matter now, Stark," Fury said. "Gone is gone."

Fury chewed his cigar in thought, then looked directly at the hero. "But who is this Madame Hydra?"

"You actually met her earlier," Iron Man said quietly. "The knockout with green hair?"

Fury gaped.

"Tell me you're kidding."

"I got played," Iron Man admitted.

"That could explain a lot—we've had reports the Supreme Hydra is dead," Fury said. "The impression we had was that they were splintered, but she must've stepped up to run New York, or the whole blamed East Coast."

Another figure dashed into the room. All eyes turned.

"We have a situation," Jones interrupted as he joined them, out of breath from jogging some distance.

"What now?" Fury asked.

"The aerial team is reporting a squad of HYDRA agents heading toward the Lincoln and Holland tunnels."

"How'd they get away?" Fury demanded.

"I saw them splinter off earlier," Iron Man said. "I thought they were regrouping, and would remain on premises. My mistake."

Fury shot him a look, but didn't say anything.

"Damn it, we thought this was their big blowout, and that they'd have all their forces here," he said. "But this was nothing more than a colossal decoy, while they launched a surgical strike where it would *really* hurt."

Iron Man agreed.

"Down that deep, they would need flawless communications, as well as equipment that would enable them to tunnel beneath the riverbed," he said. "The weapons were never the primary objective."

"If they get control of the tunnels before we can clear them, they'll really have us by the short hairs," Fury added. "We've gotta move!"

"What are your orders?" Hoekstra asked.

"How quickly can you evacuate the tunnels?" Iron Man asked. He noted the armor was at 57 percent, and it would have to do.

"At this hour, traffic is light enough that shutting them won't be an issue," Fury began. "It'll depend on how quickly the terrorists move, though, and there's no way we have enough personnel to clear out the people who live in the areas around the entrances."

"Call in New Jersey transit and the police," Iron Man prompted.

"It'll be bedlam," Fury said. "Better we shut the tunnels and stop HYDRA there."

Iron Man nodded and practically ripped his cables from the outlet.

The colonel turned to his men.

"Jones, you and Hoekstra take a team to the Holland. Shellhead and I will go for the Lincoln. Keep an open channel at all times. Have Agent 13 take charge of the prisoners." Fury paused as the men left to do as ordered.

"What's wrong?" Iron Man asked.

"Something smells, Stark," Fury said. "Threatening the tunnels is a new wrinkle, and it doesn't add up."

"I've been dealing with things not adding up for a week," Iron Man replied. "You get used to it."

Without another word, he leapt into the sky and accelerated away, heading toward the tunnel that connected New Jersey to Midtown Manhattan.

Time was short. Too short.

XXV.

As Iron Man rocketed toward the New Jersey end of the Lincoln Tunnel, he downloaded details about the structure that had fascinated him as a kid. Three tubes, twenty-one feet six inches wide and thirteen feet tall, reaching a maximum depth of ninety-seven feet.

Adjusting his trajectory to parallel I-495, he saw the brightly lit baker's dozen of toll lanes, lights green and yellow. While there was a steady stream heading into Midtown Manhattan, the three exit lanes were relatively empty.

He began flying a search pattern over the area, seeking some semblance of HYDRA activity, and felt the ticking bomb in his mind. Seeing the traffic continue to flow, he got on the horn to S.H.I.E.L.D.

Nothing.

What the hell?

He tried another frequency, then another. He accessed the Port Authority system, and all he got was static.

Oh my god! That was when it hit him.

HYDRA hadn't stolen the communications system from the boat in New Jersey so they could communicate within their ranks. They had adapted it to block the frequencies used by law enforcement. Most likely emergency responders of all sorts.

There was no way to warn those people of the impending assault, whatever form it would take.

He tried to imagine what they would use, be it explosives, the lasers, or something worse. Whatever they employed, they could cripple Manhattan. Should both tunnels be rendered useless, it would reveal just how vulnerable New York could be. If HYDRA could do this so close to a city full of heroes, then no one would be safe.

Below the helix ramps that allowed bus access, unnoticed by the Armored Avenger, a dozen men and women were feverishly at work. They worked with miniature lights that glowed brightly despite their size, courtesy of Stane's Texas operation. Under the watchful eye of agent 389, they were assembling the modular components of a pair of devices none fully understood. They worked in silence so as not to attract undue attention, but all were eager to begin spreading the terror they had signed on to create.

Iron Man had been spotted overhead, but he remained blissfully unaware of their presence, and the sight of him lent speed to their efforts.

Before long, he would learn just how powerful a foe HYDRA could be.

At the Long Island campus, Madame Masque had located the items on her shopping list, and was helping herself to a variety of radically dissimilar items, just to confuse the investigation. Her focus had been technology, but by stealing cell phones, discmen, and other more pedestrian objects, she hoped to lend her activities the air of a common burglary.

Given how focused her assaults had been for some time now, the sheer randomness of it all began to delight her, as she approached it with a lighthearted artistry. It had been a long time since she had actually *enjoyed* herself, and she smiled beneath the golden faceplate.

Since she would never again set foot on Stark Industries property, she had allowed herself the luxury of the mask. It reminded her that she was *more* than a simple thief. Indeed, she was a representative of criminal royalty, and it felt good to revel in it.

Already bagged and awaiting removal were the devices she had come for. Her last act would be to access Burstein's office and log on to his computer with his own user name and password—which of course, she had known for some time.

That done, she withdrew a floppy disk and inserted it into the drive, then downloaded a customized program she had purchased just for this occasion. It would worm its way through the mainframe and delete random files without harming the backups, which remained on digital tape and were kept off-site.

On top of her physical mischief, this digital randomness would confuse Stark, Burstein, Zimmer, and the other geeks who thought they understood the computers. This particular worm had been developed by a fifteen-year-old genius who wrote the program for her from scratch. It was perhaps the best $1,000 she had spent that year, and he had been ecstatic to receive what he thought of as a king's ransom.

Once the program was successfully loaded and had started running, she logged off and shut down the system so that everything would appear innocuous when the staff arrived in just a few hours.

Shortly thereafter, she made her way across the campus and loaded her acquisitions into the trunk of her car. Hiding the mask one last time, she drove up to the gate, which was manned by someone she didn't recognize. Before long she was speeding down the Long Island Expressway.

The personal items would be dumped in a trash container between there and LaGuardia Airport, while the real objects of her desire would accompany her home.

XXVI.

Agent 389 received the ready signal from a member of his team, and he returned the hand sign. The last few components were ready to be put into place, and then the fun could begin.

Peering out from under cover, he delighted in watching an increasingly frustrated Iron Man fly around in circles. No doubt he was trying to radio his allies, and discovering that his radio was useless.

But he quickly ducked back under cover, and checked his watch—each passing moment also meant S.H.I.E.L.D. was approaching, and for a change he and his group were badly outnumbered. If any of the dozen fell, that was the game—there were no ready replacements poised to step into the breach. No more "arms" to replace those that were cut off.

Madame Hydra had tasked everyone else to Cord's factories; a show of force intended to cripple their newfound enemies. That assault, coupled with the crippling of the city's most precious artery, would signal the era of HYDRA.

Hail Hydra!

Her methods drove him nuts, but Madame Hydra's goals matched his. He despised a corrupt state and federal government, was appalled by the sheer ineptitude of those who ruled as if they were better than the rest. Who forced *their* rules on the sheep of the nation.

There were many groups that echoed his sentiments, particularly in the center of the country, but the small hate groups he had sampled paled in comparison with the expertise HYDRA had demonstrated, and on an international scale. There was no question that they had been the right people to join in order for him to make a difference.

Remaking the world for his wife and children was a goal that had justified abandoning them. One day, he could return home and claim credit for being an agent of change.

Until then, he had to fight and stay alive.

His fellow agents were clamping the last bits of metal into place, then attaching the power packs. Everything matched the drawings, at last, and the primary machine was a thing of beauty. It was squat and dark, but spoke of power, throbbing with energy as a low hum began to build in volume.

He knew from the documentation the device needed eight minutes to power up, then it could be connected. Within twenty minutes it would be fully operational, and then they could execute their orders.

He signaled that it was time, and six agents grabbed small nodules and high-tech drills. At a second signal, they sprinted out from the hiding place and fanned out across the span of the tunnels.

Their suits were dark for the occasion, and they had just a few minutes to reach their designated spots, bury the nodes exactly thirty feet down, and vanish.

The tools stolen in Austin would bore through concrete and stone with wide, diamond-tipped drill bits, powered with experimental fuel cells that outperformed the best commercial drills. Telescoping arms would take the bits to the appropriate length in a matter of moments.

The drills whined softly in the night, and had someone been listening carefully, they would have heard and come looking. But the sounds were drowned out by the cacophony of the tunnel—the rumble of trucks, the honking of horns, and the constant drone of automobile engines—so they worked without hesitation or interruption. Once the holes were dug, the cables were lowered and dirt packed in around them.

Their tasks completed, the terrorists returned to their hiding place under the roadway. All had been trained well, and managed to remain unseen.

Five minutes remained, so 389 whispered encouragement to each of them. He instructed them to make certain their sidearms were charged and ready.

Then there were just four minutes left.

As he had expected, a trio of S.H.I.E.L.D. craft flew over the area, performing an aerial ballet with Iron Man, and then circled for a landing—but not too close to the tunnel. Each of the three craft emitted five agents, so yes, they were outnumbered.

But then again, HYDRA had them outgunned.

The woman known as 78 held up two fingers.

He nodded and signaled the men manning the device to turn it on.

When one finger was raised, 389 nodded and extended his left arm, hand open. He clenched the hand into a fist and jerked it down.

The secondary weapon was engaged, lighting up the area with brilliant yellow-white light. Beams of coherent energy shot into the sky, announcing their presence and location. They spread out, and actually seemed to coil around one another, white and yellow beams mixing in a gleaming formation.

The cascade rose high into the sky and began falling back to earth, a fountain of light raining down over the HYDRA agents.

As anticipated, this caught Iron Man's attention, and he angled down and dove at the light source, but actually bounced off the glowing canopy.

Once more the Armored Avenger struck, and once more he was rebuffed.

Quickly, he used his onboard sensors to determine what it was he was facing. The energy seemed to exist on fluctuating frequencies that formed a crude shield over the surface and kept objects out.

Iron Man was tired.

Angry. Frustrated and well past the end of his patience.

The shield, he noted, wasn't uniform in size or shape, nor did it completely cover his enemies. Instead, it seemed more of a delaying tactic than actual protection.

They were nestled under the ramp the buses used, but their rear was accessible and he doubted they could move the equipment while it was functioning. That gave him an angle of attack, and he swung through the sky and circled, seeking an entry point for a well-placed repulsor blast.

Kicking his boots into action, he jetted toward the ground, took aim, and let loose.

The repulsor struck the dirt and garbage at the feet of the trio operating the shield. A second burst grew closer and struck the machine, ripping through it and causing a shower of sparks.

Just as quickly, the larger light show ended, exposing HYDRA for all to see.

He landed and, letting his anger fuel him, waded into the group, knocking them flat in short order. He was artless in his attack, adjusting his armored blows so that they wouldn't be lethal.

There were certain lines he would never cross.

Having eliminated the opposition, he walked over to a second object, and scanned for radiation. Had it been present, his own actions might have been as deadly as anything the HYDRA agents might do.

The scan came up empty, and he gave the device a cursory glance, then decided he didn't care what it was designed to accomplish. It couldn't do so if it was rubble.

He raised his boot . . .

. . . and carefully placed explosives went off, knocking him backward with sharply concussive force.

As he regained his footing, he glanced about him and

realized that the S.H.I.E.L.D. agents had arrived. They were struggling with a half-dozen or more additional HYDRA agents near the tunnel entrance.

As he turned his attention back to the device, he saw lights glow to life and realized he was too late.

Someone had activated it remotely.

Katalin.

 **xxvii.**

Next he felt a rumble deep underground, radiating under his boots, and realized that it was another sonic weapon, akin to the one Madame Hydra had used to paralyze him.

The thrumming grew in sound and intensity, and he realized that it was sending out an ever-increasing energy pulse, one that had to be stopped.

Now.

Suddenly he was struck repeatedly on the back of his knees by a pair of energy beams, causing him to buckle.

Whirling about, he saw two green-clad agents, each firing from rifles, their barrels glowing red hot from the discharge. The force of the blows had been more distracting than anything, and steam rose into the cool air from the heated portions of his armor.

He stared at the two for a moment in disbelief, and adjusted his tri-beam emitter to let loose a concussive pulse that knocked the pair flat, eliminating their non-threat.

The vibrations below him were growing in intensity, and that did not bode well. He identified the power source, took aim, and fired a tightly focused beam that struck the generator, but left the rest of the device intact.

Sparks as his precision strike accomplished . . .

Nothing.

The damage had been done.

He wasn't a geologist, but he suspected the magnitude of the vibrations would measure on the Richter scale, and launch a state of panic on both sides of the river. The New

York area was riddled with faults, and they must have located one that ran through the bedrock.

The damage to the tunnels remained to be seen, but unless the vibrations could be stopped immediately, the panic alone could kill hundreds, perhaps more.

Stark cursed Madame Hydra all over again, because this was just mindless destruction. It had nothing to do with global conquest.

Activating his communications array, Iron Man took to the air and made another attempt to contact Fury. To his surprise, he got through.

She must want us to share in the carnage, he thought bitterly.

"*Fury here,*" a breathless voice said.

"Trouble," Iron Man began.

"*Tell me about it,*" came the response. "*Where are ya now?*"

"I'm headed into the tunnel, to see if I can clear it of vehicles. Do you have a tech genius handy?"

"*Yeah, you,*" Fury said.

"Great—I'm a little busy," Iron Man said angrily. "Who else?"

"*I'll check,*" Fury said. A moment later he returned. "*Got 'em, and he'll be here in a coupl'a minutes. What are we doing?*"

Iron Man entered the tunnel and saw lights blowing out in the ceiling. The sound was deafening as hundreds of car horns of different types blared incessantly, echoing in the space. He winced at the noise, and activated his sound dampeners.

"Have him take a look at that machine, see what it did, and what it can undo! If need be I'll talk him through it, and you need to have an alternative power source handy."

"*We're on it,*" Fury said. "*Go save lives.*"

"I can't do it myself, Fury. I'll take the center tube, you send men down the sides," Iron Man instructed.

"We're on it," Fury repeated. He broke the connection. Moments later he was back.

"Ya want some good news for a change?"

"Absolutely," Iron Man replied.

"Holland Tunnel's clear. No sign of HYDRA. They focused everything here."

"Well, that's something," Stark grumbled. "What do we have on the other side?"

"New York's finest has both tunnels closed and are trying to get everyone out. I've got a team on its way."

"Nothing like this in the manual is there?"

"Never read it," Fury said. *"I have enough trouble with all the reports."*

Stark cut the channel, focusing on the task that lay ahead of him.

He adjusted his chest emitter to act as a spotlight and flew near the ceiling, gingerly maneuvering in a narrow space between the vehicles and the tunnel's top. Most of the vehicles had stopped, and there were a handful of pileups where motorists had tried in vain to drive around. The result was that traffic was at an utter standstill.

There were a few engines smoking, but no flames had yet appeared.

Thank god.

As he reached the center of the tube, a loud cracking sound caught his attention and a section of lighting on the tunnel's side was shaken free by the vibrations, which sent it hurtling toward an SUV. He thrust himself between the falling fixture and the vehicle, whose driver gunned the engine in a futile attempt to escape. The armored figure was struck by the right fender, knocking him off course, but he managed to swat the fixture away before he tumbled to the roadway.

The tunnel shuddered.

The SUV bounced once off the tunnel's side, then came to a rest.

I have to find a way to make this work, and fast.

He scanned the vehicles closest to him, and located a large sixteen-wheel truck with an empty trailer. Recognizing that there was no time to be elegant, he dug his iron-clad hands into the rear doors and ripped them off with one smooth motion.

Activating his external speakers, he set them to maximum, linking into the tunnel's overhead speakers, as well, to make certain he would be heard along the length of the tube.

"Quiet!"

The sound careened off the walls, and in a matter of moments most of the horns had stopped, and relative silence descended.

Which made it all the easier to hear the rumbling that came from below, and was still growing in intensity.

I'd better make this quick.

"Ladies and gentlemen, this is Iron Man. Listen to me carefully. Those of you nearest the exits, please leave your cars and make your way to the surface."

He had no way of knowing if they would comply, but Fury had men at either end, and they would be able to handle the crowd.

"The rest of you, please move in an orderly fashion to the center of the tunnel. I'll have you out of here in no time."

He only hoped it would be true.

Cutting the speakers, he began to crisscross the lanes. He bypassed those who were moving quickly, and located those who needed his help, lifting them off the ground and dropping them into the trailer.

"What on earth?" an older, heavyset man said, shouting to be heard.

"No time to explain, just let me get you out of here."

He saw more cracks appear, and had to dodge falling fixtures. More lights shorted out, and suddenly the only sources of illumination were headlights and his uni-beam.

The deep rumbling sounds diminished, and actually stopped, but the damage was done. The entire tunnel was unstable, and he needed to clear it as quickly as possible.

When the trailer was filled with bodies, he ripped the trailer's connections from the cab, then crawled underneath and braced himself.

"Thrust at fifty percent."

The trailer lifted slowly, and he kept it gradual to avoid having it break in half, and to keep all of his charges inside.

"Thrust at seventy-five percent."

There was going to be an awful lot of collateral damage, but the Golden Avenger had little choice but to use the trailer as a battering ram and shove vehicles out of the way in order to save the people he was carrying. He didn't dare hit full speed, instead using sheer strength and physics to help him clear a path as he made his way toward the New Jersey exit. Nevertheless, it took him only ten minutes to reach his goal.

As soon as the badly dented trailer was emptied, he returned it to the center and repeated the process. By this time there were a lot fewer people to ferry, and one more trip, which went far faster now that a clear path existed, did the trick.

He returned to the tunnel, sweeping his uni-beam from side to side, searching for anyone who might have been injured and left behind.

A worn Iron Man pivoted and ripped a door from a twisted car, then tore off the airbag to reach the woman within. She was attractive in an evening dress, and was bleeding from cuts on her bare arms. The cool air was making her shiver, and he worried about shock.

As gently as he could, Iron Man lifted her from the vehicle, made certain she was lucid, and then took to the air.

"Are you still with me?" he asked. "What's your name?"

"Jillian," she replied.

"Are you still with me, Jillian?"

"You bet," she managed to reply.

"Here we go, then," he said and took to the air, taking the injured woman through the tunnel and handing her off to the first EMT personnel he saw.

Without waiting, he flew back into the tunnel, this time surveying the damage as he flew.

There were relatively few victims remaining, and finally the tunnel was clear and he could focus on the next task.

Stark realized that his power levels were dipping again, but there was no way he could stop. He had to clear the tunnel of as many vehicles as possible so engineering crews could enter and begin emergency repairs.

Instructing emergency crews to clear a large area at the New Jersey entrance, he activated his repulsors, setting them for wide dispersal. Then he began blasting the vehicles out of the tunnel, using the beams as battering rams. Insurers were going to love him when the claims began to roll in.

Finally the way was clear, and he shut down the repulsors. But the rumbling that had accompanied the rubble didn't stop.

The tremors were back.

Did they just start up again, or is it Madame Hydra, screwing with us by remote control? Regardless, he needed to put an end to this.

"Fury!" he called as he reversed course.

"What do you need, Shellhead?"

"To begin with, stop calling me that," Iron Man said. "Status?"

"We're making one more sweep from the New York side. Eight fatalities so far, and a slew of people sent to the emergency room, but that's not bad, considering."

"It's still too many. And the tunnels themselves?"

"A mess," Fury replied. *"Cracks everywhere and we think there are microfissures because things are getting damp."*

"What about the machine?"

"Nothing we've ever seen before."

"Then I'm making a house call."

As he flew past the crowds of people swelling around the toll booths, he noted several television trucks.

So this is what people are going to wake up to, he thought grimly. *It'll be panic for certain, and there's no telling how it'll affect the city in the long term.*

Seconds later, he landed where the machine still lay. It had been hooked up to a new power source, and its lights were aglow. It was softly humming.

He crouched low and began to study it with red-rimmed eyes. He was sore and tired, emotionally spent, and still wired from adrenaline coursing through his veins. At some point he was going to crash hard, and needed to solve this puzzle before that happened.

A quick conference with the S.H.I.E.L.D. tech yielded nothing—it was far outside of anything either of them had seen before.

He studied the general construction, and noticed what appeared to be a remote transmitter. Scanning it on a variety of frequencies, he located one that was pulsing continuously. That told him what was happening, and he simply needed to figure out how to stop it.

If the remote devices were independent, destroying the main unit wouldn't do any good, and it would just cut his link with them. The tremors would continue until the tunnel collapsed entirely.

He heard multiple helicopters flying overhead—air rescue, police, and the media, no doubt—and all adding to a buzzing sound in the air like insects drawn to nectar.

Locating the antenna that appeared to generate the signal, he dropped magnifying lenses into his eye slits and traced the circuit back, back, farther and farther into the bowels of the machine. He peeled back layers of circuitry; ever careful not to damage the device . . . just lay it bare.

At every turn he found something new. It was all raw data, and he was having to assess it on the fly, running entirely on instinct. But he did his best work on the fly, and had for years. The thought lent him the self-confidence he needed to push forward.

His hands began to work, seemingly of their own volition. More pieces were peeled back, until he began to reach the most intricate parts of the device. He carefully opened a chamber in his boot cuffs and pulled out a set of miniaturized tools. Removing his gauntlets, he combined his magnified view with a sense of touch he had developed through years in R & D.

His was the touch of a high-tech surgeon.

When a television crew tried to get close, Agent Hoekstra intervened, placing himself between camera and genius. When one of the reporters complained, he was quickly removed.

The full picture was coming together quickly, and Stark felt the perspiration run down his cheeks and then his neck, despite the armor's cooling system. He heard further noise from the tunnels, and each rumble was like the tick of a clock, counting down to something he wouldn't be able to fix.

Iron Man touched a tiny probe to a spot where two circuits met, and there was a spark. He jerked back, and was certain that only his chestplate had kept his heart from stopping right then and there.

And finally, there it was—a circuit board that regulated the frequency of the remotes, sending precise sonic pulses down into the earth and wreaking havoc on the structure of the faults.

There was something strangely familiar about that piece of circuitry, something almost elegant in its intricacy. He paused for a moment, entranced by its design, and then it struck him.

The design was *his*.

The inventor froze, paralyzed by the revelation. Somehow, whether by theft or simple purchase, HYDRA had managed to get what they needed to wreak havoc.

Stark was jolted out of his paralysis when he heard more destruction echo from the tunnels.

And he knew now *exactly* what he needed to do, in order to create a neutralizing harmonic that would counteract the sonic disruptions HYDRA had started. Fingers flew faster than ever, changing patterns, reversing the flow of information, locking components back into place until he was ready.

With a click the device was intact once again, but now it was his. He scanned the frequencies again. . . .

And sent out a remote command of his own.

Iron Man stood and listened. The tremors continued, and he wondered if the command had been received. Had he missed something? Had he somehow left a critical connection incomplete? His mind raced back through the device, circuit by circuit, tracing pathways in an instant.

Suddenly, something was different.

The vibrations beneath his feet were lessening, bit by bit, until finally they stopped.

He turned then, and a pathway opened in the crowd. He walked away from the device that had killed people whose only crime was that of being in the wrong place at the wrong time. A device that had, at its heart, his handiwork.

He found a shadowy section of ramp and leaned against it, letting the exhausted body and mind finally come to a rest.

xxviii.

Madame Masque had kept her face mostly covered with a hood and a scarf, so she didn't attract a lot of attention as she returned to the apartment with her stolen goods. She figured she could call Francois later that the morning, which was really only a few hours away at this point.

She was tired and wanted a hot shower and a cold drink before preparing for her next move. Going undercover was actually sort of fun, and she liked the notion of playing different parts. As Gabriella Marquez, she had been straightlaced and ultraserious, so for the next role she wanted something lighter and more carefree.

Maybe she'd even use her Whitney Frost name again, which reminded her of happier times. After all, there was nothing to connect Whitney with Masque.

Setting her pistol atop her handbag, she hung her coat in the closet, wrapped the scarf carefully around a hanger, and began unzipping her dark blue jumpsuit, when she heard a sound in the hallway. The building was quiet, so the noise was strange, and the idea that someone else was up at this ungodly hour puzzled her.

There was a loud *crack* and a splintering as her front door strained against the dead bolt, and metal ground against metal. While the door itself seemed to hold, the frame was set in the cheap concrete walls, and almost immediately it began to separate.

She quickly recovered and reached for her gun, while her mind turned over the possibilities. Had Nefaria sent more goons after her?

She glanced at the window, and realized she was too high up. Unless she could reach the fire escape, which was doubtful, she would just end up a stain on the sidewalk.

Another impact made a noise that was sure to wake the neighbors, and the police were certain to be called—which meant her options were disappearing with each heartbeat.

Standing with her feet apart, her body poised, she lifted the gun, flipped off the safety, and was ready to fire first if it came to that.

The door frame finally surrendered, and Garrison Quint came hurtling into the apartment. Masque was stunned to see him, and even more so when she saw Pepper Potts step lightly through the wreckage.

Her hesitation allowed Quint to lunge forward and grab her pistol, but he made no other move.

Potts was perfectly coiffed, her outfit a tasteful business suit that flattered her figure with an open-collared pale-green blouse and just the right amount of jewelry. She was dressed for a day at the office.

Potts was followed by two more SI men in their uniforms, guns out and ready. Masque was seriously outnumbered, and she made no sudden move.

"Oh good, you're in," Potts said way too cheerfully.

"What is the meaning of this?" Madame Masque replied, since she really had nothing else to say.

"I think you know," the redhead answered, surveying the apartment with a casual swivel of her head, her hair moving like something out of a shampoo commercial. "Breaking, entering, stealing company property . . . need I go on?"

"I won't deny it," Masque said.

"Good, since there wouldn't be a point." She faced Masque head-on. "I'm pretty sure Mr. Stark would like this to be handled out of the limelight, which is why we didn't bring the police." She glanced around again.

"So where are the computer chips and other items you've stolen?"

Masque just shrugged, earning her a frown. Her mind was racing through her options, and realized that they were few, bordering on none.

"How did you find me out?" she asked, gesturing to offer Pepper a seat. The redhead shook her head, and Masque just shrugged again. She was afraid it was becoming a habit.

Pepper wandered around the living room, checking out the décor, and looked unimpressed. Masque had to agree, though silently, since it had all come with the apartment. The stuff was inexpensive, unimpressive, and without character. A bad Hollywood set if anything.

"You were pretty easy to track, once I put my mind to it," Pepper told her. "Mr. Stark was so preoccupied with HYDRA, and Congress . . . and you that he really wasn't focusing on any one problem.

"I didn't have the same handicap."

Masque started following her, trying to access a hidden cache of weapons, but in such a way that Quint's goons couldn't tell. Tricky, but not impossible.

"You played the part well," Pepper admitted. "You gave him the cold shoulder, making him want you all the more. He would have fallen for you, had that green-headed bitch not showed up at the same time."

What green-headed woman?

Pepper was admiring the view of Manhattan, then she turned and appraised Masque again.

"Just who are you really?" Potts asked. "There is no Gabriella Marquez," she said confidently, stepping closer. She was making it sound like girl talk.

Masque hated girl talk.

"I'm known as Madame Masque," she replied, and Potts put her hand to her mouth to suppress a chuckle.

"Kind of a silly name," she said.

"Says the Girl Friday to someone called Iron Man," Masque said.

"My title is executive assistant," Potts corrected coldly.

"You will treat me and the Stark Industries company with more respect than you have in the past."

Feeling petulant, Masque said, "Make me."

What she never expected was for Potts—dressed in business attire—to tackle her.

The two bodies collided with a dull thud, and they fell in a tangle to the carpeted floor. Potts wasn't a trained fighter, and if Masque could get a good angle, she could snap her neck. Still, the last thing she wanted was a murder charge.

But that didn't mean she couldn't bruise Stark's flunky in the process. For the moment, Quint and his thugs stayed out of it.

Fists flailed and the redhead grabbed a handful of hair, eliciting a muffled yelp from underneath the golden mask. Potts was enthusiastic, if inexperienced, and gave as good as she received.

Masque was tired, and decided to put an end to it. She figured once the woman was gone, it would just be the guards. They seemed like trained toadies, and Quint didn't scare her at all.

She twisted around to land a solid blow, when her entire body suddenly felt a charge run through it. She went tense, then limp, and fell to the floor.

Pepper Potts rose over the unconscious body and retracted two thin electric wires. They rewound into the chunky silver bracelet she wore on her right arm. She dusted her hands off, and then grinned at Quint.

"You ever see anything like that?"

"No, ma'am," Quint said. "What did you do?"

"Tony built me this," she said, waving the braceleted arm in the air. "He said I needed some sort of personal defense, and this thing packs a wallop. The taser's electrical discharge knocked her right out."

"Nice," Quint said with a grin. "My guys should have something that compact."

"You and most law enforcement should have this stuff within the year. He's been modifying its design and power supply."

Quint nodded, then gestured for his men to secure the now-insensible form of Madame Masque. While she watched, he personally scoured the apartment, checking for stolen goods. The pile of things he found was impressive, even though they had come expecting to find *something*.

Then he addressed Pepper again.

"Can I ask why you attacked her? We had her covered."

She looked at Quint with a crooked grin.

"She had it coming, and I've been feeling the need to hit something for days. She made as good a target as any, and really, she had it coming."

"Oh, I agree. Just was curious."

xxix.

Stark awoke in his bed, his mouth gummy, his mind fogged. He couldn't remember how he got there.

He forced his eyes open and studied his bedroom, and saw his robe awaiting him on the wing chair as always. On the table beside it, in something of a heap, was the armor—all except for the boots, which were on the area rug. The gold and crimson metal was obscured with dirt and grime.

Sitting up too quickly made him feel a little lightheaded, so he stayed in place and took several deep breaths to get a grip on himself. Once the wave of weakness passed, he assessed his body. His muscles ached and his right shoulder felt a twinge of pain. His heart was beating with regularity and his chest was without pain.

He judged that he had been asleep for many hours, and he finally sought out the clock on the nightstand, which told him it was 2:34. The sunlight told him it was afternoon. Even after his worst college benders he'd never slept that late before.

And he felt as if he wanted more.

Instead, he swung his feet to the floor and waited to see how his body reacted.

Not too bad.

Beside the clock were the controls that accessed the internal communications system, and he pressed the farthest-left button, which would bring his butler. In just under two minutes the man knocked once and entered the expansive bedroom.

"How do you feel, sir?"

"Like I went ten rounds with Ali," Stark admitted. "Some coffee, please."

"Of course, sir," the man said, and he left the room.

Alone again, Stark reached for the farthest-right button and pressed it. That opened a direct line to his office. It took seconds for Pepper's lovely voice to come on the line.

"Have a nice rest?"

"Never mind that. What's going on?"

Pepper cleared her voice.

"Your work at the Lincoln Tunnel was a success, and it's still intact. It needs weeks of repair work, and New York and New Jersey are bickering over who gets to foot the bill."

"Draft a memo to both governors," Stark instructed, standing and beginning to consider what to wear. "SI will hire Damage Control, Inc. to handle the repairs, at our expense."

"Very good, Mr. Stark," she replied with an approving tone.

"I want the names of the eight people who died, and contact information. I want to go to the funerals, and pay for them," Stark said, shucking off his pajama top and deciding on a shower first.

"Of course," she said.

"Next, we need to rearrange the calendar so I can catch up. I also want to ramp up production on weaponry for S.H.I.E.L.D. I emailed the department heads on Sunday, asking them to figure out which plants can be retasked for the job. Coordinate the responses and get started.

"I want S.H.I.E.L.D. better prepared for the future. Weapons, emergency equipment, transportation, the works."

"You left some notes to that effect," she told him. "It's already underway."

"Good," he said as he entered his bathroom, the lights

turning on automatically. "Next, I want Nick Fury and Rhodey in my office today. Make it around five, if possible."

"Done."

Water ran over his toothbrush and he looked up at his reflection. The dark smudges under his eyes weren't good. The stubble made him look older, with maybe a hint of gray starting to show. This dual career was aging him, but he paused and realized his heart felt good.

That was something.

"I want a meeting with Quint to tighten security. I'm done having my place burgled and trashed."

"No problem, although I think he has that issue under control."

She was right, he realized. HYDRA had been laid low last night—well, earlier today—so that should put an end to it for the moment, even if he still didn't grasp the full scope of what they were trying to accomplish.

Remembering the expression on Madame Hydra's face, he was pretty sure he never would.

"Is the company still running?" he asked as he put the toothpaste on the brush.

"Isn't it always?"

"Well, it runs better when I'm not there."

"You say the sweetest things, boss," she said. "I'll see you later. Take your time."

Stark luxuriated in the hot water as it ran over his body, scrubbing every inch, then he rinsed and repeated. By the time he emerged from the bathroom, steam followed him out and the table had been cleared of armor and set with a pot of coffee, a china cup, and a plate of his favorite breakfast.

A copy of the *Daily Bugle* was discreetly folded by the pot, its headline proclaiming the danger of having super-humans running loose around the city. He wasn't entirely certain he disagreed.

The world let him eat in peace, and he brooded over the past few days. His actions had been rash, and he should have done many things differently, starting with keeping his head in the game and not falling for one woman, let alone two.

He'd need to let Gabriella down gently, he supposed.

Stark drank too much and got sloppy, costing people their lives. He was out of shape, and realized he was allowing the armor to do too much of the work. He resolved to drink less, and book workout time at Avengers Mansion, using its state-of-the-art equipment to improve his muscle tone.

As he sipped his coffee and caught up on world headlines, he notified Happy Hogan that he'd need a ride to the office. Hogan sounded, well, happy to have something useful to do, and he was probably smarting at the way Fury had dismissed him the previous night.

Was it really just last night?

So much had been done in less than twenty-four hours.

Feeling more human than he had in days, Tony Stark put on his best navy-blue suit over his crisp white shirt and red-striped tie. He carefully brushed his hair and then added just a touch of product to keep everything in place. He wanted to make a good impression and reassert himself as the corporate leader, first and foremost.

After all, it was his intellect that had managed to reverse the damage. It had built the crude armor that saved his life and sent him on his new path.

Then again, it was his intellect that had been at the heart of the device that had yielded so much carnage. It was a sobering thought to realize that everything he did would need to be guarded more carefully than ever before. Technology didn't have to take the form of munitions in order to kill.

Stark and Hogan chatted casually as they drove together from the mansion to the campus. The sun was already nearing the horizon as they arrived at the main gate, and at the admin building Hogan held the door as Stark emerged, sans overcoat, but carrying his briefcase.

Pepper awaited him in the lobby, without any papers but wearing a big smile. He nodded and looked around. People milled about, a guy from the mailroom wheeled his cart toward an elevator, and he could hear chatter all around, with phones ringing softly in the distance.

It felt so . . . normal.

Reaching his office, he unbuttoned his suit coat, lowered himself into his chair, still feeling the aches—his atonement—and began sifting through the pile of phone messages. Lost in thought as he composed replies and figured out whom to avoid, he almost missed the rapping at his door.

He looked up and there stood Fury and Rhodey, both looking as if they had slept a lot better than he did. They shook hands, he offered them drinks—which were thankfully declined—and then they sat in the conversation area.

"How do you feel, Tony?"

"Better than yesterday, Rhodey," he said. "Still got a ways to go."

"No doubt. You still look like you've been through hell."

"Thanks," Stark said with a grin. "Few can see through me."

"Yeah, the armor does a nice job of hiding the real you, doesn't it?"

The question struck close to home, and he avoided a quip. Instead, he turned to Fury.

"Look, Nick, I want you to know that we're working to get you guys outfitted faster than I promised. But . . ." He paused.

Fury sat back, hands on his knees, poised for something bad. His good eye glared.

"But?" he prompted.

Stark swallowed and continued.

"But . . . I want a say in how the weapons are used."

Fury's eye opened wide, and he remained silent, prompting Stark to continue.

"The Executive Council is well meaning, but they stay in their ivory tower. Like you, I'm out there," he said, gesturing toward the window. "I'm getting my hands dirty, and recognize that drastic force may be called for. But there are limits, and if we give S.H.I.E.L.D. something akin to absolute power, we have to make sure it doesn't get misused."

"You turned down my offer to be a card-carrying member of our little club," Fury said, earning him a surprised look from Rhodey.

"As I said, Colonel," Stark continued, "I already have Stark Industries, plus the Avengers, and my own personal headaches. I don't need another organization to put demands on my time. Of course I'll be available—just as I was this last week. But no, I won't want to serve as an agent of S.H.I.E.L.D."

Fury nodded slowly, though his expression indicated that he wasn't sold. Stark decided to forge ahead anyway. But before he could, Rhodey spoke up.

"Tony's got a point, and frankly, having him on the outside, keeping a weather eye on us, isn't such a bad thought."

Stark nodded in agreement, and Fury looked thoughtful.

"There's more," Stark said. Avoiding Fury's expression, he continued.

"I want to work with you on the entire operation, make sure all the international pieces fit smoothly, not be a kludge."

"Kludge?" Fury asked.

"A mess," Rhodey interpreted.

"The Executive Council made a mistake choosing Stoner over you," Stark said. "This isn't smoke up your skirt, but an honest assessment. You conceived of S.H.I.E.L.D. long before the need presented itself. There's a wealth of experience that should have been tapped from the start. From what I gather, your commandos tended to be an international operation. You understand other cultures and their needs, and how to form a team out of the pieces."

Fury nodded, his eye looking faraway, recalling something from the past.

"Just one thing you have to remember," he finally told the industrialist.

Stark gestured for him to continue.

"They gave me S.H.I.E.L.D., and I'm the director. When push comes to shove, if we disagree, you can't just take your toys and go home."

Stark seemed to consider the statement, and nodded.

"Agreed. I've seen you in action. You're cool under fire, and you I can trust," he said.

With that, they shook hands.

Fury turned to Rhodes and asked, "You sure I can't get you to switch allegiances?"

Rhodey shook his head.

"I'm really flattered, Colonel. But I made a deal. I finish my tour of duty, then cash out and go into the private sector."

"Sure, for the cushy life of a corporate lackey," Fury countered.

"Something like that," Rhodes said, then he laughed.

XXX.

The last twenty-four hours had been hellish.

Instead of widespread destruction, Madame Hydra had been thwarted at every turn. It was a degree of failure she had not experienced in many years, and it did not sit well with her.

Iron Man and S.H.I.E.L.D. had defeated overwhelming forces, and managed to round up most of her New York agents. To top it off, her Lincoln Tunnel team had failed. Her forces were seriously depleted, and fresh bodies would not be available to her for a while.

She seethed with indignation at the failure of her leadership. Her orders had been questioned, and she had placed her trust in lackeys who seemed rational and pragmatic, but failed at every turn.

Through the years she had needed very few people. She was self-made, a survivor for whom everything was a resource, to be employed for survival or utter destruction. Nothing else could be tolerated. Men or women, they were there to service her needs, and nothing more.

Which is why the lingering feelings she still harbored toward Anthony Stark bewildered her. He was the enemy, and she had played him for a lovesick fool, but they had reached a level of intimacy that confused her, because she was inexperienced with processing emotions. Every time she tried to tamp them away, they resurfaced.

Her stomach ached from his punch, and that she could understand.

It echoed what she felt in her heart.

As she made her way from Long Island back to the underground lair that HYDRA used for its New York base, she desired a shower, a hot meal, and perhaps a full day's sleep. Then she would assess the damage and begin new plans. She knew that changes had to be made.

Perhaps two dozen HYDRA agents were left for all of New York. A meager number, but if their motto was correct, those ranks would swell in the coming weeks. What global law enforcement and world leaders never understood was how to tap the common man's frustration and anger, how to stoke it to white-hot brilliance and, like a blacksmith, shape it into something hard and dangerous.

The entire complex—with its computers, weapons, bunks, and training areas—seemed unnaturally quiet. No security beyond the mechanized variety greeted her.

She tensed, ready for a fight. Over the years, she'd been trained by many of the best fighters in the world. She could bare-knuckle brawl with the best of them.

Straining her ears, she tried to detect any motion, but was rewarded with electronic humming from the equipment, and a whisper from the air systems. Taking slow, silent steps, she made her way toward the commander's office. If 269 followed protocol, he'd be there waiting for her.

Right about now, though, she suspected that protocol had been suspended in favor of a coup.

She made it another twenty feet or so before the rustle of fabric against leather alerted her. Slowing her gait, she took several deep breaths.

The attack came from two sides, which surprised her. One agent charged her with a hunting knife held high, while the other launched himself, arms outstretched to contain her.

As a result, it was easy for her merely to crouch low, avoiding their grasp. Her hands extended, fingers together and palms flat. She thrust both arms up from her position and caught both in the solar plexus, causing them to double over.

She quickly grabbed the knife arm and pinned it with her shoulder, her left elbow viciously rising and catching the man in the jaw. Then she whirled about, grabbing the other man by the cowl, and twice rammed his head into the metallic wall.

This was way too easy.

It was a warning.

Rising to her feet, she stepped over the two prone men and continued toward her office.

Without pause, she threw open the door and strode into the fully lit room. Seated behind her desk was 269, two glasses sitting in front of him, both filled about a third of the way with dark amber liquor.

"What do you mean by this?"

"A toast," he said, shoving one of the glasses toward her. He remained seated, as if without a care in the world.

"Get up, 269," she said. Her voice dripped with anger.

He finally rose, holding his glass aloft.

"To the future."

"What future? We've failed. Actually, *you* failed. The tunnel mission was a botch," she said.

"Indeed," he said, still holding the glass. She didn't understand, but refused to let it show.

"Again, why toast the future?"

"They fear you now," he said. "You threw everything you had at our enemies. You sought to strike a blow that— failure or not—sent a strong signal. Those who remain within our ranks speak of your passion, of your leadership, and all who join us will know not to challenge you."

"And you think the future will be brighter?" she asked carefully.

"A future aglow from the flames of cities on fire," he said. There was conviction in his voice, plus passion. Though she had never before realized it, he was fully committed to her cause.

"What was that in the corridor then? Your idea of a gift?"

"No," he said, and he gestured with his glass, then walked from around the desk, standing beside her, acting like an equal. "They were the last two who doubted you. I whispered in their ears, and encouraged them to try to remove you from power. I let them rig the entire thing.

"Now they know better," he added. "Shall I have the bodies removed?"

"No," she answered, and finally picked up the glass from the desk. "We need troops, until the ranks are replenished. But now they know better."

"A lesson well learned, no doubt," he said.

"For every defeat, there will be greater victories," she said, without acknowledging the toast. "And lessons learned."

"Something like, 'Fail once and two victories shall appear,' " he quipped.

"Not quite, but we compensate and come back better prepared," she said. "The stakes are higher now that S.H.I.E.L.D. is involved. It will make our victories all the sweeter."

From behind her, she heard a chorus.

"Hail Hydra! Cut off a limb and two more shall take its place!"

At a glance, she saw the corridor filled with many of the remaining agents, most of whom must have overheard the exchange.

It was the right time, so she raised the glass higher and finally returned the toast.

"To the future," she said, and swallowed the tumbler's contents in a single gulp.

As she placed the glass back on her desk, she looked at her troops.

"While our gambit failed, it has suggested another option," she began. "There are other tunnels under New York—the sewers. Through them, we may be able to strike at a much greater number of people, spreading the fear even further. We must regroup and plan so that this time Iron Man and S.H.I.E.L.D. cannot stop us. It may take months, but the results will be worth it."

The men cheered her words while she smiled at them coldly, reasserting her control. New York would tremble at her feet.

Unbidden, Stark's face flashed through her mind, and a warm spot appeared in her chest. Her hand reached for the scars under her long, lustrous hair, then hesitated and dropped.

She erased the image and crushed the feeling.

epilogue

Ever since he had invented the armored persona of Iron Man, things seemed to be moving at an accelerated speed— something that often threatened to overwhelm him.

But for now, he needed to focus on his personal area of influence. A visit to the secretary of defense, and another to Senator Byrd. A suit of armor in desperate need of repair and upgrades.

Yet he knew in his heart that whatever plans he made today, they would be revised tomorrow when something new threatened Stark Industries, New York, or the world.

Pepper came in with a sheaf of papers for his signature. She looked a little tired, which was unusual for her. She also looked rather smart in her business attire, and once more he mentally patted himself on the back for promoting her.

"Rough day?" he asked as he began signing letters that received only a cursory glance.

"Got up early," she said, retrieving each signed letter, blowing on the ink before placing it in a blue folder. "Had an errand to run before coming in."

"Well, after this, go knock off. I'm not going anywhere for a few days, so if you want, take tomorrow off."

"Thank you, Mr. Stark," she replied. "We'll see what tomorrow brings."

He signed in silence, his mind drifting backward, sifting through the last few days as lingering issues haunted him.

"Something on your mind?" she prompted.

"Actually, yes," Stark said, putting the pen down. He

indicated that she should sit, which she did, placing the folder atop his desk.

"After everything that we've experienced, I still can't get it all to fit. What HYDRA stole from Cord and Stane and Richmond and the others made sense. But the things they took from us don't fit. For some reason, they came at us— and only us—on two fronts. Some of the things they took are still unaccounted for. And we know now why they needed the communications system, but why *two*?"

"It was Marquez," Pepper said, and she sounded exasperated.

"What?" Stark asked. "*What* was Marquez?"

"She was the one on the inside," Pepper continued. "It's not even her real name, or her real face."

Slumping deep into his chair, Stark sat and listened, his world turned upside down. First he had slept with the enemy, and now this.

"But she seemed so good at the job," Stark muttered. "And Michael thought she was terrific."

"Right. It's how she got by you undetected. She *was* very good at her job, which enabled her to steal from you for the Maggia."

"The crime family?"

"Exactly. She was robbing from you, selling off the goods, and making a tidy sum."

"Plus, she had benefits," Stark mused.

"Never hurts in this day and age," his aide agreed, and she continued. "Marquez walked off with the gyroscopes, and instigated the gas attack."

"Then she was responsible for Drum's death," Stark said, and he frowned, remembering the anger.

"You kept thinking every robbery was about HYDRA, and that muddied the picture you were trying to form. It never once occurred to you that there might be parallel strings of robberies going on at the same time."

"Not once," he admitted. Suddenly he realized—more than ever—how formidable Pepper Potts truly could be.

"So what became of her?"

Pepper hesitated, and then decided something in her mind and continued speaking.

"Once I figured her out, I worked with Quint, and we rigged extra security around her office. I wanted her caught in the act, and sure enough, last night it worked. She even put a virus in the system, but I alerted Mr. Burstein and he had it removed before serious damage could be done."

Stark sat stunned. All along he kept saying he'd do everything possible to preserve his family legacy, and here he had missed so much.

"We trailed her last night and, well, it's been taken care of."

"Where is she now?"

Now it was her turn to frown. Finally, she tucked a stray lock of hair behind her left ear and spoke once more.

"We didn't want to involve the police, so she was being held at the security offices, and . . . well . . . she escaped."

"How?"

"She wasn't as helpless as she seemed, and when only one man was watching her, she struck and put him down.

"He's fine," she said quickly. "A little embarrassed, but okay.

"I'm very sorry," she added.

"Don't be," Stark said. He walked around his desk, sat beside her, and leaned in close. "You did what I couldn't, and for that I'm grateful."

They sat in companionable silence for a while, then she spoke again.

"Mr. Stark," she began hesitantly, "I took the liberty of meeting with the department heads yesterday. I asked them to begin crafting a series of checks and balances that will establish separate security protocols for each division of the company. This means that, even if someone is able to get inside, they won't be able to move freely from one division to another. And the IT people are working on a program to give them instant control over any computer that tries to utilize stolen Stark technology."

Stark peered at her, stunned again.

Maybe I should step down, and let her run the place.

Seeing his expression, she looked worried.

He grinned, and she smiled back, looking stunning.

"Instant control," he muttered, and he let his mind wander in new directions as Pepper handed him yet another letter to sign.

historical note

This book is loosely set in the first years of the Marvel Universe, embracing situations found throughout Marvel Comics, mostly 1966–1969. For example, Madame Hydra was introduced in *Captain America* #110, somewhat after Whitney Frost/Madame Masque was introduced in *Tales of Suspense* #97, and both occurred after *Strange Tales* #135, wherein we first learn of S.H.I.E.L.D. (set between *TOS* 64 and 65). However, it has been subsequently revealed that Madame Hydra had been around for many decades prior to her arrival with HYDRA. Similarly, James Rhodes was grafted onto Tony Stark's backstory in the 1980s, and that change is reflected here.

Our one divergence, to fit with the modern comic-book reader's understanding of the character, is that the public in this novel knows that Tony Stark is Iron Man. While he is associated with S.H.I.E.L.D., as he has been from the start, he is not the organization's director.

The Marvel Universe is approximately eight to ten years old, so, following a rolling calendar, this would place the story around the year 2000, and the Marvel Universe's technology reflected those modern-day sensibilities, with cell phones aplenty and nary a vacuum tube in sight. It's also a less populated universe of heroes and villains at that time, which will explain the absence of certain familiar colleagues when things go horribly wrong.

This time frame also allowed us to set the story at a dramatic point in history, as global violence has put the world on edge. The rise of HYDRA leads to the creation of a counterbalancing organization, S.H.I.E.L.D., and we set our story in the early days of the operation.